Lottie Phillips worked as a teacher before turning her hand to fiction. She was brought up in Africa and the Middle East and then – as an adult – travelled extensively before moving to London and finally settling in the Cotswolds with her young son. When she's not writing, you will find her scouring interior design magazines and shops, striving towards the distant dream of being a domestic goddess or having a glass of wine with country music turned up loud. As a child, she always had her nose in a book and, in particular, Nancy Drew. *Sunshine at Daisy's Guesthouse* is her second romantic comedy but she also writes psychological thrillers under the pseudonym Louise Stone. Readers can find Lottie Phillips, otherwise known as Charlie Phillips, on Twitter @writercharlie or at www.writercharlie.com

Also by Lottie Phillips

The Little Cottage in the Country

Sunshine at Daisy's Guesthouse

LOTTIE PHILLIPS

ONE PLACE. MANY STORIES

This novel is entirely a work of fiction. The names, characters and incidents portrayed in it are the work of the author's imagination. Any resemblance to actual persons, living or dead, events or localities is entirely coincidental.

HQ
An imprint of HarperCollins*Publishers* Ltd
1 London Bridge Street
London SE1 9GF

This paperback edition 2018

First published in Great Britain by
HQ, an imprint of HarperCollins*Publishers* Ltd 2018

A catalogue record for this book is available from the British Library.

ISBN: 9780008310080

MIX
Paper from responsible sources
FSC C007454

This book is produced from independently certified FSC™ paper to ensure responsible forest management.

For more information visit: **www.harpercollins.co.uk/green**

Printed and bound in Great Britain by
CPI Group (UK) Ltd, Melksham, SN12 6TR

To my Dream Team, thank you

Prologue

Amsterdam, 1997

Daisy adjusted the focus on the camera and zoomed in. He was waving his hands about as if to say 'ta-dah, look at us, in Amsterdam, without a care in the world'. He made her laugh when he tried to be the joker. He wasn't a joker at all, he was quiet, reserved, and serious, but her heart soared at his efforts to always make her happy, and she clicked the shutter over and over again, as if wanting to impress this moment on her mind forever.

'Beautiful lady, what are you doing standing over there?' He smiled at her and then, much to her horror, and in a very un-Hugh-like manner, he gestured to a man busy making his way to work, his briefcase in one hand. 'Isn't she one of the most gorgeous women you've ever set eyes on?'

The man grumbled, looked momentarily in her direction and gave a small smile and a nod.

'Hugh!' she shrieked, dying internally of embarrassment whilst also secretly enjoying the attention.

'Well,' he called over the cobbled street to her. 'They all need to know!' He paused, fumbled in his pocket. 'You think that was embarrassing, wait for this!'

Her heart quickened. What was he doing?

He stopped, looking briefly serious and said more quietly, 'Daisy, come over to this side.'

He brushed his foppish fringe out of the way with his free hand, the other remaining firmly in his pocket. 'Curtains' he had told her gravely, 'they're called curtains.' She knew he was dying to cut them off but, again, he wanted to fit in with her friends.

'How can a hairstyle be called *curtains*?' he'd asked the day before. 'I mean that's a house furnishing, not a haircut.' She had kissed him all over, inhaling deeply the scent of Ralph Lauren Polo and told him he should have the haircut he wanted. Eventually, he agreed; post-Amsterdam, he would visit his favourite barber and get rid of said house furnishings.

She watched him steadily now, refusing to go over to his side, teasing him. She swallowed a laugh as he shuffled from side to side impatiently in his Skechers. Skechers had been another display that he was a 'man of the time'. The fact that they were still alarmingly white and new made them even more conspicuous. They didn't suit him and he hated wearing them but as he told her, 'I don't want you to think I'm just some boring finance guy who wears chinos and boat shoes.' Even though they both agreed that he was in fact all of the above. Maybe not boring, just *well behaved*. Daisy, on the other hand, was a party animal that flitted between the gym, clubbing – she had to show Hugh 'big box, little box' – and the odd lecture. Why exactly she had chosen French, she had no idea – and as she had pointed out to her main lecturer, her classmates *were* French; where was *le justice* in that?

'Excuse moi, uhh…' She had paused, given herself time to think with the old 'uhh' trick and said, 'Mes amis…'

Her lecturer had cut in, smiling kindly. 'Just speak English.'

'OK,' she agreed. 'My classmates are all French, where's the justice in that?'

Mr Faron smiled. 'Why did you choose French?'

Truthful answer: she thought she might finish the three years as a cultured, thin, beautiful, long-fingered, cigarette-smoking woman who rattled off the language to her sexy French friends.

'I want to go into business with the French,' was what she had actually said.

What her teacher didn't understand was that she came from the back end of beyond, in other words a farm in Gloucestershire, and she had never really had a penny to her name. So she had wanted to better herself.

It was partly the reason she had fallen for Hugh. He was intelligent, very serious and could talk about stocks and shares and GDP something or other in his sleep; actually, come to think of it, Daisy knew he actually did talk about those things in his sleep.

She brought herself back to the now, and after a moment or two more of watching Hugh, she couldn't bear it any longer. Why *did* he look so nervous?

She jogged over to the other side of the bridge towards Hugh, who went to take her hand, but instead she teasingly dipped down to sniff a display of perfectly formed yellow tulips. As she bent over, she was aware of Hugh's eyes on her and she pretended to study the flowers. She knew he was undressing her with his eyes. Not much guesswork involved, really, as she wore a crop top and bike shorts. She was lucky, she guessed, that she hadn't piled the weight on at university – she was, as Hugh affectionately called her, a gym bunny. They had met in their second year; the most unlikely couple, according to her friends. Yet, here they were, at the end of their three-year degrees, in Amsterdam, carefully avoiding the subject of what they planned to do next.

Eventually, she looked up and took a sharp intake of breath; it was as if he had read her mind.

'Hugh, what are you doing?'

He was down on one knee holding open a box. Inside, lay a simple silver ring with a diamond.

'Hugh!' she squealed. 'What on earth are you doing?'

He still hadn't spoken, red creeping up his neck.

Finally, he cleared his throat. 'Daisy, would you do me the greatest honour and become my wife?'

She stood, mouth agog. Her life flashing in front of her. Wasn't she too young? Hadn't they only just left university?

She shook her head and his face crumpled but then she grinned; he looked confused. What was she thinking? She loved this man. They could spend the rest of their life together, have children, live happily.

'Yes,' she shrieked and hugged him so hard he wobbled and fell onto the pavement. 'Yes, you silly, funny, beautiful man. I will marry you!'

She had lost all previous inhibitions and smiled at the now small gathering of onlookers who clapped her decision.

Hugh gathered himself, relief written across his features and he took her into a firm embrace, kissing her deeply.

'We'll be together forever,' he whispered and she melted into his arms, as she breathed in the smell of cologne on his skin. She thought she could die happily as long as she was never separated from Hugh.

She had never felt so safe in her life.

Of course, she didn't know that she would lose Hugh to cancer twenty years later.

Chapter 1

'I have no idea why I let you talk me into this, Lisa,' Daisy grumbled as she wiggled to and fro on the small changing-room stool. She had fallen for the *Levi's for Curvy Women* bumph and now she would never be able to leave this store again.

No, really. She was officially stuck in the jeans. Oh, she had got as far as below her knees but then her generous size sixteen thighs and bum had decided she was beyond even Levi's. Great.

'Lisa, get in here now.'

She could hear giggling on the other side of the curtain and then, 'Oh, I love them, they're perfect.'

Daisy, now with a beetroot red face, looked at her sweaty, bloated body in the mirror and rolled her eyes. 'Lisa, I'm so happy for you that your size ten self fits so wonderfully well in jeans from the *normal* Levi's section, but if you wouldn't mind helping me remove my cargo ship ass from these ones, I'd be so grateful.'

Eventually, Lisa could be heard moving her curtain across and then she shimmied into Daisy's changing area. Lisa, looking amazing in her straight jeans and bra, took one look at her friend and burst into laughter, quickly righting herself when she saw tears in Daisy's eyes.

'Oh, Daisy, I'm sorry.' She gulped. 'I didn't mean to make you feel bad. You're beautiful.'

'No.' Daisy waved it off. 'It's all this. I can't do it. I've lost *me*. Does that make any sense?'

Lisa nodded. 'I thought it might make you feel better.' She paused. 'You know, getting out and going shopping.' She hung her head. 'I'm sorry.'

Daisy brushed her tears away and conjured up a smile. She didn't want to make Lisa feel bad. She knew it had been well over a year, surely she was meant to be feeling better by now? Hugh would have thought up some mathematical equation in which someone's spouse dies and the point at which they should start to feel normal, even happy.

Lisa sat on the floor now, gently tugging at the jeans, but they wouldn't budge.

'You're going to have to pull harder,' Daisy instructed, and an image popped into her mind of her mother telling her the very same thing when she had often tried, but failed, to get the cows onto the transporter.

'I'm like a heffer,' Daisy said and Lisa bit her lip, trying not to laugh. 'I'm like a heffer in jeans. Now *that* would sell. I must remember to phone Levi's marketing deparment.' Lisa, now in a leaning-back position, as if readying herself for tug-of-war, pulled harder and harder on the jeans until they eventually broke free, sending Lisa cascading through the curtain and into the seating area (for bored men).

Lisa could be heard apologising to a man for landing at his feet.

'Bet you thought all your dreams had come true!' she said in a singsong voice and backed herself through the curtain. She and Daisy both fell about in fits of laughter.

After a few minutes of laughing so hard that they were almost silent except for the odd painful squeak – their stomachs threatening to turn to six-packs from the pain – they got a grip. Well, not quite. Daisy wiped her eyes and realised she was doing a laugh-cry.

Lisa wordlessly took her into a firm hug and stroked her hair. 'Daisy, I'm sorry. This was a bad idea. I just thought it was time you had some fun.'

'It has been fun,' Daisy said. 'I haven't laughed like that for months. I'm just a bit of a wreck. One minute laughing, the next minute crying.' She paused. 'It's like being a pregnant woman. I imagine it is, anyway.'

They left the store, Lisa carrying her new jeans, and Daisy grateful for her free-flowing wide leg trousers. Who wanted to be *contained* in skinnies anyway?

'Coffee? Cake?' Daisy suggested.

'Absolutely.' Lisa nodded and they headed to one of the mall's central coffee bars.

'I'll get them in,' Daisy said. 'You find us a table.'

Daisy eyed up all the cakes, the last hour's events already being purged from her mind, and she chose a large slice of chocolate for the whippet-like Lisa (life *was* unfair) and she went for the carrot cake (there had to be at least one or two of her five-a-day in there).

Once they were both ensconced in a corner, Lisa turned to her friend. 'Listen, I'm worried about you. I don't think it's healthy you living alone in that enormous house.' She softened. 'I mean… you know, you need to…'

'Move on?' Daisy arched a brow.

'Well, no, not *move on*. That sounds so harsh. I just mean it might help you to recover if you moved away from the house, sold it perhaps.' Lisa refused to make eye contact, her gaze fixed on her fork stabbing at the cake.

'Lisa.'

'Yes?' She eventually looked up, like a naughty school child waiting for their punishment.

'Lisa,' Daisy repeated, 'Hugh died over a year ago of cancer.

Now, don't get me wrong, yes, I knew it had been coming for over two years so some might argue I'm not in shock, I should bounce back faster.' She paused, a lump rising in her throat. 'Only, it doesn't work like that.' A tear slid down her cheek. 'Knowing he was going to die for two years built the whole thing up in my head.' She looked at her cake and pushed it away, suddenly losing her appetite. 'Because after he had been diagnosed and stubbornly refused all treatment, I thought that every day he lived, maybe he wouldn't die from cancer. I was so angry with him, so angry for refusing treatment. There's a time and a place for pig-headedness I used to tell him, and that wasn't it. Sometimes I thought that maybe—' she gave a short, self-conscious laugh '—maybe they had got it wrong. Then, on the other hand, I knew it would get him eventually and so every day he was still here, I realised how much I would miss everything he brings…' She gave a slight shake to her head, and corrected herself. '*Brought* to my life.'

Lisa nodded, her own eyes welling, and put her fork down. 'I know, I'm sorry.'

'So I guess I'm trying to get over three years' worth of grieving, does that make sense?' She paused though, knowing she was being untrue to herself. 'I know that Hugh and I had our problems. We loved each other passionately but he could be controlling.' She nodded. 'Like he wanted me all to himself. Which is why…' She looked at her friend and blushed. 'Do you think it's wrong that I feel kind of like I want to move on already? Like I want to meet someone? I'm not sure if I'm allowed to feel like that but I would love to be in a care-free relationship… but then a part of me thinks I shouldn't be allowed to be happy again, does that make sense?'

'Yes.' Lisa nodded. 'It does, which is why I just thought if you didn't live in that house, that maybe you could try and build new memories.'

Daisy shifted irritably. 'I don't want to *build new memories*, Lisa. I am very happy with the old ones.' She bit her lip. 'Most of them.' She thought about her twenty-year marriage. 'It was all-consuming, our marriage, filled with passion but I've now woken up to its faults too.'

'Look, I'm just looking out for you but, of course, you know best.'

'I know.' Daisy smiled gratefully. 'And I've thought about it more and more, I think I'm ready to move on. I think I *need* to move on.'

Daisy looked at the next table. A man and woman had chosen to sit side by side, instead of opposite one another, and they were holding hands, laughing at something on his phone. Their easiness and happiness sent a pain through her heart. She didn't want to be the woman who grew old, begrudging other people their lives. Her friends had all done so much for her since Hugh closed his eyes for that final time in January last year. He had died at home, and she had luckily been by his side, only because her gut instinct had told her not to go and visit her mother that day. She had been all ready for her bi-weekly coffee with Mum but a feeling of unease had gnawed at her, forcing her to cancel her plans.

Her phone buzzed, snapping her out of her thoughts and she fished it out of her bag. The screen saver was a picture of Hugh in Amsterdam back in 1997, just before he proposed. He had his arms up in a 'ta-dah' kind of a way.

She looked up and caught Lisa staring at it. No words were exchanged but she knew what Lisa was thinking. Until she made some changes, she wasn't going to live her life again. And that probably included uploading a different screensaver. Maybe Lisa would be happier if she put up a picture of a flower or a puppy.

It was a text message from James, her and Hugh's best friend. Her heart lifted. She enjoyed any contact with their oldest and closest friend.

Hi Daisy, hope you're doing OK. Can I pop by later with something? I think it's time I gave it to you. Maybe 4ish? J X

She was surprised, having seen James many times since the funeral; she couldn't imagine what he might want to give her.

'It's James,' Daisy said, and she read the text aloud. 'He wants to give something to me.'

Lisa snorted and arched a brow. 'Sorry, I mean, a bit forward, don't you think?'

Daisy giggled. 'Lisa, your mind belongs in the gutter!'

'Got you to smile again though.' She shrugged. 'Maybe it's something of Hugh's. James mentioned before he had some old photos, didn't he?'

Daisy furrowed her brow. 'But he says "it's time I gave it to you". I mean that does not sound like a bunch of photos, does it?' She smiled. 'James was amazing throughout those last years with Hugh, not sure how I would have coped without him. All of you.'

'Well, let's get going then as there's only one way to find out. And Daisy?' Lisa slid her hand across the table, clasping her friend's. 'Listen, we're all here for you, however you want us to be. OK?'

Daisy smiled. Lisa stood and looked at her watch. 'I'll drive you back home then head onto work.'

Chapter 2

Daisy was grateful when they pulled off the M4 and away from the madness of Bristol. There had been a time when she loved nothing more than heading into the city with her friends or Hugh and soaking up the buzz of the cosmopolitan hubbub.

Now she couldn't cope with it. She wanted to scream at everyone that they were being too noisy, too energetic, too alive. The countryside was quieter, allowed her to think, enabled her to remember Hugh properly, although Lisa believed she needed to make new memories. As she had pointed out, she was just fine with the ones she had. It was all she had, and she didn't want to let go of them – but was it time?

Lisa drove quickly in her convertible, top down even though it really hadn't warmed up enough, towards Atworth where Daisy lived – had lived – with Hugh. Hugh had become an incredibly successful banker and bought an enormous manor house on the outskirts of the village. Daisy had never, growing up, imagined she would live and own such a glorious pile with its creamy sandstone walls, and ivy and wisteria creeping ever higher up to the tiled roof. The front garden alone was so picturesque it often took her breath away to this day, with its aged stone benches and cherub spouting water into the lake. It was actually just a big pond but Tom, her other best friend, said it was a lake. He was quite sure of it.

'A pond, Daisy darling, is the size of the paddling pool we had in our student house, yours could take a rowing boat. Catch my drift?' To which he fell about laughing at his own wit.

The back garden was sublime. Wild roses and an oak tree that Hugh adored. He would often sit for hours at a time on the weekends (he was rarely around in the week), reading his *Financial Times* and snoozing. He never knew but Daisy used to watch him and fall in love with him all over again. Hugh had worked so hard to buy the house and to keep her in a lifestyle that her own mother, a farmer's wife, had thought was too grand for the likes of her daughter.

'Well, Daisy, don't forget it's was me and your father putting our hands up sheep's asses that allowed you to go to university, you hear? Don't you ever forget your roots.' She had a strong Gloucestershire accent – you could almost smell the grass and taste the cheese when you listened to her.

They drove up to the house and Lisa turned the ignition off.

'I'm afraid I have to go and feed the red-trousered folk of Cirencester.' She pulled a face. 'So that should mean an evening of over the top laughter and women claiming the crudités are "so filling, darling, couldn't eat another morsel", and then the men will drink their whisky and talk golf and skiing.' She laughed. 'It's a joy.'

Daisy smiled. 'You know, I feel your luck is about to change.'

Lisa giggled. 'Why, have you found me some rich banker friend? Because if you have, I don't even care what he looks like.' She snorted. 'You know it's best to have sex in the dark anyway. You just imagine they're George Clooney, job done.'

Daisy grinned and got out of the car. 'You, Lisa Davidson, are my best friend and a gem.' She paused and indicated the length of Lisa's body. 'You have kept in such good shape and look great, Tom is probably one of the best-looking gay men on planet earth,

James is just,' she smiled, 'lovely… and I've… got a good sense of humour.'

'Good sense of humour?' Lisa shrieked with laughter. 'That's what fat people say when they're advertising themselves on dating sites.'

'Exactly.' Daisy winked. 'don't forget I'm bubbly too.'

Daisy was suddenly hit by the fact she hadn't said anything about Hugh. For a second, she felt quite breathless – maybe she was beginning to move on.

'And Hugh,' Daisy said quickly, looking up at the sky, 'is up there looking down at us.'

'Thinking, James is a dish, Lisa's still a complete loser, Tom is over the top, and I love Daisy.'

Daisy's eyes teared up. 'Oh God, get out of here before I cry again. My mother always told me not to make a scene and look, I now spend my life making scenes.'

'Bye, beautiful lady. I'll ring you tomorrow. Find out what James has up his sleeve.' Lisa started up the car and swung it around, speeding out the drive, a cloud of dust behind her.

It amazed Daisy to this day that Lisa was still single. She was gorgeous, fun and flirty. Wasn't that what men wanted? In fact, Daisy used to be like that herself but marrying Hugh so young meant she had felt comfortable early on. Even as she piled on the pounds, he loved her and she felt good for it. In fact, he would often encourage her love of baking. She was not good at it but he always politely and solemnly tried her day's bake. Lisa and Tom often tried it too.

Hugh's reaction would be, 'Darling, that is marvellous.'

Lisa and Tom, however, would be stood behind him pretending to put their fingers down their throats and then come up all smiles. 'Yes, *darling*, it is… words just can't describe it!' James would just give her that look, a look she had never been able to describe, and smile at her.

Hugh did over time learn to relax around her other university friends and it had felt like they belonged to a club. They would, especially in the last two years of Hugh's life, when he would have periods of being very tired, help each other prepare kitchen suppers and then dance and drink to whatever tunes were on the radio. It had been oddly perfect when she could forget about the future, about what would happen, about what did eventually happen over a year ago.

She reckoned *grieving* (she hated that term) would have been easier if they had had children but they didn't try for the longest time. They didn't want to break their happy bubble, however, she had always lived with a nagging feeling that they should have been trying for children. But then she had convinced herself that it was okay to be an older mum and what was the rush? Plenty of women were having children in their late thirties and early forties. Despite her doctor telling her she was *geriatric* when it came to having children, even three years ago.

'Jesus,' she had said to Dr Sawyers. 'I am not geriatric, I'm in my prime.'

Dr Sawyers nodded sagely, his plethoric face not looking up from his notes. 'You may be having the time of your life.' He paused. 'But your ovaries are not.'

With that, aged thirty-nine she told Hugh they had to go at it like rabbits. Admittedly some of the romance was taken out of the moment with statements like that but this was a matter of urgency; a time bomb no professional could disarm. She had to get pregnant.

Only, as if Sod had laid down his law, a month later Hugh found out he had terminal cancer. Suddenly she didn't want children, she just wanted to spend every moment she could with her husband. He would become so tired and immobile, that she couldn't bear to watch. They hugged and kissed like each day was their last together but children were soon swept from her mind. That wasn't to say she didn't wish she could keep a part of Hugh here, with her, but she was consumed with guilt about bringing children into the world under those circumstances.

Daisy was abruptly brought out of her reverie by the sound of another car coming up the drive and realised she hadn't actually moved since Lisa left.

James, in his Maserati, roared up to where she stood and hopped out. He walked quickly over to her and took her in a warm, comforting hug.

'Daisy, how you doing?' He eyed her bag. 'Been out shopping? That's good.'

She wanted to point out that she was still able to dress herself, eat and move. Hugh's death hadn't taken those facilities from her, but she knew, deep down, he was just being kind and she was being entirely unreasonable. She always wanted to look like a strong woman around James, when in fact, right now, she wished he would just hug her again.

'Yes,' she nodded. 'Lisa thought it was a good idea to go to the shopping mall in Bristol. She bought jeans which make her already stunning body look more… stunning.' Daisy smiled. 'I, on the other hand, was beached on the shore of Levi's Land and decided make-up was probably a better bet for someone like me. Oh, and wide trousers.'

He laughed, his kind eyes lighting up, but when Daisy's eyes fell to what looked like an envelope in his hand, he immediately stopped and grew seemingly tense.

'What did you want to give me, James?' She almost dared not to ask. 'Is it that envelope?'

She heard his breath catch. 'Yes.' He indicated to the house. 'Shall we go in? Only I think it's best if you're sitting down.'

She nodded in agreement, her heart quickening. They walked towards the solid oak front door. She opened her bag and found the key. Daisy didn't like to open the door when she had company; the dull ache she felt every time she realised Hugh wouldn't be there made her feel quite light-headed.

'Are you OK?'

She felt James's hand on her arm, warm and firm.

'Yes,' she murmured, a lump in her throat. 'I just find certain things a bit hard still.' She looked up at James who nodded and bit his lip; almost as if he was dreading showing her whatever was in that envelope. 'Let's go through to the kitchen, have a cup of tea.'

She felt happiest there and, at this time of year, she could see the snowdrops scattered across the lawn.

As she busied herself filling the kettle and placing it on the Aga, James sat and nervously handled the envelope.

'So anything new?' She knew it hadn't been easy for him either, losing both a best friend and colleague. 'Any girlfriend on the scene?' She always asked this, braced for him to one day confirm he was seeing someone. She could only describe the feeling as jealousy but why should she be jealous of James loving another woman? They were just friends…

'Nothing new.' James's face grew grim. 'I miss him at work, the whole place changed after Hugh's death. It's probably as it always has been but I can't even look at the water cooler without thinking about him. I know he wasn't there for quite big chunks of time towards the end anyway but just knowing that…' His voice trailed off. 'Well, I don't need to explain it to you.'

She turned and appraised James. He looked older, with deeper lines around his eyes, since Hugh's death, but he was still as rugged and gorgeous as ever. She and Hugh had always joked that he should have been a model and not hidden away in the world of banking.

'No,' Daisy agreed and put a mug of steaming tea in front of him. 'You have every right, though, to feel as cut up as I do. Anyone who knew Hugh does.' Daisy smiled tenderly at James. 'You know he had such a great effect on so many people's lives. And he could, also, be the most boring old fart on two legs.'

James barked out a laugh and then grew self-conscious as though he felt he shouldn't allow himself to be happy.

'Laugh, James, when you can. We are allowed to laugh.' Daisy had no idea when she had become such an expert but maybe she was beginning to come through some initial phase of grieving. She was paraphrasing the book she had been given by Tom: *Stop Crying and Pull Yourself Together*.

Tom had presented it with such a flourish she hadn't had the heart to tell him that the title was a bit harsh. That being said, she had actually read it and it had made her laugh aloud so, who knew, maybe it worked?

'In fact,' she continued, 'I was talking to Lisa today about... moving on.'

He raised his brows. 'Moving on? As in...'

'Yes, I don't want to spend the rest of my life by myself.'

'Hmm.' He nodded, sipping fast at his tea. He then pushed the envelope across to her.

'It's a letter.' He averted his eyes. 'If you say you're ready to move on, maybe I was right in thinking I should give it to you today...'

She nodded.

'From Hugh,' he went on.

Her heart skipped a beat and her mind went into overdrive. Had he been having an affair and now had countless children – the children they'd never had – with another woman or more? Had he decided to leave his money to someone else, was his will a joke?

She put a cool hand to her forehead and breathed deeply.

'Are you OK?' James asked, suddenly by her side. 'It's not actually bad, if that's what you're worried about. He just asked me to give it to you when maybe you felt a bit stronger.' He gave a small shake to his head, and pushed it at her again. 'Sorry, I'm making it sound awful. Just read it.'

Slowly, Daisy picked up the envelope, her hand visibly shaking, and with her forefinger, she sliced through the top. The sight of Hugh's handwriting even on the envelope was like a warm, comforting hug and she drew out a piece of manila paper, the very kind that Hugh had kept in a small pile on his desk. His neat and precise writing filled the page. She brought the letter up to her nose, hoping to smell him but there was nothing.

James excused himself, told her he would be by the oak tree when she wanted him. He took his mug and left her alone.

Chapter 3

My dearest Daisy,

Firstly I want to tell you I love you. You are my world, my rock, my life.

I have asked James to give you this letter when I hope the rawness has faded a bit. Even better, maybe you are bloody relieved to have got rid of the boring old sod! Hopefully you are having parties every night and living the life you want and deserve. Keep laughing, I adore the way your nose wrinkles when you laugh, I adore the way you sometimes laugh so hard, there isn't a sound! How is that possible?!

I am writing this in the present tense because I'm still here for you but that being said, I want you to have fun, live life to the full, and maybe, hopefully, find love again.

I only have one wish because really this was our wish. We dreamt and often talked about setting up a bed and breakfast at Atworth Manor. I know you're thinking you won't do it without me. You're stubborn like that. Try it though. For me? See what adventures it brings you. I have left you, as you will know by now, the house and everything that ever belonged to me. If you want to follow our dream, I am there with you every step of the way.

James knows about our dream and says he will help in any way he can. He wants to be there for you, to look out for you. Please let him, he's a good man.

Keep this letter and read it when you feel like you can't do something. You can, Daisy Ronaldson, you are the most amazing woman I've ever had the honour of knowing and I still can't believe you said 'yes' in Amsterdam.

Say 'yes' again, let's make our wish come true.

Love and kisses,

Hugh xxx

Daisy put down the letter, tears streaming down her cheeks, and tried to breathe through the onslaught of raw emotion threatening to drown her. James entered the room quietly and sat down next to her, taking her hand.

'Holy shit, James,' she said. 'There was never a right time to give me this, the silly sod.' She smiled through her tears. 'And I am not stubborn.'

She waited, the gasps of her fast breathing the only sound.

'James, have you read it?' He nodded. 'You see, the B&B was our dream. *Our* dream. It was after we watched that couple in France doing up that chateau. I remember we had had a couple of bottles of something Hugh had found in the cellar and we talked like we could do something like that here, in England.' She snorted with laughter, tears still pooling. 'But even though we often joked, if we were ever to have done it, it would have been *together*.' She looked up once more. 'Good lord, Hugh Ronaldson makes me angry. Why does he lay this idea at my feet and expect me to run with it? I don't do as I'm told.' James nodded his agreement with a wry smile on his face. 'I know, I know, I've never done what anyone's said. Well, there you go, I don't plan to start now.'

She looked at James through blurry tears. 'No offense but I

don't need you to look after me. I'll be just fine.' She circled the knots in the wooden farmhouse table with her finger. 'In fact, maybe, just maybe I'll move to France and meet some baker and eat croissants for the whole of my life and use that bit of French I vaguely learnt at university. I mean, as you know, James, I have five minutes on *Le Front National* down pat.' She giggled. 'Look, if those two off the telly box can manage, then so could I.'

She hung her head and let out a long shaky breath. He let her keep talking.

'Shit me, James, why did he do it? Why did he go and leave me? We were meant to be together forever. That was the deal. I even changed the words at our ceremony. *Until arguing over house furnishings do us part.* Remember?'

James laughed with affection and grabbed her hand, holding it up to his cheek.

'Do you also remember how appalled my mother was at our ceremony? She wanted to know why we had all this posh food, when we could have had her hog roaster for free…'

Daisy smiled, brushed more tears from her cheeks, and rose from her chair, her legs unsteady beneath her. She had not been expecting that. The grief suddenly felt so fresh and acute, the breath knocked from her lungs.

'Do you know I sometimes talk to the ceiling?' She smiled, wiped her nose with a sheet of paper towel. 'Because I let myself believe he can hear me.'

James smiled kindly. 'I've done that too.'

'Well, we're as barmy as each other.' She drew a deep breath. 'Listen, James, this all feels quite odd actually.' She held up the letter. 'You see, many years ago Hugh and I watched this programme…'

'I know.' He nodded. 'The couple in the French chateau. I saw it, Hugh told me you had been quite serious about this dream.'

'He was very serious but I always thought it was a crazy idea.'

In her head, it had been more of a fantasy in which she would have never-ending guests who sipped G&Ts on the veranda and admired her peonies. She would, of course, wear a floppy hat and have a smudge of dirt from gardening on her left cheek as she greeted her regulars who would claim that the house was *'looking more and more beautiful year on year and how did she stay looking so young too?'*

Anyway, now Hugh wasn't here, why would she even think about it? More to the point, why would she set up the B&B with James? She loved James dearly but this was such a huge commitment.

James cleared his throat. 'Listen, he had just found out about the Big C so told me about this dream. I think he had started to think about you and how you would cope afterwards.'

Daisy lifted her head, and a familiar irritation at Hugh's needing to control everything, even from the grave, flooded her body.

'What? How I would cope? I am coping just fine, thank you. Good Lord. Why are men like that? Why do men feel they can just *solve* everything? So he thought he would get me to set up a B&B with you in order to get over my grief?' She gave a sharp shake to her head. 'God, a mathematician to the end.' She gestured wildly with the letter. 'I mean, don't get me wrong, I'm grateful to both you and Hugh for surmising that a sodding bed and breakfast would be a good idea but the thought, now, of anyone in my home is an abhorrent one, so the answer is no.

'Anyway,' she continued, 'don't you have a job to get on with? You have, after all, just been promoted, haven't you?'

His face flinched with hurt and he looked at the ground before looking back at her.

'Sorry,' she said. 'I'm not annoyed with you, more annoyed with Hugh. He knows I'm the sort of person who feels so guilty if someone asks me to do something. What about your job in London?' she pressed.

A small smile appeared at the corner of James's lips; he tried to hide it. 'I quit a week or so ago, I didn't enjoy it anymore anyway.' He looked again at her face set in a defiant pose. 'I'm actually not sure why I'm laughing but it is quite funny, but you look so lovely when you're angry.'

'That is not even funny.' But then, she, too, felt a small bubble of laughter and she giggled. Once she started to giggle, James snorted as he tried to hold back his chuckling and then they started to laugh uncontrollably. James leant his hand against the wall as his broad frame convulsed with laughter.

Daisy wiped away the tears and realised how good it felt to let go like that.

Once they had both caught their breath, James smiled, resting his hand assuredly on her arm. 'I didn't quit my job because of this letter; I quit because I couldn't bear working where Hugh had once been, the office wasn't the same. You know?'

'Yes,' she said, calm now. 'I know. I live in this house every day, remember?'

He nodded, his voice quiet. 'I think that's what Hugh was worried about, he thought you would stay here and perhaps feel you had to because it had been your home together. Then we agreed that there was no way you would ever consider selling it, so the next best option is to change it, invite people in.'

Daisy furrowed her brows. 'You're doing it again.'

'What?' Confusion crossed his face.

'Being a man. Trying to solve it.' She looked around her. 'I love this house because it's *my home*. I don't need to invite strangers into it.' She dipped her head. 'Actually, if anything, I think I would resent that.'

James nodded. 'Well, you know what's best and you're probably right but if you did want to try and you needed someone to look after the office side…' He stuck his hands in the air. 'I'm your man.'

'Otherwise, what? You find another job in the city?'

He shook his head. 'No, I thought I'd try moving.'

'What? Out of London?'

'No.' He smiled. 'Further afield. Australia. There are some great opportunities there at the moment and it would just mean properly getting away, starting again.'

Daisy's heart skipped a beat. 'Oh, I see.' She was, for once, speechless. She knew he was right to want to move on but another country? Though why should it bother her? James was just a friend. Friends did that; they got on with their lives.

She stared hard at the ground, contemplative. Maybe it was because it felt like everyone else was moving on and she was stuck. Stuck in the thick quagmire of grief and memories that threatened to drown her. She couldn't, however, stop other people from saving themselves.

'Oh, that sounds wonderful,' she said but she could hear the forced appreciation in her own voice.

'You don't sound that happy about it.' James searched her face. 'Sorry, it's not that I'm abandoning ship, it's just… you know.'

'No, absolutely.'

Suddenly, there was the rumble of a car coming up the drive. She didn't need to turn around to know it was Tom. The giveaway was the faulty exhaust pipe; it sounded like a Boeing 747 coming into land.

'Hello darling Daisy,' came a booming voice behind her and shortly the doorway was filled with the tall and athletic frame of Tom, wearing bright pink chino shorts and a Hawaiian shirt.

'Oh my, Daisy.' He air-kissed her cheeks then looked at James, grinning broadly. 'If only I had known that James was here. I'd have put on my very special—' he elongated this word '—cologne. This one is so understated and I hate to be understated.'

James, ever the gentleman, held out his hand. 'Good to see you again, Tom.'

Tom clung to his hand like ivy to a wall. Daisy eventually had to tell him to let go.

'Oh sorry, darling Daisy, it's just this man has left me hanging since university days.'

That was the thing about Tom: not a shy, retiring bone in his body.

'Why are you dressed up for some sort of New Orleans street party?' she asked, eyeing his loud and proud outfit.

'Well, darling, I've decided I'm not getting any…' Once again, his eyes walked the length of James's body who Daisy noticed flushed ever so slightly. It had taken her twenty years to not flinch at some of his statements. 'So,' he continued, 'I think it's because I've been wearing drab, wintry, but ever so chic, clothes. Now is the time to break free and show people my spring and summer wardrobe.'

Daisy giggled. 'How's it working out for you?'

'Well, so far, some builders asked me when the parade started…' Tom mused, grinning. 'Anyway, more to the point, Lisa sent me.'

Daisy narrowed her eyes. 'Oh, she did, did she?'

'Yeah, she said you had big news and I was to find out what the big news was…' He waited expectantly, like a puppy.

'There is no news,' Daisy interrupted quickly. 'None.'

'No, no news,' James agreed, catching her grateful smile.

Tom put his hand on his hip. 'OK, not being funny. You two are so up to something.' He grabbed the piece of paper from Daisy's hand and turned his back on Daisy who madly tried to scramble it away from him.

'Tom, give it back to Daisy, come on,' James said, like an ever-patient schoolmaster.

Eventually, Tom turned back to them both and beamed. 'This is wonderful. This is so wonderful.'

Daisy wrenched the letter from his grasp and held it to her chest. 'It's not happening.'

Tom wasn't listening; he was already on his phone.

'Lisa?' He smiled at his audience and Daisy just stared on in horror. 'Daisy is going to set up a bed and breakfast at the house.' Daisy could hear a muffled voice on the other end of the receiver and she went to grab the phone.

'It's not true,' she managed to say quickly before Tom had it back off her.

'Yeah, *and* James is going to help her which means he's going to live at the house. *How* good is that?' He indicated his outfit. 'I knew, when I put this on, something special was going to happen today.' He touched Daisy's arm tenderly, phone still pressed to his ear and then with a nod of his head to James, he said, 'Come on guys, group hug. I'll put you on speakerphone, Lisa. We are more than happy to help out, aren't we, Lisa? We'll be doing it in the name of Hugh.'

Daisy quickly found herself ensconced in a mass of male limbs, quickly noting that James wasn't refusing and putting Tom right. No, he was *fully* involved in the group hug.

'Um, guys…' She disentangled an arm and waved her hand around like a white flag. 'Um, I actually said no, I wasn't going to do it.'

James and Tom moved in closer and she was well and truly trapped in a sandwich of testosterone, hairy chests and Tom's sickening cologne. God, she couldn't imagine what the other cologne – the special one – was like; she would have needed a gas mask.

'Um, James, didn't we just agree that we're not doing this crazy idea and you're heading to Australia?' Her voice sounded small as they still refused to let go and she remained trapped.

'Shouldn't we at least try, Daisy? Isn't it what Hugh would have wanted?' Tom said.

'Exactly,' Daisy heard Lisa say.

'Um, actually if anyone's doing it, it's me and James.'

'Nah, you need all hands on deck,' Lisa said and Tom murmured his agreement. 'I mean who's going to change beds and cook eggs.'

'I'm not sure I want everyone here all the time *plus* guests.' Daisy was growing ever hotter. 'Can I get out of this hug? I mean this is craziness.'

'No,' Tom said. 'Darling, you are staying there until you agree. At least give it a go, then we can always stop if it turns out badly and James—' he delivered a fake sob '—could then go and tan his beautiful body on an Australian beach and discover he was gay, after all, but can't afford the return journey home so he will never have me in his life…' He stopped, genuinely caught up in his own fairy tale. James shifted uncomfortably.

'And Lisa and I could go back to waitressing in the bistro, talking to the tweed brigade. And you, you could continue to do it is whatever you do.'

Silence descended on the huddle, Lisa included, and Daisy realised that, unbelievably, he was right. What did she have going on? She didn't have children, she barely spoke to her mother and she didn't work. Maybe Hugh had been offering her a lifeline, and maybe, annoyingly, the boring old sod was right.

No one had spoken since the end of Tom's presidential speech; they were waiting on her.

She clutched the letter and held it to her lips. 'Categorically no.'

Tom huffed. 'Lisa and I will cook you guys dinner. I'm going to pick her up now anyway and let's see if we can't persuade you this evening.' Tom gripped his phone. He hadn't stopped smiling. 'There is *so* much to talk about.'

Daisy felt uneasy as she watched Tom head back to his car. James, sensing this, squeezed her shoulder.

'You OK?'

She nodded, forcing herself to smile.

He nodded and walked outside, leaving her alone in the hall as she caught sight of a silver-framed picture of herself, Hugh and James taken at an outdoor concert three years ago. Hugh and James hugged her close. Maybe that was why she hadn't entirely written off the B&B idea in her head: James was the closest she could be to Hugh. The thought of him on the other side of the world had made her feel panicky, unsure. She couldn't let go of any more of Hugh. Not yet.

Chapter 4

Daisy looked at each of them in turn over the rim of her glass and inhaled her wine. Tom had gone to town over supper. He had remembered that the B&B idea stemmed from a reality show set in France and so red, white and blue bunting fluttered across the ceiling, the table was laden with salami and casserole and some sort of terrine with *actual* animal hair poking out of it (rustic she had been told), beset on top of a paper red gingham tablecloth and, of course, there were carafes of red wine. It looked glorious and simply perfect. Her eyes flitted towards the ceiling and she was glad Hugh (who, to her mind, was now a permanent fixture of the ceiling or sky) could feel a part of it with the bunting. She discreetly held her glass up to him.

'Salut, dear Hugh,' she thought and fearing another onslaught of tears, said, 'Gosh, it must be hot in here,' and offered her glass to Tom for a refill. 'Fill her up, please.'

She was trying to get drunk because she could see where the conversation was going; they wanted her to set up the B&B. But, she thought, what about her quiet, controlled world where she just about *coped*: what would happen to that? The thought alone of losing the tranquillity was awful and she snorted inadvertently into her glass, wine escaping in all directions.

James eyed her kindly. 'You OK?' he whispered from stage left, his voice barely perceptible above Tom's booming laugh, and his hand briefly touched her own. 'You know, it is *your* house, you can always say no.'

However, she might have known that nothing got past her friends and Tom stopped talking as both he and Lisa turned to her.

'Oh, come on, obviously it's your decision, but we're sure you can do it. Of all people!' Lisa pouted. 'I can help out and quit my job, and Tom can quit his. There's a reason they call us casual labour.'

'I know but it's so rash, so sudden…' Daisy's voice trailed off.

She studied Tom's hazel eyes dancing with happiness, Lisa, who was positively glowing, and finally James, who had somehow in the last few hours lost some of the grey pallor that comes from months of heartache. Why couldn't she be so positive?

'I'm not saying no as such,' she said quietly. 'I'm just scared.'

'Listen.' Tom stood up, cleared his throat and pushed his chair backwards causing it to scrape loudly over the flagstones. 'I'd like to propose a toast to Daisy for being such a gem and, I know she doesn't feel it right now, but we only want what's best for you.' He looked at her. 'This could be the making of you, of us.' He puffed his chest out in an almost Napoleonic fashion and started to sing, quietly at first. Daisy could see his mind whirring as he adapted the lyrics and it took her only moments to figure out the song, her finger already tapping out the drumbeat.

'*Do you hear your friends sing? Singing the songs of… Atworth Manor?*' Then his smile grew wider as the next line fit into place. '*It is the music of the Daisy crew who will laugh and smile again!*'

Daisy grinned. They all knew *Les Miserables* was her favourite musical and Hugh had taken them all, everyone sat at her table tonight, to see it at the Bristol Hippodrome the Christmas before last, a month before Hugh died.

'*When the beating of your heart, echoes the beating of the manor, there is a life about to start!'* He lifted his hands. 'Come on! Again!' He ripped his second Hawaiian shirt of the day (this one even louder with a giant palm tree enveloping his back) open, shooting James a look of 'look at me, I'm a god' and held his wine glass way up high, the liquid sloshing over the side. 'Let's do it again, people, and let out your inner campness!'

Lisa stood, her hand struck across her chest, followed by James and then Daisy, giggling, also rose to her feet. They swayed in time repeating each line Tom boomed at them as if they were in fact revolutionaries. Daisy's giggles manifested itself in side-splitting laughter and within minutes she was swaying and drinking along. Daisy realised, for the first time in months, maybe years, she felt lighter and somehow different.

After a few minutes, Tom collapsed in a chair. 'Christ almighty, I'm out of practice.' He wiped the sheen of sweat from his forehead. 'But, you see compadres, we will win this. We will win back laughter!'

James did laugh. 'You've got a very good voice.'

Tom looked at him. 'Some say good voice when they mean fine body.'

Daisy punched Tom playfully on the arm. 'No, I think he actually meant your voice.'

'Daisy, darling, you read things so literally.'

Lisa poured out more generous glasses of wine. 'It'll be like being back at uni.'

'But no Hugh,' Daisy whispered.

James shifted next to her. She realised she must stop doing that: making others feel uncomfortable, like they were unwanted replacements. James was very much wanted and she glanced at him and smiled. 'I'm glad you're here.'

Daisy felt eyes on her and looked up sharply. Lisa winked, and she flushed, guilt washing over her. Then seconds later, Tom was pushing catalogues on her.

'What are these for?'

'I picked them up earlier when I was in Cirencester.'

Daisy eyed them gingerly, not liking where this was going. 'And…?'

'And I think some of your rooms need a bit of a spruce up if we're going to have guests staying.' Tom drank deeply from his glass.

'No, I haven't said yes yet.' She stood, her heart fluttering. 'This is my house, this is the house I did up with Hugh, I'm not just going to *redecorate* and erase all that.' She saw James nod briefly out the corner of her eye, perhaps even gesture to Tom to take it easy.

'Daisy, darling, I am not trying to upset you. It's just an idea. I know how much you love interior décor.'

She knew he was right: ten of the sixteen rooms remained starkly furnished, as they simply hadn't got around to doing them. Perhaps, in her heart, she hadn't thrown herself into the house over the last couple of years because she knew she would end up living alone in the depths of its corridors and shuttered windows. Shutters she had closed the day Hugh had been diagnosed. She had wanted to shut the world out: just Daisy and Hugh. It was safer that way. Only now she was being forced to confront those dark crevices and she wasn't sure she could do it.

'Listen,' Lisa said, more gently now, 'Dais, if you want to go ahead, how about you choose what you would like. You have the best taste after all.' Daisy gave a small smile at this compliment because she knew it to be true but also she had seen the state of Tom and Lisa's rented accommodation.

'Are you trying to tell me, Lisa, that after all these years you haven't come to love the leopard print, velveteen cushions and the life-size framed photo of *The Nude Man*?' Tom grinned broadly. 'I even bought you zebra print under sheets for your birthday, you ungrateful cow.'

Daisy snorted with laughter and she looked at James who sat there wide-eyed.

'Is that all true?' he asked Daisy.

She nodded. 'Yes, all true. Every single word. But, most importantly, Tom has forgotten to tell you about his love of an artist who paints... um, man parts.'

'Lucky you!' James furrowed his brow. 'Man parts, huh?'

Daisy laughed, her mind returning to the idea of the B&B. It was true, she did love a project and if it involved anything to do with interior décor and was moving in the direction of being the next Kelly Hoppen... maybe this was what she needed, otherwise, as Tom so often bluntly pointed out, what else did she have?

'OK, just say I was to say yes...' Lisa squealed and Daisy smiled. 'I get to choose the décor and there's one rule: no one goes into Hugh's office or our bedroom.'

They nodded solemnly.

'That's the one place I can be with Hugh, it means the world to me.' Her eyes glassed over. 'OK? It really would mean so much to me if I can trust you to stay out of his office.'

The gathering nodded in unison.

'In which case...' She grinned broadly. 'OK, what have we got to lose?' She frowned as everyone jumped up to hug her. 'Well, probably a lot but it is exciting.'

'First thing tomorrow morning before Mum comes for lunch I will go into Cirencester and start ordering furniture and curtain material.' She paused. 'Then I can tell her our plans.' Daisy visibly flinched. 'That's going to be a treat.'

James looked confused. 'I thought she loved Hugh.'

Daisy nodded. 'Don't you remember me telling you? Hugh wasn't the problem. Mum never agreed with me marrying Hugh. She said that I'd grow too big for my boots living in a house like this. I was a farmer's daughter and farmers' daughters don't marry men like Hugh.' She grimaced. 'To this day I can't tell if it's because she genuinely believes that or almost doesn't want me to be happy.' Daisy shrugged. 'Who knows? She's a complicated thing, dear Mum. Anyway, here's to Atworth Manor and our plans.' Daisy clinked everyone's glasses in turn and looked at the ceiling.

'I hope you're happy, Hugh, you silly sod,' she whispered.

The next morning, nursing a boisterous hangover in which it felt as if the drums behind Tom's song were still going strong, she geared herself up to face her demons: the tour of her own house. Tom and Lisa who had already claimed their rooms at the top of the house, where they always stayed anyway when nights socialising rolled into morning, had returned to their flat to officially hand in their notice; the landlord wouldn't care. He had wanted rid of Tom and his leopard print many moons ago. She had met the landlord once; a gentleman dressed head to toe in tweed, even his brogues possessed tweed fabric inserts, and the owner of the most horrid Jack Russell on planet Earth.

'Nigel.' He had proffered a limp handshake. 'Oh, you're another friend of Tom's, are you?' he had said, his voice so far back, it was probably being wired over from a previous era. 'Well, any friend of Tom's is no friend of mine.'

'Charmed, I'm sure,' she had said, resisting the urge to slap him across the face.

His mangy mutt stood at his owner's feet, baring his teeth and looking like he wanted to eat Daisy for his breakfast.

'Gosh,' she said. 'Don't you and…' She indicated the dog.

'Bitsy.'

'Ah.' She forced a smile and looked him the eye. 'Don't you and Bitsy look so alike.'

Nigel nodded and then pulled a face. 'Yah, I suppose we do.'

Her phone buzzed in her pocket: James. He too was already halfway to London, apparently to collect more belongings. He had been very happy to stay on the sofa last night until rooms were sorted. Daisy had already decided he could have the one next to hers. It would make her feel safe knowing he was near.

He was to keep his apartment back in London; he owned it outright and Daisy was grateful. That was one less person to entirely financially support. She loved Tom and Lisa to bits – they were as much family to her as her own had ever been – but to think they would quit their jobs, albeit jobs in a restaurant and bar, and now they were giving up their shared home too. It didn't bear thinking about and she had to remind herself that if it didn't work out, which she suspected it might not, they could all go back to how they were. She was sure the restaurant would want them back. On the other hand, she was positive the landlord wouldn't want them back polluting his Cirencester house but there were *other* rented houses out there. She nodded; yes, they were grown-ups and really, they could make their own decisions.

Her phone beeped again. Tom.

'Daisy, darling, have dropped credit card down the outside drain trying to break into house. Could be longer than expected.'

They still only had one key between them, she realised, and shook her head in disbelief.

'Don't worry, taking tour of my own house. Scared.'

Moments later: 'Don't be scared. We love you.'

She smiled and felt a surge of strength. Now, standing at the top of the stairs, she bypassed her and Hugh's bedroom and walked to the first unused bedroom. She drew a deep breath and pushed the door open. It squeaked loudly on its hinges and a rush of stale air hit her square on. Tiptoeing, as if not to disturb its dormancy, she made her way to the window and pulled open the internal shutters letting the light flood in. She turned and looked back at the room, her eyes immediately stopping at the fireplace. How they had argued over that fireplace! The thought sent a shock of pain through her and her breath caught.

'I think we should rip it out,' Hugh had said adamantly. 'I mean, it's not functional.'

'No!' She crossed her arms. 'We are *not* ripping it out, that would be like ripping out someone's heart. It is part of the fabric of this house. We just clean it up and it becomes a feature.' She had closed her eyes, wishing that Hugh had some sort of mind that didn't involve maths. He would not be subtracting this one from the room, not whilst she lived in the house.

Then she had felt a kiss, ever so gentle, on her nose. 'You funny thing. If it means that much to you, we keep it. You know best, after all…'

Daisy returned to the present, her eyes smarting with these fresh memories. She supposed that would keep happening. The remembering stuff.

The question now was could she do this? Was she strong enough? Maybe Tom, Lisa and James were wrong; maybe she was herein meant to be a sombre widow who would grow old in the quiet pattern of the life she had adopted since Hugh's death. But then, a movement at the window caught her eye. It was Mr Robin: a gardener's best friend and, to her mind, Hugh's best friend. As Hugh gardened, no matter the time of year, Mr Robin would appear. She felt for the latch on the window and gently pushed it open. Mr Robin stayed put.

'What do you think, Mr Robin? Can I do this?'

As if to answer he bobbed closer and to her utter amazement, he entered the room and sat delicately on the wrought iron radiator. He cocked his head and even when she put his hand closer, he didn't move. Then, moments later, he moved back out onto the windowsill.

'Extraordinary,' she muttered. 'Maybe you're Hugh?'

With that, she felt once again lifted, and a bit like peeling a plaster off, she moved quickly from room to room, opening the shutters both inside and outside, letting the light flood once more into Atworth Manor. With each window she opened, the robin flew nearby and she grew almost exhilarated at how liberating the whole process was. Dust clouds danced through the air with her quick and determined movement and with each window she opened, the spring air outside appeared to smell sweeter and fresher.

When she had opened up every single room in the house, she took the catalogues Tom had given her and a pen and made notes on each room and the feel she wanted. Atworth Manor, she realised, was turning into a very calm and beautiful French chateau as she chose white, pale grey and dusky pink linens, white metal frame bedsteads and, she sighed happily, she would put flowers everywhere. Flowers in every room. People would arrive and feel *alive*. She wanted that. She needed that. Who knew, maybe other widows would arrive and they too could benefit from the energy?

Just as she had written the last item down to be ordered and wiped her brow at her morning's efforts, she heard the familiar clunkety-clunk of her mother's Land Rover (the kind, Daisy thought, that proper farmers kept with no heating, appalling steering and barely a roof). She looked out of the windows on the final floor's landing and yes, it was as she had thought; Jenny, her mother, dressed in wellies and overalls, just come from her own morning of hard work.

Daisy moved quickly down the flights of stairs and arrived at the bottom as her mother knocked, somewhat aggressively, on the heavy front door.

Daisy clutched the catalogues and notes to her chest like a comfort blanket and pulled open the door with her free hand.

'Mum,' she breathed. 'So good to see you.' She went in for a hug but when her mother didn't reciprocate, she pulled away quickly.

'Not sure why we couldn't have met down Hilda's Coffee Shop on the edge of town or, even better, your old family home?'

'I thought you might like me to make you lunch here.' Daisy pulled the door further open and nodded for her to come inside.

'Well, Daisy, you know full well neither you or me belong in houses like this.' She had never lost her broad Gloucestershire accent even with the influx of 'yuppies', as Jenny called them, to the area. Though Daisy was glad of it because on the odd occasion when her mother was in a softer mood, it sounded glorious to her ear and reminded her of days out in the fields together tending to the animals or, on the rare day off, her mother making a huge picnic for them all, including her father who was still alive then.

Daisy often tried to recall when her mother had become quite so bitter; she reckoned it must have been after her father died. He had a heart attack one day, out on the farm, and that was it. So sudden. He had been fine that morning eating his two rashers of bacon and two poached eggs with a wedge of buttered toast. In fact, she often thought guiltily, how at aged sixteen as she was becoming highly aware of her body she had ribbed her father over his diet and how, if he wasn't careful, it could be the end of him. Then, one morning, the man she adored with his laughter lines and rough, calloused hands just dropped down dead.

Daisy and her mother were both widows, only in Daisy's case, her husband died over the course of a few years. She had never been able to figure out which way out was best. Maybe it didn't matter; both left gaping holes in lives.

She realised her mother was still stood in the hall and so she herself had to move towards the kitchen, otherwise they might be there all day.

'I've got soup I made a few days ago, your favourite? Tomato. And some bread I put in the bread-maker this morning. Does that sound OK?' Daisy looked at her mother who was eyeing up the antique French kitchen dresser and the granite work surfaces. She didn't even need to ask what she was thinking. Granite was for posh people, apparently. What was wrong with a bit of Formica?

'Sounds fine,' her mother eventually answered, sitting awkwardly on the edge of the carver chair.

'Great, perfect,' Daisy remarked through gritted teeth. As she set to heating up the soup and slicing the bread, she wondered how she was going to tell her mother about their hare-brained idea.

She needn't have worried.

Her mother's beady eyes had already clocked the catalogues and list on the table.

'Tell me you're not redecorating? You know, you might be quite well off but Hugh's money isn't going to last forever.' She paused. 'Life is expensive when you're relying on yourself.'

Daisy continued stirring the soup, turning ever so slightly from the range.

'Actually—' she forced a smile '—you won't believe this…' Her mother flinched as if Daisy were about to inflict pain upon her. She had spent her life relaying her plans and goals with the utmost of care, never expecting a warm reception. Especially after the death of her father, he had been her go-between. 'So I'm opening a B&B with Tom, Lisa and James.' She turned quickly back to the soup.

The silence lay heavy and ominous.

'Well, I suppose it would do you good. Ground you.'

Daisy took that as a seal of her approval.

'Actually, it was an idea Hugh and I had years ago but not here, not in this house.'

'Where then?'

Daisy poured the soup into the bowls and placed her finest bone china soup dish in front of her mother. Her mother's arched brow told her that she would have been happier with Tesco's own.

'France.' Daisy sat down, busied herself with cutting more bread needlessly.

'Well, that really would have been a stupid idea. You in France? We all know how well French went for you at university.'

Daisy pushed down the lump in her throat. 'Actually, I had been relearning and I'm almost fluent,' she lied, pushing the far too hot soup into her mouth. Anything to avoid talking about it any further.

'I'm amazed,' her mother started after taking a mouthful of soup, giving an almost imperceptible nod of approval, 'that James would want to stay here. I mean James is obviously from a house like this so that bit doesn't surprise me but to stay here with the likes of you and your friends. It doesn't make sense.'

Daisy lifted her chin defiantly. 'What does that mean? "The likes of you"? I may not have been born into a house like this but it doesn't mean I can't live in one.'

'Oh, Daisy, don't be silly. I've told you all along you should have stayed with me on the farm. I needed your help and you insisted on going to university, which, frankly, was a total waste of time and money because then you married above your station. You just tried to make me look bad.'

Daisy buttered her bread, pushing the knife this way and that with such force she thought she might break the knife. 'You'll never be any different. I don't know what happened, Mum, but when Dad died you changed and you pushed me away.' She pouted. 'Anyway, maybe I can make a success of this. Imagine that. Imagine your own daughter actually running a successful business.'

'Well, we'll see about that.' Her mother spooned the last of her soup into her mouth and stood. 'Thank you, I think I'd better get back to the lambs that have arrived early.'

'Oh, have they?' Daisy's prickly mood softened. She had adored lambing, watching new life enter the world. 'Do you want me to come over? Help?'

'No,' her mother said stiffly. 'You stay here and look up cushions. Much more important.'

With that, her mother bustled from the kitchen, her wellies leaving a trail of mud to the front door, and got into her jeep, roaring off down the drive.

Daisy continued to sit, almost numb from the visit, except for one thing. Her mother had left a burning desire somewhere deep in the pit of her stomach, a desire to make the business not only work but be a raving success.

Chapter 5

Daisy's mood had entirely shifted in a twenty-four hour period. This time yesterday she had felt as if the plans for the B&B were at best, mad, at worst, catastrophic. But something had changed. She had sensed it even in the sunrise this morning. It had appeared brighter, more hopeful.

She rose early and made everybody breakfast. Well, she said everybody: Tom and Lisa. James hadn't returned last night as he had promised. He had texted her saying he had some unfinished business. Daisy felt momentarily panicky at this news. But why should she? He was his own man. Maybe it was because James had given her the letter, set this whole ball rolling, that she felt he needed to be there every step of the way. When her more rational self took over, she knew that of course he had unfinished business: he had just quit his job, he had an apartment in London to close up for a while, he had… a girlfriend? The thought jolted her. She shook off the self-righteous feeling of ownership and they had a quiet breakfast of omelettes, hangovers still very much present.

However, over the next two weeks, and with each passing day, she felt fresh and raring to go. She had phoned Laura Ashley and other interior shops in Cirencester asking them to deliver. In fact, on the final morning of deliveries, she was just about to call up to Tom and Lisa with the bell in the kitchen, when she heard the beeping of a lorry reversing.

Tom and Lisa ambled down the stairs, clearly woken rudely by the sound of deliveries and sat heavily at the table. Daisy looked at them with affection, it was as if they were still at university. The only giveaway was Tom's peppered hair, Lisa's accentuated laughter lines and in her case… well, just about everything had gone south. Her friends with children often talked about how it all went 'pear-shaped' after having children. She hadn't needed sproglets for nature to take its course.

Daisy had dealt with the various deliveries that had appeared in the last forty-eight hours and had used the barn at the back as a storage area. She imagined the neighbour, a very sullen man in his eighties who had never taken a liking to her or Hugh, would imagine she was having some sort of post-Hugh crisis, spending all his money wildly in an attempt to fill the void in her life.

When she had signed on the last dotted line and the barn looked like a warehouse, she walked to the kitchen, her cheeks flushed with the excitement and anticipation, in order to find Tom and Lisa.

'Gosh, I hope you two like my choices!' She poured herself a glass of orange juice, barely noticing the silence. When she had drained the glass, she eventually looked at her friends. 'Guys?'

They were staring at her, smiling broadly.

'You look positively radiant, darling,' Tom gushed. 'Goodness.'

'She does, she really does,' Lisa agreed and took Daisy in a big bear hug before standing back once more.

Daisy smile immediately faded. 'Maybe I shouldn't be so… you know, I mean maybe it's not respectful…'

Tom placed his hands firmly on her shoulders and looked her squarely in her eyes. 'Whose idea was this?'

'Hugh's,' she mumbled, pushing down the panic and sadness in her heart. 'He wanted me to do it.'

Tom nodded. 'Exactly. He wanted you to do it and he wanted you to be happy. I imagine he's looking down on us now.'

Daisy nodded; she knew so too. He was looking down, peering over his ridiculously expensive specs, and smiling.

'Yes, you're right.' Daisy nodded again and then indicated outside. 'Come and see?'

She was hesitant. It felt as if she was baring her all showing her friends her ideas for the rooms. They walked to the barn and she opened box after box, explaining the various French toile curtains, the linen sheets, the white bed frames. Eventually she came up for air and waited for their reaction.

'Well…' Tom said, his voice brimming with concern.

'What?' Daisy stood more upright, her heart fluttering. Why had she ever thought she could choose the right furnishings for Atworth Manor?

Tom grinned. 'I can see you've decided to dodge leopard and zebra print which might be your downfall…'

Lisa snorted. 'It's bloody beautiful, Daisy. Bloody classy.'

'Yeah, it really is.' Tom pulled Daisy in for a congratulatory hug. 'You have so many hidden talents, you beautiful woman. Hugh would be so proud. Hugh *is* so proud.'

Daisy felt her heart lift.

'Good thing you got it sorted so soon because—' Tom winked '—I took it on myself to sign up Atworth Manor with some exclusive agents throughout the country and Europe as James said it was worth paying a premium so…'

Daisy stared, wide-eyed.

'We are officially a boutique B&B with 5 stars.'

'What?' Daisy screeched.

Lisa joined in now. 'Yeah, you pay quite a lot of them for the ranking so…'

'What?' she screeched again, realising she sounded demented but she felt as if she was being hit from all sides.

'And,' Tom said gleefully, 'we have our first guests arriving in…' He looked at his watch. 'Three days and five hours.'

'Holy…' Daisy's voice was shrill. 'What on earth were you two thinking? We have to make plans, set things up, think about the accounts.' She was struck by something else. 'None of us have ever done this before and you've already got people coming! I haven't even got sodding eggs!'

'Well, lucky for you,' Tom said gallantly, 'I have got a few of my friends, beautiful muscles, beautiful physiques, Gloucestershire's finest if you know what I mean, to set up all the furniture, Lisa will make beds as we go and you, dear Daisy, are off to the mecca of Bed and Breakfast Land…'

She waited, expectant. Daring not to breathe.

'Waitrose!' he announced.

'What are their names? Are they from the UK?' she asked. Maybe, she thought, if they came from Iceland they might want salmon, if they came from Japan they might need sake. OK, she agreed with herself, maybe too much for breakfast but she needed to offer them a night cap. She'd been to some fabulous bed and breakfasts throughout the country with Hugh and the service never stopped at just a bed and a breakfast. In fact, she remembered Hugh getting pissed on whisky at an honesty bar in Scotland, but forgetting to pay. It was added to his bill; he had been necking a one-thousand-pound bottle of vintage whisky.

'Relax, Dais,' Tom said smoothly. 'Just do what clearly comes so naturally to you.'

'But I haven't even been into a supermarket since Hugh died,' she realised aloud. 'I've been getting them to deliver. I mean, I don't know who I'll meet and I can't bear the looks of sympathy and pity.'

'Well, time to face the music, Daisy darling, and get that fridge full!'

Just as she was about to protest, a minibus pulled up the drive, a dust cloud in its wake. The bus was pink with a leopard print strip around its centre.

'What on earth?' she breathed. 'Is this our guests?'

'No,' Tom announced happily, waving enthusiastically at the bus, undoing one more button on his shirt. 'This, ladies, is heaven.'

Out of the bus, one after another, stepped six drop-dead gorgeous men: all chiselled, all with impeccable physiques and…

'The tightest shorts I've ever seen,' Daisy whispered aloud.

'Yes, here is my dream crew ready to build your furniture and dress your house. Dave set this company up a couple of years ago when a woman he does DIY for said she wished there were more like him; men who are good with their hands and who women feel safe around.'

Daisy looked at Lisa who she expected was having a similar surreal experience herself but, in actual fact, Lisa had started to trot down the drive, greeting each and everyone by name.

'Dave, hi!' Lisa chirped. 'Gary, how's the knee? Didn't they tell you not to slide down the pole like that…'

Daisy smiled at the team as they approached and went to shake their hands. They all shook her hand in turn and Dave, the leader, gave her the lowdown as if she were the queen.

'I introduce to you, the Dream Team.'

'You are very welcome,' Daisy said, smiling. 'So very welcome!'

Daisy spotted James's car pulling up – he had been opening a business bank account in Cirencester – and she suppressed her laugh: now this she wanted to see.

James parked his car and got out, making his way towards the crowd now standing outside Atworth.

'James!' Tom shouted, the excitement evident in his voice. 'This is James, the guy I was telling you about!'

Six, seven counting Tom, Athena poster model men from the Eighties turned to James who held his hand up awkwardly in greeting. 'Hi all!'

The men flocked around James, and Daisy and Lisa laughed until they cried and only laughed some more when James arrived at their side, his usually carefully placed hair ruffled.

'Well, they all seem lovely,' James said, his voice genuine if not dazed.

'The account all sorted?,' Daisy said, only semi-jokingly.

'Yep, all in order.' He touched her arm gently. 'You look radiant today.'

Daisy found herself blushing and she didn't know why. She was glad when Lisa dragged James to the barn to show him the new items for the house.

Chapter 6

Three days later, having helped assign furniture to various rooms and overseen the making of the guesthouse, Daisy had realised she had to face the sea of tweed that was Waitrose in Cirencester. A bed and breakfast was not much good without the breakfast part. She had been surprised at how easy it had been and was now safely ensconced in her own kitchen. She began to unpack all the ridiculously elaborate goodies she had bought. James, who was to be their accountant, had told her just to have fun with it, budgeting was for down the line.

'How did that go?' James's voice behind her and she turned to find him in the doorway.

'Well,' she said, holding up two boxes of eggs, 'I'm pretty sure these are just eggs but as everything else in the store has been seeped in Madagascan vanilla pods or been allowed to have the sea breeze of Antigua rush over them, I wouldn't be surprised if these eggs aren't just eggs but eggs from a hen with its own masseuse and pool.'

James chuckled. 'Yeah but our guests will be appreciative, I'm sure.' He smiled. 'In fact, I can hear a car now.'

Daisy's heart started hammering. What on earth were they doing? People were traveling *to* them: the pressure was immense!

But, also, somewhere deep down something shifted, a kind of unwillingness to let go of her space even further. It was one thing to allow her friends in but strangers…

Then a thought occurred to her. They didn't even have a sodding reception desk! She hurtled past James who followed closely behind. Tom was ushering the dream team out the back door, their shirts draped casually over their buff shoulders. She waved politely and then addressed Tom. 'We haven't even got a reception desk!'

'You don't need one,' Tom said as he checked off something else on his clipboard.

'I want to feel like we've got this covered,' she said and in one fell swoop, grabbed a sideboard in the hall, twisting it into position, took a vase of flowers from off the other table and James handed her an ancient Indian bell – an anniversary present from Hugh – just as their guest entered the hall. She moved from around the sideboard and stepped forward to greet the man.

'Oh. My. God.' A voice boomed across the hall. 'This is unbelievable.' The accent was not English but the most amazing drawl of a real-life Texan. Daisy's heart flipped with excitement. They had *international* visitors.

A man with a cowboy hat and boots with actual spurs stepped forward, his baby-blue gingham shirt just about containing the overhanging waistline, helped by an opal-encrusted belt thread through his jeans' belt loops.

'Hi, I'm Bob,' he said assuredly. 'Bob from the Hamptons.' He smiled, a smile so wide it filled the frame of his face. 'Actually, I lie. I'm from Texas but I live in the Hamptons now.'

Daisy held out her hand. 'Daisy – welcome to Atworth Manor.'

Tom pushed himself forward. 'I loved *Dallas*,' he enthused and James nodded in agreement.

'*Dallas*, huh?' Bob said. 'Yeah, that was shot down the road from where I used to live.'

Lisa skipped down the stairs, talking loudly as she went, her face a sweaty mess, totally unaware of their guest in the hall. 'I've just finished. Oh my God, Tom, what were you thinking inviting people to stay before we had even furnished the…'

Daisy had fixed a grin to her face and was giving Lisa a hard stare.

'What's up, Daisy? If looks could kill…' She turned her head to the mountain of a man blocking out the natural light. 'Oh, holy crap, *this* is our guest, isn't it?'

Daisy nodded.

Bob let out a roar of laughter. 'Only just finished! You mean to say that this pretty little lady here—' he indicated Lisa with a warm smile '—has been rushing her tiny, English feet off to get ready for me?' He paused. 'I'm a cowboy at heart, folks. I would've been happy under canvas in your back yard.'

'Probably not a fair swap for your money,' Daisy offered. 'But thank you for…' She realised Bob and Lisa were staring at each other in a strange manner and she coughed, breaking up the moment. 'Anyway, shall I show you to your room?'

'That'd be great, honey.' Then he tapped in his head. 'I tell you what, if this weren't screwed on… I've forgotten something. And that something is my other half.'

Daisy nodded and Lisa excused herself.

'I'll only be a tick,' Bob laughed. 'That's what I learnt from some English folks this morning. A tick!' He chuckled. 'Isn't that what dogs get…' He paused. 'Oh, speaking of, I'll go and get my little lady love.'

Daisy watched the hulk of a man leave and she turned urgently to the others. 'Is everything ready?'

Tom crossed something off on his list with a flourish. '*Be charming as hell to guest*. Done.' He nodded. 'All done, dear Daisy, and James and I are just about to lock ourselves away and discuss budgets.'

James looked vaguely alarmed at the concept.

'You look frightened,' Daisy commented.

'Worrying for a man who worked in the city!' Tom hooted.

'I don't think that's the bit that's scaring him.' Daisy laughed as Bob walked back in with just a bag.

Tom and James excused themselves and Daisy indicated the lack of wife.

'Um, did you forget your, um…'

'Oh, she's in here.' He held up his leather weekend bag.

'Right.' Daisy nodded, wondering if it really was wise to open one's house to complete strangers with perhaps a variety of issues.

Then, much to her surprise, the bag moved and she stared at the opening. Suddenly a soft chestnut-coloured Chihuahua's head popped out.

'Here she is, my little lady.' Bob kissed her on the head. 'Her name's Barbara. Had to bring her to England with me so she could see the sights, drink tea.'

'Oh,' Daisy laughed, almost relieved. 'How lovely. Does she like other dogs because we've got a couple of border terriers, Ant and Dec, hanging about.'

'Well, if they're male, she'll like them.' He winked. 'She's named after Barbara Cartland and she's a highly-sexed little pooch, though I can assure you she's been *dealt* with if you know what I mean.'

'Has Barbara enjoyed herself so far?'

'Hell yeah,' Bob hooted. 'She's seen Buckingham Palace and I showed her a picture of the Queen with her corgis. She thought that was awesome.' He trailed off and Daisy couldn't be sure if he was pulling her leg or not.

'Brilliant. Lovely.' Daisy felt so British and formal next to this man, she wished she could offer him an American welcome with cheerleaders and a BBQ, but it would have to do. 'Let me show you your room.

Lisa reappeared at the top of the stairs, a strange smile on her face. 'I'll show you, just follow me.'

Daisy went to excuse herself: Lisa was clearly keen to show

Bob herself but Lisa, reading her thoughts, said, 'Come, too, Daisy. It's your house after all. Come and see what me and the boys have done.'

They duly followed Lisa up the stairs and towards the very first room Daisy had opened up yesterday. Lisa pushed the door open and stepped back and Bob, as if he knew this was a momentous moment for them all, on so many levels, took off his hat.

The room was beautiful. The white bedstead adorned with the greys covers looked warm and inviting, the tartan curtains made it cosy and Lisa had even thought of reed diffusers and soft lighting.

Daisy's breath caught as she thought she could almost hear Hugh sigh with contentment. He would have been happy.

'Are you alright, Ms Daisy?' said Bob, noticing her moist eyes.

'Yes, sorry, fine.' She brushed them away. 'Just a big moment, you being our first guest and…' She didn't finish. This wasn't the time to explain her life story.

'Well, I sure am honoured,' he said, his face serious and eyes filled with compassion. 'And to you, Miss…? He looked at Lisa.

'Lisa,' she said, blushing.

Daisy had finally twigged. She hadn't seen Lisa this lost for words in well… never. Lisa had fallen in love with their first guest.

'I'll head back downstairs. Do shout if you need anything…'

'Yes, thank you, Ms Daisy.'

She gave a small smile at his polite affectation. He was certainly the loveliest first guest they could have wished for.

'Lisa will let you know about keys and breakfast and so on…' Lisa wasn't really listening but Daisy could see from the new lock on the door and sheath of keys hanging from Lisa's pocket, her friends had all the details under control.

She decided to head down to Hugh's office. She had told everyone the room was off limits so she knew she could gather her thoughts there.

She smiled at them as she turned on her heels and went down

stairs. Alarmed, she thought she heard voices coming from Hugh's office and picked up her pace as she made her way towards the familiar oak door. That couldn't be right; she had told them to stay away.

She pushed it open and, to her horror, James and Tom were sat on the leather chesterfield in the corner, papers adorning the coffee table. They didn't even notice her, they were laughing so hard about something – she thought she heard snippets of Dallas storylines – that it was only when she was stood over them, they stopped.

'Hey, Daisy, everything OK?' Tom said.

Her body was rigid with anger, her fists in tight balls at her side. 'I told you,' she said in a heated whisper, 'to stay out of this room.' Her voice caught and tears began to cascade down her cheeks.

James immediately leapt up, his face ashen. 'Oh shit, I'm so sorry, Daisy, I completely forgot.'

Tom nodded, shuffling the papers together. 'Yes, we forgot. It was my idea. I guess I wasn't thinking.' He paused. 'The door was open…'

James started, 'We had a key—'

'I've got the only key…' She shook her head, distress fizzing at edges of her thoughts. 'Get out,' Daisy breathed quietly, her voice strangled with emotion. 'Get out.'

They moved past her. Tom tried to put his hand on her arm and she shook him off.

'Just go.'

Once the door had been firmly shut behind them, she collapsed onto the sofa sobbing. She felt as if she was losing her connection with Hugh, like he was slipping from her grasp and with every person in her house and every person moving about Hugh's space, she would lose sight of him altogether.

They had moved Hugh's favourite bowl from Indonesia to the side as well as the the drinks mat that Daisy knew he kept on the left-hand side of the table. Hugh would lie across the sofa, cup in easy reach, stop reading and admire the oak tree outside as its leaves changed from season to season. Quite often she would bring him a fresh coffee late at night, when he was working on figures for a client, and find him asleep, his specs dangling from one hand, the quiet purring of sleep as his chest rose and fell.

She placed her hand on the cool leather now and wished more than ever that she could feel Hugh's warmth, his life.

Daisy rose from the sofa, put the bowl back as it was, realigned the mat and went to sit at his desk. She'd actually never sat there when he was alive. She knew it was his space and he needed that but now, she would do anything to feel close to him, and so she sat there and wept.

She hoped their guest, Bob (and Barbara), wouldn't hear her. He had been invited to a boutique B&B, not a wake.

That was when she noticed it; she had never seen it before. A box. A steel metal box, the kind you might file important papers in, under the desk. She bent down to retrieve it but it was too heavy to pick up, so instead she crouched on her hands and knees to see if it would open.

It was locked shut, requiring a small key. Hugh had never mentioned such a box and surely, of all the people in the world, he would have told *her* its contents. She needed to get inside but, without a key, she would have to smash the lock and that felt like sacrilege.

She sat up again, her brows furrowed, and felt a twinge of guilt at even contemplating breaking into it. It was Hugh's box and she was sure that whatever was inside couldn't have been that important. Maybe it was information for some high profile clients.

Daisy looked at it one last time and decided to forget she had even come upon it. It was no more her business now than when Hugh was alive.

She pushed her shoulders back, checked the room had been fully restored to how it had been and looked at the ceiling.

'Sorry, Hugh. They weren't meant to come in here. It won't happen again.' She cocked her head to the side and gave the ceiling a wry smile. 'Love you.'

She left quietly, glancing at the leather Chesterfield and whispered, 'I'll bring you a coffee later.'

Shutting the door, she barely noticed James sat on the stairs. He shot to his feet when she came out.

'Shit, Daisy, I wanted to say I'm so sorry. I don't know what we were thinking.' He looked shaken. 'I really am sorry.'

Daisy's heart melted, it was hard to resist James's boyish face. She put her hand on his arm. He looked up quickly at her and they held each other's gaze for a moment or two before Daisy felt compelled to break the moment.

'Um, look it's fine. It's just I need to hold onto something, you know?'

James nodded, then a heartbeat later said, 'By the way, we've had loads of interest and we have a whole group arriving tomorrow for the weekend.'

'Cripes.' Daisy pulled a face. 'This is really happening.' She studied James, a thought suddenly occurring to her. 'Aren't you incredibly bored doing something as tame as a B&B? I mean I know that it's a million miles away from life in the City.'

His face twisted with pain. 'I just need time away from my old life and actually I think this is going to be fun.'

She smiled. 'Well, we already have a real-life Texan so what's not to love?'

'And tomorrow we get a group of ten. Lisa spoke to the woman who's organising it. She's from London. Marylebone, to be exact.'

Lisa bounded down the stairs and hugged them both tight. 'Eek! I love this. We're actually doing it guys!'

Daisy smiled and disentangled herself. 'Do I think someone's fallen in love with Bob?' she whispered.

James pulled a mock-surprise face at Lisa whose cheeks were now on fire.

'Don't be ridiculous,' she said, and then smiled slyly. 'But he is quite handsome.'

Daisy laughed and caught James looking at her, a fleeting expression of sadness crossing his face. Or was it sadness? She didn't know but was grateful that Lisa continued to ramble on.

'Anyway, James has probably told you that tomorrow we have ten arriving for and I quote—' she put her fingers in the air to demonstrate '"—we are so looking forward to our hashtag holibobs, darling!"…'

'Holibobs!' Daisy snorted. 'Holibobs!' She realised she was laughing and how good it felt to laugh. Perhaps Atworth Manor and its guests would be the best medicine, after all.

Chapter 7

They worked tirelessly throughout the rest of the afternoon to ensure the final rooms really were finished and Daisy had to hand it to her friends, they had certainly done her and Atworth Manor proud. No one would believe that only a few weeks ago she hadn't even received the letter from Hugh.

By six o'clock the rooms were sparkling, beds made, towels in place and keys in locks. It looked and smelt glorious. Bob and Barbara had been intrigued by the bustle of activity and offered their help too. At one point, Daisy had stood back to take the scene in. She saw Tom up a ladder, cracking a joke about queens and light bulbs, his shirt off and his toned body on show. Lisa held the ladder in place, her eyes never leaving Bob who helped James drape the heavy, tartan curtains. Barbara and Ant and Dec were running around the room in frenetic circles. Even with all the hustle and bustle, she had realised how good it felt to be surrounded by friends, old and new.

At six o'clock, they collapsed onto the floor of the final room and Daisy announced she would make supper for everybody but first it was time for gin and tonics. Bob went to excuse himself but Lisa stopped him.

'No,' Lisa insisted. 'You worked as hard as anyone here, you can have supper with us.' Lisa looked longingly at Daisy.

'Of course! I meant you too, Bob,' Daisy agreed.

They gathered themselves up from the carpet and made their way downstairs.

They congregated in the kitchen: Lisa and Bob were put on gin-and-tonic-making duties and Tom helped Daisy cut up potatoes for the cottage pie.

'Daisy...' James stood by her side, his voice low. 'Can we have some time together outside?'

'Of course,' she agreed, searching his eyes but realised that no doubt he needed a bit of time away from the mad house. She of all people understood that. Once they had put the final touches to the pie, she put it in the Aga, grabbed her drink as well as one for James and made her way out of the kitchen to find him. She knocked quietly on his bedroom door but he wasn't there. She tried everywhere and was about to give up when she caught sight of a glow of light from the garden. James was sitting beneath the oak tree looking at his phone and, for a moment, her breath caught: it could have been Hugh sitting there. She had to give herself a moment to remind herself of who it actually was.

She made her way across the dewy grass towards James. The air was crisp and she realised her shirt was flimsy against the early spring frost.

'For you!' She handed him his drink. 'Made by Bob's fair hands.' She smiled. 'Think it's three-quarters gin, one quarter tonic.'

James laughed and took it gratefully. 'Thank you. And thanks for coming outside, I just wanted to chat with you. Feels like we don't have much time to ourselves.'

'No, I'm grateful actually.' She breathed out deeply. 'It's nice to get air and stop.' She leant into him, their shoulders touching. 'And to spend time with you.'

He didn't speak and even though he was looking directly ahead, she saw the movement of him nodding.

'Hugh used to sit under this tree all the time,' Daisy said. 'For a moment… for a moment, I thought you were him.'

'Sorry.'

'Don't be.' She hugged herself against the cool breeze. 'It's comforting having you here.'

Again, he nodded.

'You know, I have something for you.'

She shifted. 'What do you mean?'

'I mean I was given this—' he held up an envelope, another envelope '—by Hugh. Today's…'

'Today's…?' She furrowed her brow and then it hit her with full force. A sob escaped her lips. 'Oh my God, it's our anniversary. I forgot, I fucking forgot.' She put down her glass and wiped away her angry tears. 'You see, I knew I would start to forget stuff.'

James drew her into him. 'You didn't forget, it just wasn't at the forefront of your mind and that's okay. That's more than okay.'

Daisy felt his body shift next to hers and a fluttery feeling stirred in her stomach.

She glanced at the envelope through a haze of tears. 'What is that?'

He handed it to her and she took it, carefully slicing the top open with her finger. She drew out a card, an anniversary card and laughed because the card was so unlike anything Hugh would ever have bought.

'This cannot be from him.' She looked at James who gave her a small, knowing smile. Hugh, the man who didn't believe in cards had for the first time in their entire marriage bought an actual anniversary card from an actual shop. The irony wasn't lost on Daisy who snorted through her tears.

'He dies and *then* buys me a card.'

James laughed, squeezed her shoulders with tenderness.

Daisy read the card out aloud. 'Dearest Daisy, I know what you've just thought. He's actually bought a card! Well, I didn't want to shuffle off this mortal coil and not visit Clintons. That really would have been a crime. Seriously, though, I hope you're okay. I know James will be looking after you.' Her voice caught and she stopped, looked briefly at James who didn't flinch. 'Keep going, my darling. You're doing so well. I love what you're doing with the house. All my eternal love, Hugh.'

James stretched his legs out in front of him, and drank deeply from his glass.

'It's like Hugh's still here, like he's watching me.'

James nodded. 'He wanted you to know he's still here.' He took Daisy's hand and placed it gently across her own heart. 'He'll always be here.'

'But how… the house? I mean, I could have said no to the whole bonkers B&B idea and then this card wouldn't have made any sense.' She paused. 'Did he write another one in case I had said no?'

James smiled and shook his head. 'That's the only card he wrote.' He drank again. 'He told me he knew you would do it because he knows you're a fighter and made of stronger stuff than any of us.'

Daisy's eyes smarted once more, a lump developing in her throat. 'You're like a messenger.'

He nodded. 'Yes, just the messenger, always the messenger.' James stood, almost abruptly. 'We should go back inside before everyone wonders where we've got to.'

Daisy nodded, unsure of what she had said wrong, and wondered about his sudden change in mood, before she stood herself. They were inches apart now and the air between them was thick with emotion. She kissed him on the cheek then used the back of her hand to softly wipe the same spot. He appeared to soften at her touch and she said, 'Thank you.'

He nodded and together they made their way inside. The others were already tucking into the pie and the bottle of botanical gin was almost empty.

'We wondered where you two had got to,' Tom said. 'Come and eat.' He stopped when he noticed Daisy's blotchy face. 'Oh God, what's happened?'

'Nothing,' she smiled. 'It's just I forgot it was our anniversary today. But James had been keeping a card that Hugh wrote…'

Lisa piped up, 'Hugh wrote and bought a card! Holy crap.'

Daisy laughed. 'Exactly what I said.'

Bob invited her to sit next to him. 'Well, your folks here have just been filling me in on Hugh and he sounded like a fine gentleman.' Bob held up his glass, his cheeks flushed with the warm food and drink. 'To Hugh!'

They all held up their glasses and gave three cheers. James sat next to Daisy and took her hand, giving it a small squeeze. She smiled at him. He was a good man. He was a good man, with divine looks, she thought, as the candlelight cast shadows over his chiselled features.

'So, what I'm dying to know,' Lisa said, 'sorry, not dying… what I mean is…'

Daisy laughed. 'It's alright, Lisa, stop walking on eggshells!' She smiled. 'Come on, spit it out.'

Lisa blushed. 'I am *interested* to know what other surprises James has up his sleeve?'

Daisy hadn't thought of that but then she didn't want to think of that; James was proving to be her connection to Hugh and she wanted that to go on forever. She gave James a smile and he smiled tenderly back at her.

'This is lovely, guys,' James said, piling the pie onto his fork and taking another mouthful.

Lisa didn't even notice he hadn't answered her question as she was too busy talking to Bob about a local shop where he could buy a Cotswold Tweed jacket for Barbara.

But Daisy did notice and she watched James as he ate and joked with Tom. How much more had Hugh given him to pass on? She knew one thing: she didn't want it to end, and James made her feel safe. She realised then, as James looked up and caught her eye, smiling, that he was keeping her going. She felt herself falling in love with him.

The next morning, after they all made breakfast together, Bob announced he would love to stay a couple more nights if that was possible.

'Oh, I thought your plane was leaving later today?' Daisy said. 'But let me just check the book…' She scrolled down. 'No, that room is free, well, forever at the moment.' She smiled. 'So, yes, please stay.'

Lisa bounded in from outside. 'I'm going to show Bob the sights of Cirencester. You heard he's staying?'

'Yes.' Daisy arched a brow and smiled knowingly. 'I heard.'

'Great.' Lisa ignored her friend, making her way to the door. 'We won't be long.' She paused and turned back. 'The Holibobs crew will be arriving at lunch.'

'I look forward to it.' Daisy was genuinely excited to see the B&B filling with guests. She felt more alive than ever.

James joined Daisy in the hall and watched Lisa and Bob head towards the Jeep Cherokee Bob had rented.

'Love is in the air,' James sang quietly and Daisy laughed.

'I have not seen Lisa this manic about a man since Reginald the Rapper.'

'Who the hell is Reginald the Rapper?' James gave a small disbelieving shake to his head.

'You *don't know* who Reginald the Rapper is?' She feigned shock and placed her hands on her cheeks. 'Reginald the Rapper was the regular entertainment on a Sunday night at the local pub. Lisa was a waitress there for a year or so and she fell hard for the man.'

'What happened?'

'He decided to write and dedicate a song to Lisa.'

'Oh, that's good, isn't it?'

She smiled. 'A song that he didn't run past her before he delivered it to his regular audience. It went something like this.' She rounded her shoulders and adopted what she believed was an urban-rap-like-pose.'You are my Mona Lisa, I am so pleased to meet ya, you ain't perfect but that's what I've come to expect, I like the way you move, do you want to spend your life in my groove.'

James let out a deep growly laugh, tears rolling down his cheeks. 'I can't believe it and I can't believe you memorised it!' He paused. 'You are amazing, do you know that, Daisy?' He hugged her and as he pulled away, she felt the same connection as she had done last night. It was electric, every inch of her skin tingled with anticipation.

She laughed, breaking the moment, and tried to ignore the butterflies in her stomach. James had this effect on her that she couldn't even put into words.

'We have spent *many* a night watching Lisa perform that one so it's etched on my mind.' Daisy grew serious. 'Needless to say, Lisa felt she could do better and dumped Reginald.'

Just as Daisy was about to perform the second act, a navy Jag drove at speed up the drive, followed by three Range Rovers.

'Oh,' Daisy said, 'this must be the Holibobs brigade.'

James looked quite alarmed and Daisy laughed. 'Don't worry, James, I'm sure they don't bite.'

A woman in pale pink cut offs and the crispest white shirt on Earth hopped out of the Jag and walked, no bounced, her way towards the front door. Her perfect coiffed blonde, highlighted bob rose and fell with every bounce but there was never a hair out of place. Daisy put her hand up to her own hair involuntarily and pressed it down.

'Darling,' came the voice like a loud tiger purr from the entrance. 'We are here to have our like, hashtag, holibob!' She beamed. 'You must be Daisy. I'm Annabelle.' The woman poured into the room, her hand extended and shook Daisy's, then James's hands vigorously. 'I'm afraid, darlings, we're early because Agamemnon's piccolo lesson was move to the 8 a.m. slot and I told the troops that, well, we may as well sit in on his lesson and head straight off from there.'

Daisy noted she said 'there' like 'tharrrr'.

'Nice to meet you,' Daisy eventually said. 'The rooms are made up so you're very welcome to settle in now.'

'Oh, you are such a gem. I knew when I spoke to your maid, Lisa, that you were going to be such a gem.'

'Lisa isn't the maid,' Daisy corrected. 'She's my friend.'

'Oh, we all think our cleaners are our friends!'

Daisy went to correct her but the remaining Holibobs troops quickly descended on the house. They looked like the Boden catalogue come to life.

'Here come the brood,' Annabelle said, standing back to make way for the crowd.

As the remaining guests tumbled through the door, they introduced themselves and Daisy and James shook all their hands in turn.

'Well, I've already told you I'm Annabelle.' She flicked her lifeless bob into action and it quickly took up its original position. 'But we also have my husband Rupert or Rupy-Poopy… my son, Agamemnon, or Aggers…' A man in chino shorts and a pale blue sweater stepped forward, shook their hands and stepped back, followed by a boy who was a glowing icon of everything Enid Blyton. The list went on and Daisy and James met daughter Hermione (Hermes); friend Fenston (Fenny); wife Cecilia (Sissy); twin daughters Gwendolyn (Gwennie) and Mauve (Mau-Mau). Finally the friends, 'boarding school' rugger lads, arrived in the form of Fitzwilliam (Flighty Fitzy) and Cuthbert (Bertie).

Daisy eventually spoke once she realised roll call had finished. 'You are all very welcome. We'll show you to your rooms and then I can suggest some local attractions. You might like…' Daisy wracked her brain. 'You might like the local English vineyard. It's just opened up for this season, they're showing people how it's made…'

Rupert, the husband, snorted. 'Bloody English trying to make wine, what a joke!'

This was met with a barrage of snorting and giggles.

'Well said, Rupy-Poopy!' Annabelle laughed. 'No, actually, we might just sit in front of your fire and play in your garden.'

Everyone nodded as though that was fair game and went off to collect their bags.

Daisy looked frantically at James. 'Fire? Play in the garden?'

James frowned. 'Well, I guess we hadn't thought about that bit.'

Daisy nodded. 'No, well, you go and make up the fire in the sitting room and I'll go and look for the Giant Jenga under the stairs.'

Half an hour later, the guests had been shown their rooms and were now downstairs and, as far as Daisy was concerned, they were running amuck through her house. But it was no longer just her house; she knew that. These were paying guests and surely it was fine that Hermione, or Hermes, had found that if she leapt from the middle landing towards the chandelier she could just about to touch the crystals with her hand. Annabelle, glass of Prosecco in hand (at 11 a.m., Daisy noted), giggled and held her glass up to Hermes.

'Darling, probably best you don't jump from there…' Again, 'there' sounded like 'thar'. 'Maybe try jumping from the other side of the landing, yah?' Annabelle turned to Daisy. 'You have such a beautiful, little house going on here, don't you? It's absolutely so sweet.'

Daisy raised a brow. 'Little?'

'Yes, darling, I mean it's just so cute.'

'You live in Marylebone? That's a lovely area of London. House prices very expensive.'

'Hmm…' Annabelle sipped her drink. 'Yah, I suppose they are.

Hadn't thought about it. We own two houses, knocked into one. Just lovely. But, of course, we own other houses too.' She chuckled. 'I mean I've always wanted a house in the country but Rupey says that there's no point whilst we own half of London!' She laughed heartily at her own wealth.

Daisy nodded, irritation flooding her body. 'Well, thank you for admiring my home.' My *hovel*, she thought dimly.

James reappeared with more logs for the fire and Annabelle skipped over to him.

'Oh, James, you are being ever so helpful.' She brushed his shirt with the tips of her fingers causing Daisy's stomach to turn. *Was Annabelle flirting with James?* 'You really are a gem.'

'Oh, Annabelle, it's nothing honestly. We just want you to be happy here.' He grinned at her. 'All part of the service.'

James's eyes flicked towards Daisy, but Annabelle continued unabashed. Annabelle put her glass on the sideboard and leant down to readjust her trouser leg, clearly flashing her cleavage at James. Daisy noted the way he ever so slightly blushed and she moved forward.

'Annabelle,' she said rather more abruptly than she had planned, 'why don't I show you and the children the Giant Jenga I've put in the garden?'

Annabelle gave her a black look but quickly smiled and then placed her hand firmly on James's forearm. 'Hope to see you later, James.'

Over my dead body, thought Daisy but then, as quickly, wondered why on earth she was getting so riled and realised it really was nothing to do with her. However, she thought resolutely, she wanted to uphold some sort of professionalism at Atworth Manor and flirting with guests was not adhering to that policy. She would inform everyone, especially James, later on…

Annabelle duly followed Daisy out the back door. Daisy could not relax around this woman, she wasn't sure why but there was an air of ownership about her; this was someone who got what she wanted.

'Well, here you are.' Daisy pointed at the Jenga game as if she expected Annabelle to start playing at her command.

'Thank you, darling.' Annabelle wasn't even looking at the Jenga, however. She was staring back through the sitting room window at James stoking the fire and putting on fresh logs. Rupert could be heard through the closed windows telling everyone the story of his rugby triumph as a young boy at Eton.

'If I hear that story one more…' Annabelle muttered through gritted teeth. 'Anyway, thank you, darling Daisy, I will let the children know.' She inspected her nails. 'So James tells me you've only just opened up your quaint B&B because your husband…' Her voice trailed off.

Daisy looked her in the eyes. 'Yes, that's right. My husband died just over a year ago.' Daisy forced a smile. 'And, it's going very well so far.' *For day three*, she thought, *but actually I wish I hadn't opened my house to snobs like you.*

James appeared in the doorway and Annabelle held out her glass. 'Would you, James? Get me another Prosecco. I have a pounding head and it really is the only thing that will cure it.'

James furrowed his brow momentarily and smiling, took the glass. 'Of course.'

'We brought our own fizz, darling. We didn't know if you country bumpkins would have a bar.'

'Well, we don't because we are a bed and breakfast, not a full board hotel,' Daisy pointed out, her shoulders stiffening.

'Yah, of course.' Annabelle smiled as James approached with her full glass. 'You really have quite a man here working for you.'

Daisy's breath caught with annoyance. 'He is a friend, actually. We all work together.' She looked at James to gauge his reaction and to wait for his support. Instead, she was surprised to find James appear to grimace at her words. 'James? That's right, isn't it? We're all good friends.'

'Yes, just *friends*, as Daisy keeps saying,' he said, looking at Daisy and nodding. 'We're just friends. A group of us decided to set it up after…' The shadow that had previously crossed his features lifted and the old James was reinstated. He smiled tenderly at Daisy. 'After Hugh, our dear friend and Daisy's husband, died.'

Annabelle, Daisy noted, clutched her glass increasingly tightly. 'Well, sometimes, don't we all wish to be single again?' Laughter erupted from her small mouth like tinkling glass. 'Here's to moving on!' She held her glass up and Daisy and James pretended to hold up their own.

Rupert, as if on cue, appeared at the door.

'Oh there you are, Annie.' He noted the glass in her hand. 'Didn't notice you had cracked open a bottle?' His words appeared to be emphatic of a previous argument.

'I have one of my headaches.' Annabelle barely looked at him as she spoke.

'Well, can you come inside, please? Aggers wants to know if the maid packed his Jack Wills sweatshirt. He keeps complaining of being cold.' Rupert looked at James. 'Despite your splendid fire, old chap.'

James nodded and smiled.

'Well, it is a draughty house,' Daisy said. 'I'll advance the heating. Maybe that will help?'

'Oh, well, we'll pay extra, of course, if that's OK with you?' Rupert nodded gratefully.

Daisy was just glad to be able to leave them and she walked off quickly to the kitchen. There, she found Hermes sat on a chair at the kitchen table. She coughed as she approached, even though it was her house, and Hermes looked up at her with disdain. Like her mother, Daisy thought.

'Hi, Hermes,' Daisy broached as diplomatically as she could. 'Guests aren't really allowed in the kitchen.'

'Why? Mother and Father have paid you a bucketload, I don't see why I can't sit in your sodding kitchen.'

Daisy threw her head back with surprise. She knew she hadn't spent much time around children but surely this wasn't normal for a girl who could be no older than twelve.

'How old are you?'

'Eleven.' She rolled her eyes. 'Please don't try and make small talk with me.'

Daisy had had enough. 'Right, Hermione, please leave my kitchen. I've had quite enough.' Daisy pushed the advance button on the boiler and turned back to the girl, quite expecting another mouth full. Instead, she was confronted with an eleven-year-old in floods of tears. 'Oh dear God, I didn't mean to sound horrible!' Daisy rushed to her side, put her hand on the girl's hand. 'I'm sorry, do sit if you want to, it's fine.'

The young girl snivelled and looked up at her. 'Don't tell Mother and Father I'm here.' Her eyes rounded. 'Please. I'm just so sick of their arguing and Mother's drinking.'

Daisy's heart softened and she pulled a chair up next to Hermione. 'Oh, listen, do you like cake?'

Hermione gave a half-smile. 'I'm not allowed cake.'

'What?' Daisy pulled a mock-tragic look. 'Not allowed cake? That's illegal.'

Hermione laughed. 'Mother says I have to keep my GI level down and something about cleansing my colon…' The girl looked at Daisy in earnest and Daisy, in turn, did everything she could not to snort with laughter.

'Well, I tell you what…' Daisy stood. 'I am going to close this kitchen door and get us both a slice of chocolate cake.' She smiled. 'I didn't make it, you'll be glad to know, you can ask my ex-husband about my baking skills.' The word *ex* made Daisy stop in her tracks.

Hermione looked at her. 'Ex?'

Daisy cleared her throat. 'Yes, he died recently. Well, just over a year ago so not that recent.'

'I'm sorry to hear that.' Hermione bowed her head reverentially.

'Thank you.' She took a deep breath. 'I guess we both need cake.'

They sat together, unspeaking, eating their cake, drinking squash and Daisy realised she felt quite calm once again.

'Thank you, Hermione. You've been great company.'

'So have you, Miss Daisy.'

'I tell you what, you can come here whenever you like, just don't tell anyone else.'

Hermione rose from her chair and pushed it under the table. 'I won't tell.' She grinned, her cheeks rosy from the warmth of the Aga and no doubt, Daisy thought gleefully, sugar was buzzing around her tiny frame. *Bugger the GI index and the sugar dodging purists*, she thought, *there was more to life than weight and bloody skin complexion.*

She thought of her own mother who would have had none of that. In fact, Daisy remembered the time she quoted some super food diet in her *Glamour* magazine at her parents; it had been met with grumbles of the youth's lack of appreciation of the work that went into food. And therein, her move towards a diet had been stamped on and she had never thought about the D-word since. She had been a gym bunny at university – mother had claimed it *unnatural* – but since then, and since marrying Hugh, she had returned to her curvier self.

James strode into the kitchen and caught her eating the remaining morsels of her cake. She pushed it away guiltily, as if her mind's meanderings could be read on her face.

'That looks yummy.' He sat where Hermione had just been sat. 'I just saw Hermione and she whispered to me, "You've got a good one there." What did she mean?'

Daisy blushed despite herself. 'I have no idea. We barely spoke. She needed some respite from her family and I told her she could sit in here with me and eat cake.' Daisy laughed. 'First slice of cake she's been allowed in years, she'll be bouncing off the ceilings.'

James smiled affectionately at Daisy. 'Well, maybe she's right, you are a good one.'

'Oh, you soft git.' Daisy smiled. 'I'm not sure about any of that. I'm not sure I'm a good one and I'm not yours.' She laughed, getting up. 'But there you go.' She started to clear the plates into the sink.

He fell silent and Daisy turned to look at him. 'Are you okay?'

He nodded. 'I could be yours, if you wanted.'

She laughed, almost nervously, unsure of what he meant. 'You mean because Hugh's given you the job?'

'No, because…' He faltered. 'No, because…'

'She started scrubbing unnecessarily hard at a plate. 'Because?' She realised she wasn't breathing; her heart wouldn't be still either.

'Because…' She turned again at his voice. 'Because I care about you.'

Daisy smiled, trying to hide her disappointment. 'As I do you.'

He smiled, rose and squeezed her shoulder with his strong palm. 'My dear Daisy.'

She returned the smile, their eyes searching each other's but it was only once he had left that she inhaled deeply and tried to calm her shaking hands.

Chapter 8

The hashtag Holibobs crew took themselves off to the local pub for supper. Annabelle popped her head around the kitchen door as they made their way out.

'Any sign of James? Haven't seen him all day.' She smiled sweetly at Daisy. 'Wanted to thank him for all his help.'

By this point Tom, Lisa and Bob (and Barbara) had all returned and they were tucking into Daisy's homemade lasagne. Daisy had filled them in on the unlikely Marylebone crew.

Annabelle's eyes surveyed the others. 'Is it normal to have your staff to supper, Daisy?' She asked this question quite innocently.

'They're not staff. That's what I was saying earlier. They are my dear friends. As in they *really* are my dear friends.' She pointed in turn. 'Here's Tom.'

Tom stood, wearing a new Hawaiian shirt that was one or two sizes too small, and thrust out his hand. 'Ah, you're the famous Annabelle. Hope you're settling in OK.'

Annabelle ignored his hand. 'What are you wearing? Is it Halloween?'

Tom jutted out his jaw and pouted. 'Uh, no need to be rude with a capital R.' He sat back down sulking.

Daisy sighed inwardly. 'This is Lisa and Bob.'

Bob stood up and also stuck out his hand. 'Good evening, ma'am.'

Annabelle finally obliged and shook his hand. 'Do you come from some ghastly place in the US? You don't sound English.'

'Correct, ma'am.' Bob cocked his head. 'I'm from glorious Texas.'

Annabelle actually pulled a face of disgust and Daisy wished she would just leave.

'Anyway, James isn't here but I will pass on your thanks.'

Annabelle hovered momentarily and then left without another word. Daisy heard the front door slam and closed the kitchen door once more, breathing a sigh of relief.

'That woman gets under my skin.' She looked at her friends. 'I'm not sure about this anymore. I don't know if I want people taking over my house. It feels wrong somehow.' She paused. 'I mean, she was all over James.'

Tom raised a brow. 'Are you surprised? The man's a god. I'm amazed we're not having to fight off the mobs outside.'

Daisy grew irritable. 'Oh for God's sake, Tom, he's just a human.'

Lisa and Tom exchanged a look. 'You know, it's okay to find men attractive again,' Lisa said quietly. 'You are allowed to move on.'

Daisy turned her back on the group around the table and poured herself a stiff gin and tonic. She knew she had to get a grip and that she had no reason to be annoyed with anyone but for some reason she felt as if she was spiralling out of control. She gulped back the drink, silence looming behind her and realised that sadly the ground wouldn't swallow her up so she turned back to the table.

Bob was clutching Lisa's hand and Tom was holding Barbara's paw.

'Love you, Daisy,' Tom said his face filled with concern. 'Maybe it was a daft idea. I shouldn't have left you guys today to deal with that lot.' He indicated the London crew.

'Yes, we should have stayed,' Lisa agreed.

Bob nodded solemnly.

Daisy looked at them all with affection, her eyes wandering once more to Lisa and Bob's hands. 'Are you...?'

Bob grinned and Lisa blushed.

'Well, congrats...' Daisy said holding up her glass. 'Here's to love.'

They all affably joined in. 'To love.'

'Where has James gone?' Daisy said, realising she hadn't seen him since her cake with Hermes.

Tom looked up. 'Said he had to go to London to sort out some business stuff. He says he'll be back tomorrow.' He shrugged. 'He's very James Bond, isn't he? Quite shady.'

'Well, I suppose we all have our own lives and we need to remember that.' She paused. 'Especially for this to work.'

'In which case, darling Daisy,' Tom said, 'you go upstairs and have a long soak and pamper yourself. We'll clean up.' He smiled kindly. 'Also, James says that he's sorted the cleaning company for the rooms and they'll come in every day at eight to sort everything out.' He came over and put his arms around her shoulders. 'So you just have to be the lady of the manor.' He kissed her nose. 'Which you already do so impeccably.'

Daisy smiled and, suddenly feeling so overwhelmingly tired, decided to take them up on their offer. She wished them all a good night and headed upstairs. Once she had set the ancient roll top's tap to hot – she knew it would take an age to fill – she decided to go and sit quietly in Hugh's study.

She sat on the leather sofa and caressed the space where Hugh would have sat with her hand.

'Listen to Tom and Lisa,' she whispered, 'talking about it being okay to find other men attractive.' Her eyes filled with tears. 'How can I find other men attractive? I mean that's not right, is it?'

Of course, she was met with silence but still she ploughed on.

'I want to be yours forever, Hugh.' She pinched the leather now, emotion swelling inside her. 'Why did you leave me? Why couldn't we have gone together?'

She gazed around the room, her eyes blurry, and noticed a bright Post-it note had been left on top of a piece of paper on Hugh's desk. Daisy sat bolt upright and stood, staring at it, almost too afraid to pick it up. It was as if Hugh had come back and written her a note but as she picked it up gingerly she recognised it to be James's writing. Irritation bubbled inside her: she had told him quite categorically that he wasn't allowed in Hugh's office and yet, he was here leaving her notes.

Dear Daisy, sorry for leaving so suddenly – business called. I know you didn't want me to come in here but I knew you would and I wanted you see this. I printed it off – an email from Hugh. Hopefully you can see that you really are special. James xx

Why would he ignore her wish? She'd simply asked him not to go into Hugh's office; it felt sacrilegious. Her eyes flicked to the piece of paper behind. How was this meant to be helping her? Every time she saw more words from Hugh, she felt a fresh wave of grief move through her.

With a trembling hand, she held the piece of paper and murmured aloud:

Dearest Daisy,

I hear you're questioning yourself again.

She held her free hand up to her mouth, shocked, and looked around her. It was as if he was in the room.

I asked James to give you this letter whenever you started questioning how special you are. You are special and moreover I want you to find love again. Please, Daisy. There is no point in waiting until we meet again. I want you to be happy now. If you find love, which I am sure you will, grasp it and don't fight it. You're stubborn by nature but you deserve happiness. Do it for me. Love always, Hugh x

'Oh, Hugh, it's as if you are with me. How do you know I'm thinking these things?' Daisy sighed deeply and sat in Hugh's office chair. 'How can I move on? Why would I want to?'

She mindlessly caressed the paperweight she had bought Hugh the day he had proposed. It looked as tacky now as it did then but it was still so special with its Dutch flag and I LOVE AMSTERDAM emblazoned on it. Maybe she should move away, she mused. Go and live in an entirely different country, set up a whole new life.

Her thoughts were interrupted by a piercing scream. She dropped the letter and ran from the study down the stairs, and found Annabelle hanging off the bannister, her dainty, ballet-pump adorned feet hovering above the stair. Daisy looked at the carpet: a large spider stood stock-still. Daisy pushed down the laughter bubbling up inside her.

'What is that?' Annabelle nodded towards the spider. 'It's gigantic. We don't get those in London.'

Daisy narrowed her eyes. 'Are you sure about that? Spiders don't live exclusively in the countryside.'

'Oh, no, we definitely don't.' Annabelle remained hanging off the bannister. 'Can you just get rid of it?'

Daisy bent down and gently picked the spider up in her hand. She wasn't entirely in love with the creatures but she would sooner get rid of this one than admit that to Annabelle. As she stood straight, Annabelle floated back down to the carpet and said, 'James... Gosh, I was told you had gone to London.' She brushed past Daisy and gushed, 'Would you like a night cap? I've just come back from the most delightfully quaint pub. It had these extraordinary beams and although it was a bit mucky, we thought to ourselves how amazing it will be to tell everyone back in London about this. You know?' She smiled effusively at James who gave her a polite nod and smile.

'You alright, Daisy?' He stared intently at her. She knew he was referring to the note and the letter.

Annabelle moved herself closer to James, blocking his view of Daisy.

Daisy shook her head and tried to dismiss the strange twisting in her stomach. Why did she care if Annabelle flirted with James?

'I'll just put this fella outside.' She indicated her hand, and because she couldn't help herself, she walked towards them both opening her hand briefly near Annabelle's arm. 'Annabelle didn't like him, so off he goes.' Daisy giggled and exchanged a look with James; she saw the twinkle in his eyes and smiled.

Annabelle was now almost on top of James. 'Oh God, Daisy, can you please just put him outside… he's vile.'

Daisy nodded. 'Will do.' She walked to the back door and set their non-paying, but favourable, guest free.

When she returned to the hall, she saw Annabelle had managed to usher James into the sitting room and he was pouring out two glasses of whisky. She felt a pang of sadness. Then she shook herself and remembered it was her house: she would join them.

'So, Annabelle,' Daisy started as she entered the room, ignoring the black look she received from her spider-hating friend, 'where's everyone else?'

'Oh, I came back early but the others were enjoying the absolutely sweet-sounding local beer.'

'Sweet-sounding?' Daisy echoed.

'Yes, it had a name about Gloucestershire pigs. Delightful.'

'Oh, you mean Gloucestershire Spotted Cow?'

Annabelle swigged some of the whisky James had handed her. 'Oh, Daisy, that's no way to talk about yourself!'

Daisy, her back now to both of them, gripped the whisky decanter, her knuckles whitening. James came up and gently touched her arm. 'Ignore her, she's had one too many.'

Daisy turned. 'Annabelle, they do have another beer that you might like to try…'

James headed towards the sofa opposite Annabelle.

Daisy continued, 'It's called London Old Maid. It's honestly matured for so long, it's amazing, and it's incredibly bitter.' She smiled broadly. 'Just like some women I know...'

Annabelle peered at Daisy and nodded. 'It sounds OK but I imagine it wouldn't be to my taste.'

Daisy nodded. 'No, quite right, me neither.' She glanced at James who was biting hard on his lip in an attempt to control his laughter.

Daisy poured herself a drink and sat in the armchair.

'So, Daisy darling...' Annabelle started and Daisy inwardly cringed. 'We were hoping to stay for the week actually.' She glanced over at James and flashed him a coy smile. 'Would that be OK? I mean the children are on Easter anyway and it's such a bore having to try and keep them entertained.' She guffawed, her perfect mouth and bright-white teeth flashing James another smile. 'I mean there's only so many times you can take them to Harrods before they're like, "Mummy, this is getting boring."' She paused. 'Anyway I feel like we're at home here.' She fluttered her eyelashes at James at which point Daisy stood and sat next to James, leaning her shoulder against his protectively.

'I think we're full,' Daisy said; the lie came so easily.

'Oh,' Annabelle looked perplexed. 'It's just I ran the idea past Tom already and he said you had plenty of room in the coming week.'

Daisy flushed ever so slightly. She'd been caught out. 'Well, that's because I forgot to tell him about the party who are coming here to renew their vows.'

'Oh.' Annabelle arched a brow. 'You're registered for that sort of thing, are you?'

Daisy, like a rabbit in headlamps, stood abruptly. 'No, not really. Anyway, if you'll excuse me.'

'And what about staying?' Annabelle prompted as Daisy left the room.

Stopping by the door, she took a deep breath and turned. 'Of course, you must stay. I must have got the wrong week. Tom's better at these things than me.'

Daisy rushed to the kitchen, tears smarting her eyes. 'Good God, woman, pull yourself together,' she muttered as she angrily brushed the tears away. She closed her eyes and willed the ground to swallow her up; why did she feel so vulnerable around Annabelle?

A gentle hand on her back made her jump slightly and when she opened her eyes she found herself looking into James's green eyes, which were filled with concern.

'What happened in there?'

Daisy's cheeks reddened. She knew she had made a fool of herself. 'I thought we were full up next week,' she said lamely.

'No you didn't.' He shook his head and smiled. 'You gave as good as you got though.' Daisy gave him a small smile. 'Don't let her get to you, she's a paying guest, that's all.'

Daisy nodded. 'Yes, I know.'

James gave her shoulder a gentle squeeze and left her once again alone in the kitchen. She could hear James talking to Tom in hushed tones in the hall and then Tom arrived in the kitchen, flinging the door wide open and then shutting it with such dramatic flair, Daisy couldn't help but laugh.

'Daisy, James told me you're having some sort of nervous breakdown? What is going on with my dear friend?'

Daisy rolled her eyes, leaning against the granite counter. 'I am not having a nervous breakdown.' She smarted. 'Did he actually say that?'

'No.' Tom smiled. 'He was much kinder. His words were something like, "Daisy might need you. Think she's a bit upset," and I thought, Christ almighty, she's having a breakdown. No doubt a sophisticated one with class but still she's on the edge.'

Daisy chuckled. 'Tom.'

'No, seriously, my sweet, what is going on?'

'I don't know. I just don't like that woman,' she whispered and indicated the other side of the door.

'Who? Annabelle?'

Daisy nodded.

'Surely she's just a customer, you don't need to like her.'

'That's what James said,' Daisy admitted.

'Well, he's right and you should listen to him because not only is he beautiful to look at but the man has the brain of Einstein or similar.'

'Why don't you just tell him how you feel, Tom?' Daisy mocked. 'You're being far too subtle.'

'OK.' Tom put his hands in the air. 'She's fine. She's not having a nervous breakdown. Her tongue is still forked.'

'Oh, give over.' Daisy turned back to the sink to pour herself a glass of water.

'I mean you know he's clearly madly in love with you.'

Daisy stiffened. 'What?'

'He's clearly madly in love with you.' She turned. 'Tell me you're not actually surprised by that.'

Heat rose across her chest and up her neck. 'Well, that's ridiculous because James is our old friend. He can't love me.' Her heart had started to drum in her ears. 'Can he?'

'I don't know, Daisy, can he? Can't he? Are there are hard and fast rules when it comes to love?' He raised a brow. 'I think there probably aren't.'

'Well, I mean, I can't…' she stammered. 'I mean, no…'

'Daisy, darling, stop being so hard on yourself. He clearly fancies the pants off you and I'd go as far as to say he's madly in love with you.' Tom grew serious. 'You know Hugh always wanted you to be happy. You are *allowed* to be happy.'

She nodded, silent.

Hugh had reiterated over and over again in his letters that he wanted that for her, to let James, or whomever, into her life. Maybe he really had given her approval to move on.

'I might go and find him,' Daisy whispered and Tom smiled affectionately. 'Just to chat, mind you.'

'Of course.' Tom fluttered his camel-like eyelashes.

'It's a pity we couldn't…' she joked, indicating her and Tom. 'I mean we'd be so good together.'

'Oh, darling, I would think it would be a disaster.'

Daisy laughed and left him alone. She searched the ground floor of the house, a small lamp in the hall the only light on – left for guests returning in the evening. Then her gaze caught a glimpse of a shadow in the garden, someone sitting alone. She could see the outline of James sat out on the terrace and her heart leapt.

Taking a deep breath, she quietly pushed open the French doors and called out to him. 'James?'

'Hey.' She thought his voice sounded forced but put it down to her own nerves. 'You OK?'

'Yeah, I was just wondering if we could have a…' She stopped and listened. A female voice giggled and ran out of the bushes.

'I found another one, James, sweetie.' She proffered something to James who as yet hadn't spoken. 'What a fun game.'

Annabelle looked up at Daisy. 'Oh hello, we thought you'd gone to bed.'

Daisy tried to ignore the lump in her throat. 'Oh, you did, did you?' She knew her voice sounded strained.

Annabelle didn't pick up on her tone at all and waved her lit up phone at Daisy. 'I'm searching for tulips.'

'Um, why exactly?'

'Because,' Annabelle guffawed, 'I said to James I haven't seen any tulips yet this year and then James made the funniest joke ever.'

'Really?' Daisy said drily. 'Try me.'

'He said that the tulips grow as they look for the light…' She grinned. 'So I thought brilliant, get the old iPhone out and flash it about the place, you know?' Daisy wondered how many more whiskeys Annabelle had actually had. 'So I've found a few bulbs with green bits poking out the top.'

James turned hurriedly to Daisy. 'I will put them back in the ground tonight.'

Daisy didn't know whether to laugh or cry. Annabelle flung her arm around James's shoulders and kissed him squarely on the cheek.

'You know,' she said, 'if I wasn't married…'

'Yes, well, don't let me interrupt you.' Daisy turned on her heel, her stomach churning. She slammed the French doors a little too hard and stormed into the hall.

Tom stood by the front door, his fingers flying over the keys of his phone. 'Just letting the Dream Team know there'll be more jobs around the house for them.'

'Well,' Daisy seethed, 'you can start by getting them to plant the bloody bulbs back into the soil.'

Tom stopped, looking confused.

'And Tom?' His eyes widened. 'Don't give me relationship advice again. I've just gone to find James, and he and Annabelle are having a bloody delightful time digging up my garden like dogs on heat.'

Tom snorted so loudly he nearly dropped his phone.

'Pardon?'

Daisy knew her voice was shaking but continued unabashed. 'Yes, little sweet Annabelle is rooting around in the foliage for tulip shoots whilst James looks on.' She laughed an empty laugh. 'And I thought romance was dead? Turns out it's all about night time gardening sessions.'

She stared at Tom who was trying so hard to compose himself.

'OK,' he eventually said, a tremble of amusement still present in his voice. 'I'll tell the Dream Team they need to do some gardening.'

'Yes,' Daisy nodded firmly, 'and you can charge that little blonde thing out there for their labour.'

Tom looked hard at her.

'Don't give me that look, Tom. You know she's like some excitable Chihuahua.' Daisy barely took a breath before ploughing on. 'Actually I don't want to belittle Barbara.'

'Daisy,' Tom said, looking furtive.

'What, Tom? Am I now not allowed to voice my opinions in my own house?'

She followed Tom's gaze and turned slowly to find Annabelle staring at her open-mouthed.

'Oh Christ,' Daisy breathed. 'I'm...'

Annabelle looked at Daisy, tears filling her eyes. The silence was deafening, only the sound of the grandfather clock and Tom doing his nervous throat-clearing exercises.

'Annabelle,' she started, unsure of how she could explain away her rant.

'Daisy, you said I look like a Chihuahua?'

'I didn't mean... it came out wrong,' Daisy whispered. 'I'm really sorry.'

Then much to her surprise Annabelle ran up to her and hugged her. 'You are adorable. My friend, Tilly, in London once told me I look like a Great Dane. Can you imagine how humiliating that is?' She surveyed her audience. 'Have you seen a Great Dane? Bloody enormous unsightly dogs.'

Daisy, Tom and James looked on in amazement.

'Yet, you're stood there telling me I look like—' her voice turned to saccharine goo '—you're telling me I look like a cutey-beauty Chihuahua. Oh my God, that must mean my macrobiotic diet is working a treat.' She smiled happily. 'Actually I'm mixing macro bio's up with high protein. It's what they're all doing dans LA. My nutritionist, Javier, is such a fan and goodness, the man is right, I am losing pounds left, right and centre.' She pulled a face. 'There's only one downside to it and that's that it plays havoc with your guts.'

Her audience of three pulled a face at the same time and

then tried to disguise their disgust at Annabelle's over-sharing.

'So, thank you, Daisy, you are the perfect hostess.' Annabelle kissed Daisy on the cheek, a definite reek of whisky wafting in front of Daisy's nose and then skipped up the stairs. 'I'm going to get my beauty sleep so I continue to look like a cute little pup.'

They smiled at her, Daisy in shock that she had actually got away with the whole thing. Just as Annabelle retreated from view, Tom opened his mouth to speak, but then her petite face peered over the edge of the bannister.

'Actually, Daisy-Doo, I tell you what. Shall I put Javier in touch with you so you can shed a few of those pounds?' She blew Daisy a kiss. 'Just a thought.'

Daisy, open-mouthed, knew she had no right to be angry but her weight was a no-go area.

James laid a hand on her shoulder to placate her. She softened under his touch.

'Let it go,' James whispered. Once they heard Annabelle's door close, Tom ushered them silently to the kitchen. He closed the door behind them and turned. They exchanged looks with one another and James chuckled, setting Daisy off and then Tom. For a good few minutes there was no exchange of words except breathless murmurings of 'Chihuahua' and 'dogs on heat'. Daisy literally thought she might pull a stomach muscle; her abs hadn't seen that much exercise for a good while.

As their laughter subsided, she said, 'I literally can't believe I got away with that.'

'You are one lucky lady,' Tom agreed. 'It's a good thing she's not the brightest penny…'

'But then to say I need Javier,' Daisy said sternly, suddenly remembering how the meeting with Annabelle had ended. 'Javier can stick his macrobiotics up his what's-it.'

James looked at her kindly. 'You're perfect. You don't need to change at all.'

'Anyway, we'd all prefer you didn't gas the house out with your good bacteria…' said Tom.

Daisy, who had barely gathered her composure, was set off again and she went to bed happily that night, dreaming about her upturned garden, macrobiotics and Chihuahuas.

Chapter 9

Daisy had entirely forgotten that Easter Sunday fell early this year. On one hand, since Hugh's death she was painfully aware of time and, on the other, days like this appeared to spring out of nowhere.

She had just made a cup of coffee and was staring out the study window, trying to hang onto the clarity of Hugh's face in her mind. It was often said that with time, grief grew easier but was it just because the starkness of memories and feelings grew blurred? Maybe, Daisy decided, as she stared into the middle distance, her feet up on the windowsill, that was how the human race survived. It was the mind's ability to forget the bad, focus on the good. She couldn't pretend to herself that her marriage had been perfect. This revelation had only occurred her to recently. For months she had told everyone that her marriage had been flawless, full of love, but there *had* been tension, particularly about not having children. It now compounded the emptiness – it was one thing when you still had a partner but then to lose that and have no children; she did feel very alone.

She screwed her eyes shut and tried to put the whirl of negativity to bed. There was no point thinking like this. She reopened her eyes and closed them quickly again, thinking she must be dreaming. But then Daisy stared out the window once more.

Annabelle was skipping around the garden dressed in a bonnet and a ridiculously clingy silk dressing gown. Daisy looked briefly at her coffee and frowned; she hadn't put whisky in there, had she? She looked up again. No, Annabelle was definitely dressed as a raunchy shepherdess and then out of nowhere children appeared with rabbit ears on their heads or fluffy sheep tails attached to their bottoms.

'Bloody hell,' she muttered to herself.

Then she watched James walk over to them and Annabelle guffawed loudly at whatever it was he said. Daisy gave her a hard stare. That woman was incorrigible and now, much to Daisy's horror, Annabelle readjusted her dressing gown so her cleavage had a better vantage point and her waist looked unrealistically small: Daisy decided she must look into surgery – a gastric band.

Tearing her gaze away from the pastoral scene being played out on her lawn, she realised then that it was Easter Sunday. Normally she would have made a huge Easter lunch and begrudgingly invited her mother. Because which daughter doesn't love their mother gracing her table with comments about dry chicken and poncey gravy?

As if walking further into the surreal dream that was her life, she thought she heard her mother's voice at the bottom of the stairs. Possibly talking to James. She crept out of the study and peered carefully over the bannister and yes, indeed, her mother was stood there in her finest which basically meant her cleanest cords and an aubergine-coloured mohair jumper she had had since the Seventies.

Her mother looked up the stairs at that exact moment.

'Hello, Daisy, it's a good thing you've got Tom here who remembered to invite me for Easter lunch.'

Daisy shot Tom a look who was now pretending to hang himself behind her mother's back, mouthing 'sorry'.

'Well, to be honest, what with everything I didn't even remember it was Easter.'

Her mother's mouth tightened. 'So therefore you've forgotten that it was at Easter your father left me.'

Tom nodded sympathetically now that her mother's attention was entirely focused on him. 'Where did he go?' Tom asked.

A pregnant pause filled the room and then, 'He died, Tom. Died.'

'Oh.' Tom reddened. 'Sorry.'

'I would say that it's a bit late for sorry all these years later.'

Tom looked at the floor.

'Good God mother, he was only trying to be nice.'

Her mother's face momentarily softened. 'Yes, he is very nice unlike my daughter who forgets to invite her own mother to lunch.'

'I didn't do it on purpose!' Daisy righted herself. 'I didn't even remember.'

'Um, Daisy?' Annabelle was suddenly there too.

Daisy leaned over the bannister. 'Yes?' She forced a smile.

'I'm organising a chocolate egg hunt as you can see.' Annabelle showed off her entourage of bunnies and sheep. 'Do you want to join in?'

'Um…' The truth was she'd prefer to be roasting a chicken so it became inedible and putting poncey Waitrose gravy in the microwave. 'I really must help with lunch.'

'Don't worry,' Tom proffered, 'I've got it under control. You go and have fun.'

Daisy rolled her eyes to herself. Fun. Genius.

'Thanks, Tom,' she said through gritted teeth. 'How good of you to be so organised. What would you like me to do, Annabelle?'

Annabelle grinned and whipped a paper bag from under the hall console table, skipped up the stairs and pushed it towards Daisy.

'Shall we see you outside in ten?'

Daisy dared not look and started to make excuses when she

caught Hermione's gaze. The poor girl looked so miserable as her mother once again took over proceedings.

'OK,' Daisy said and smiled at Hermione. It broke her heart to think any child was sad but under her roof she wouldn't allow that to happen: no matter what extraordinary get-up was inside the bag.

A mere five minutes later, Daisy had managed to jiggle herself into a full adult-size bunny outfit.

'Don't think the playboy mansion will be adopting that costume any time soon,' Lisa laughed as she walked past.

'Thanks, Lisa.' She indicated the zipper. 'Can you help?' Daisy caught a glimpse of herself in the mirror. 'Christ, I look like an oversized, fluffy marshmallow.'

'Sexy, my friend. That is what I call sexy.' Lisa patted her firmly on the arm. 'You're a sport.'

Daisy looked glum. 'It's actually because I feel bad for calling Annabelle a dog on heat and I feel for her daughter.'

Lisa giggled. 'Yes, I heard about that.'

'How's Bob?'

Lisa smiled coyly. 'Fine. He's the same as before…'

'Only a tiny bit in love with our English rose?'

'Maybe.' She blushed. 'He's talking about marriage…'

Daisy squealed and the over-sized rabbit grabbed her friend and hugged her. 'That's crazy but amazing! And you? What do you want?'

Before Lisa could answer, a certain petite blonde had jogged up the stairs and beamed at Daisy.

'Oh, you are a darling rabbit.'

'Thanks,' Daisy said drily.

'You ready?'

Daisy nodded and followed Annabelle through the sitting room and towards the French doors. It wasn't until Annabelle had pushed the door open that she realised Annabelle hadn't just been talking about the Holibobs crew. Her garden was slowly filling with a herd of locals. They waved at her cheerily as they made their way through the side gate and in the direction of a table of jellies and meringues.

'Um,' she said, 'what's going on?'

'Well, I went to church this morning and met quite a few of the locals on the way. Good God,' Annabelle drawled nasally. 'They do have the most extraordinary accent around here.'

'It's just the Gloucestershire accent.'

'Yes, but they don't pronounce all the syllables.' Annabelle shook her head in disbelief and ploughed on, 'So I said they should all come here, bring their children for a bit of Easter fun.'

'The food?' Daisy stood bewildered, rooted to the spot.

'Oh, I got the husband to go to Waitrose and Tom got a table from your barn.'

Daisy took a deep breath. Bunting adorned the trees in pastels and she could just make out Tom running around hiding chocolate eggs.

'Right, you ready?' Annabelle beamed, no apology on the horizon, Daisy noted. She clearly thought it was quite normal to take over someone's house without permission.

She saw her mother standing awkwardly in the middle of the amassing crowd.

'So what am I actually doing?'

'Well, I'll introduce you as the Easter Bunny and then all you need to do is hop around the garden and get the children to look all over for the eggs.'

'What are you doing in the meantime?' Daisy quizzed.

'Oh, I've got bubbly arriving for the adults.' She narrowed her eyes. 'But you can't have any until you've done your duties so don't give me those puppy dog eyes, sweetie.' She laughed.

Daisy stared at her, tongue-tied, irritation fizzling in the pit of her stomach. She started to turn on her heel. No way was she making a fool of herself like that, not whilst Annabelle quaffed Prosecco. But Annabelle had already launched herself outside onto the terrace and boomed at the sea of tweed, gardening and mucking out clothes.

'Good morning everyone!' she hollered. 'So the egg hunt is about to begin, my friends, and I would like to introduce the Easter bunny.' Annabelle looked back over her shoulder and shot Daisy a look.

Daisy caught James's eye and wanted the ground to swallow her up. How on earth did she go from being the lady of a beautiful guesthouse to a sober-as-a-judge rabbit?

Daisy stepped outside hoping the rabbit's neck and head disguised her. She knew it was wishful thinking, confirmed by the laughter and Mr Smith from the farm up the road shouting in his broad local accent, 'Wahey. Here comes Mrs Ronaldson. Doesn't she look like a playboy bunny?'

A titter of laughter rippled across the crowd.

'Lots of farmers here,' Nigel from the post office joined in. 'Make sure you don't get shot, Daisy love!'

Daisy looked back at James who smiled at her kindly and then Annabelle trotted over to him with a glass of something bubbly and he took it graciously, turning his back on Daisy and laughing seemingly uproariously at one of her jokes.

Daisy jutted out her jaw. She wished the farmers would take a pop at a certain blonde.

'Come on then, bunny rabbit.' Annabelle smiled at her. 'We're waiting.'

Daisy took a step forward, then another, sweat trickling down her back from both embarrassment and the sheer weight of the ridiculous costume.

'Jump,' Annabelle hooted. 'You're a rabbit!'

'Actually I'm not,' Daisy pointed out and James smiled at this.

'Yes, but,' Annabelle hissed, 'you are for now. I'm not stupid you know, I know you're not actually a rabbit.' She nodded seriously.

Annabelle told all the children – about twenty faces – to start hunting and the rabbit would come and help. They scattered like marbles across a table. Annabelle looked at Daisy.

Daisy took one tentative hop. She knew it was small and barely recognisable as a skip – it looked more like she had a stone in her shoe.

'That's not hopping.' Annabelle came over. 'Like this.' She squatted and rocketed herself into the air before landing back in a crouched position. Daisy had to admit she made a good rabbit.

'See?' Annabelle smiled. 'God, I tell you what, that yoga and Pilates plus Javier has done wonders for my core.' She looked pointedly at James. 'I have a *strong* core, James.'

Daisy frowned. Could rabbits go to prison, she wondered, for murder. Then as the adults now swilling fizz waited for her to push off once again, she squatted, wishing she had used that gym membership after all. She counted to three in her head and pushed herself off leaping about half the height of Annabelle but, she thought, she hadn't been given much of a chance to practise.

'That'll do,' Annabelle said, gesturing for her to continue.

Daisy rolled her eyes and jumped again sending everyone into a round of applause. By the time she reached the first child of about eight years old, she was completely out of puff.

'Have you found an egg?' she breathed heavily, wiping her brow with a paw.

She recognised him as one of the Holibobs.

'No, I bloody haven't. You are a rubbish Easter bunny, did you even hide any chocolate?'

Daisy looked hard at him. 'How old are you?'

'Nine.'

'Do you think it's okay to swear and to talk to me like that?'

The boy laughed hysterically. 'Brilliant.' He called over to Annabelle. 'Mum, the Easter bunny has got a chip on her shoulder. She's getting narky.'

Annabelle luckily hadn't heard, as she was too busy flirting with James who was smiling broadly. Daisy turned back to the child.

'You afraid of anything?'

'What do you mean?' The boy eyed her. 'You mean like spiders and ghosts and stuff?'

Daisy nodded.

'Well, I mean I'm not afraid of anything but I hate ghosts.'

Daisy grew serious, dropping her voice to stern whisper. 'That's a shame. You know the house has a family of ghosts. I speak to them and they respect me. There's a little boy about your age, actually. He can't bear rudeness and if he hears people being rude to me. He gets very protective…' She left a long pause. 'Anyway, enjoy the hunt.' Smiling, Daisy jumped off, more bounce in her action this time, the boy's mouth agog.

Daisy eventually started to enjoy herself. Most of the children – most – were actually nice and sweet, reinforcing her own pang of regret at not having had her own. One little girl she recognised from a house in the village, all of age six, whipped out an iPhone and asked for a selfie with Daisy. Daisy obliged; it would probably be her first and last chance for any sort of fame. Just as she was showing off her tail to three children, she turned to find James stood in front of her. The children behind were squeezing her tail and then one got a bit carried away with his hitting and whacked her on her actual bottom.

'Ow!' Daisy squealed and she looked back at them. 'Rabbits do have feelings, you know?'

'Sorry,' the boy said, abashed.

She turned back to James and grinned. 'I'm pretty sure there'll be complaints. I've disciplined most of them…' She spotted Annabelle's son just then. '…And scared one of them half to death.'

James laughed. 'You actually suit it.'

Daisy narrowed her eyes. 'What, my fat suit? Is that because you actually can't notice that much difference? Fat and unshaven?'

James snorted. 'If Hugh could see you now.'

Daisy grew serious, reality hitting home. 'Why do you always do that? Why did you bring his name up?'

'Oh, sorry.' James looked at the ground. 'I didn't know you…'

'Every time I start enjoying myself, start to feel like my old self, someone brings up Hugh's name and it makes me feel…' She trailed off. 'It makes me feel…' She wanted to say guilty but what was she guilty of? 'It makes me feel sad.'

'Sorry,' James mumbled again. He looked quite thrown and Daisy regretted her words.

'No, it's fine. We must keep talking about him, we need to keep him alive, don't we?' Her voice sounded strained and she kept a smile plastered on her face. But then she caught sight of Bob and Lisa kissing under the big oak tree and her heart felt wrung out.

'OK,' Tom shouted, withdrawing his head from the inside of a shrub. 'The last egg has officially been found! Well done kids, and a big well done to our Easter bunny.'

Daisy dipped her head modestly as everyone whooped and wolf-whistled. She caught Annabelle's eye and smiled but Annabelle was looking grave, her eyes on James.

Tom indicated to James that glasses needed refilling and James set off to help. Daisy, still floundering and wondering why she felt so strange about the mention of Hugh, didn't notice Annabelle approach.

Annabelle, she noticed, had drunk a few glasses and her cheeks were flushed. 'Must be hard,' she said.

'Hard?' Daisy asked.

'Being with all these children when you haven't had your own.'

Daisy's heart started to hammer, her head buzzing. 'Not at all.'

'That's not what I heard,' Annabelle said, looking her straight in the eyes. 'James says you and Hugh couldn't have children. So ironic really that everyone's hunting for eggs. Symbolic, yes?'

Daisy shook, her body tingling with tension and as the tears slid down her face, she allowed the sob building in her chest to escape. James looked over from where he was pouring the vicar another glass, his face filled with concern.

'Annabelle, I'd like you to leave. I'd like you and your family to leave.'

Annabelle gave her a wry smile. 'Oh, come on, Daisy it was just a little joke.'

'Joke?' Daisy spluttered. 'Just get out of my house…'

'And what would your business partners say about that? Look at what fun they're having and we're paying a lot of money to stay here this week.' She paused. 'A lot of money. You can ask James, I offered triple.' She smiled. 'We *love* your house and the people in it.' She searched for James and catching his eye, smiled, fluttering her hand like the Queen. And I am just overjoyed that we managed to put your comments about me looking like a dog behind us.'

Chapter 10

That night Daisy tossed and turned, the sheets twisting in a sweaty mess around her. Images of Annabelle and James flitted through her mind as well as slow-motion videos of Hugh in Amsterdam; he was looking for her but he couldn't see her, she was right in front of him, screaming in his face but he looked straight through her.

At 2 a.m. she came to very quickly, sat bolt upright, her heart pounding; it was beating so loudly she could still hear it. She concentrated on her breathing.

'Daisy, don't be ridiculous, he's dead. Hugh is dead.' She wiped away a solitary tear and nestled back under the sheets but there was her heart again. How could she still hear it? Now wide awake, she got up and realised it was someone knocking at the front door. No one else had stirred so she slipped on her dressing gown and crept down the stairs. Maybe one of the guests had locked themselves out but just to be on the safe side she grabbed an umbrella from the stand. The person at the door cast shadows across the hall floor.

'Who's there?' she called out, debating whether or not to get James or Tom. No, she decided, she didn't want to look weak in front of James and she had already seen the way Tom handled burglars. When they house shared many moons ago, a man in a balaclava broke into their digs and had Lisa's wallet and Daisy's computer. Tom who had drunkenly fallen asleep at the kitchen table woke up and thought it was one of his friends and invited him in for a night cap but on realising his friend wouldn't speak, screamed like a girl and started chucking scatter cushions at the intruder. Daisy had risen to find Tom blaspheming at the man for stepping all over his polyester zebra rug. The intruder, perhaps shell-shocked, realised it wasn't worth burgling a crazy students' house and dropped the wares, fleeing out the door. Daisy rang the police and Lisa slept through the entire event.

So, no, she wouldn't call Tom either.

'Um, who's there?' she asked, forcing herself to sound confident. 'Did you forget your key?'

'No,' came a male voice. 'Sorry, I know it's really late. Only I've just driven down from Scotland overnight and was really hoping to stay the rest of the night if you have a room free. I Googled you and you're the first on my list but if you haven't got space then I'll try elsewhere.'

Daisy opened the door and peered through the crack, tentative.

Her heart leapt. The man on the other side of the door was well over six foot tall and broad-shouldered. He was dressed in a blazer, white shirt, jeans and boots.

He smiled at her and her already beating heart nearly jumped out of her ribcage. The man was beautiful. She wanted to ask his name and if he had said Adonis she would not have been surprised.

'Alistair.' He extended his hand.

She took his hand and was surprised by the strength behind his grip.

'Daisy,' she eventually managed to get out and as realised he was trying to withdraw his hand, let go. But she continued to stare, mesmerised, into his piercing green eyes.

'Um,' he said, smiling. 'Do you have a room? I really am so

sorry for getting you up at this ungodly hour. I thought I'd be able to drive on but I'm too tired.' He rubbed his eyes as if to make his point. 'I'm heading to London but if I could stop here tonight that'd be great.'

'Of course.' Daisy, suddenly self-conscious, pulled her robe tighter around her waist, well what she had of a waist. 'Please come inside.'

He strode into the hall and by the light of the lamp she had to hide her gasp. The man was even more beautiful than she had realised. His chiselled cheeks and strong jaw line were traffic-stopping. Realising she really needed to try and act normal, she shuffled over to the registration book and checked which rooms had not been taken over by American Bob and Barbara or the Holibobs crowd. An unwanted image of James and Annabelle popped into her head and she pushed it to the back of her mind. Looking up again, she smiled at her new, very welcome guest and said, 'Yes, we have a room on the first floor. I'm afraid it's small but it's en suite and hopefully to your liking.' *To your liking?* she thought to herself. She sounded like she was selling the poor Scotsman a sofa at DFS.

'I'm sure it will be perfect.' He smiled again and, realising she was rooted to the spot , Daisy forced one foot in front of another.

'I'm sorry about my appearance,' she said as they walked up the stairs. 'Normally, I'm much better dressed.'

What was she wittering on about? It was the middle of the night. And, no, she wasn't normally better dressed, he was lucky he had got her pink fluffy robe and Snoopy slippers because he could have had the baked bean-stained T-shirt of Hugh's that she insisted could not go to charity. So, whether he could believe it or not, this was the glamorous Daisy.

Once they reached his room, she unlocked the door, walked in and switched on the lamp. A soft glow fell over the double bed made up in crisp white linen, and fluffy towels sat invitingly at the end. She lifted her gaze from the bed to the ridiculously good-looking Celtic dish who had a wry smile on his face. She reddened. It was probably not a good idea to stare longingly at a bed when Mr World was stood on the other side.

'Anyway,' she mumbled, 'it's all yours and of course breakfast is included.' She made a mental note to get up earlier than normal and practise cooking eggs. Though, as he was Scottish, maybe he wanted porridge? Or haggis?

'Do you want anything in particular for breakfast? I mean if you're from Scotland, would you like porridge or stag?'

He laughed. 'Coffee and toast is perfect. Thank you.'

She nodded and shuffled from the room. The flip-flop of her Snoopy slippers dragging over the rug and wooden floorboards was the only sound until she turned in the doorway. 'Anyway, welcome and see you when you wake.' She patted the doorjamb with her hand, regretting those words as she imagined her guest lying in bed.

'Och aye…' she said in a terrible Scottish accent and he belted out a laugh, immediately putting his hand over his mouth as he realised the hour.

'Very good impression.'

She giggled, blushing. 'Awful but thank you for being so kind.' Daisy turned and quietly shut the door behind her, leaning up against it. She could almost feel his electric presence through the wood. A movement off to her left caught her eye and she saw James emerge from the dark.

'Everything OK?' His voice did not sound at all friendly.

'Yes, why?' she whispered, moving towards him.

'Who was that?'

'A new guest. Alistair drove from Scotland overnight and needs to get to London but he's too tired to drive any further.'

'You seemed to be getting on well.'

Despite the poor light, she could see James frowning.

'Well, I mean, he's been here for all of five minutes and I think it's only right to be welcoming.'

James's voice softened and he stroked her arm with his hand. 'Yes, quite right.' He paused. 'You going back to bed? Or do you fancy a late night cocoa?'

She smiled. 'Well, there's an offer I can't refuse.'

They padded quietly down the stairs, into the hall and through to the kitchen. Only once the door was shut and the standard lamp switched on, did they talk. She realised it had been a long time since she had seen James out of a suit or jeans and a shirt. He wore a white T-shirt and long plaid pyjama bottoms. The T-shirt was stretched tight across his chest and she remembered his olive skin and how toned he remained to this day, his pecs rippling as he carefully placed mugs on the table and started to warm milk on the Aga.

'I like your slippers.' He smiled warmly. 'Cute.'

Cute. Why was she always cute or bubbly? As she had said to Lisa, these were adjectives for those women carrying one pound too many.

'I have some very demure leather slippers upstairs and a silk kimono.'

'Really?' He raised a brow, unable to hide the look of disbelief on his face.

'You know I don't,' she sulked, 'but I like to pretend there's a sexy, classy side to me.'

He stirred the milk with his back to her but at her words, he turned, his face serious. 'You are beautiful, Daisy, never think otherwise.'

The atmosphere grew thick with a heavy tension. Daisy shifted in her chair and for the second time that night tightened the belt around her dressing gown dreaming of a slim waist like Annabelle's.

James spooned out cocoa and added the warm milk, before stirring the drinks and handing Daisy a delicious looking cocoa. There went another centimetre of her waistline, she thought, but not caring too much as she sipped at the velvety chocolate drink.

'You are a fine cocoa maker, I will give you that.'

He smiled and sat in the chair next to her. 'Ah, that's the joy of many a late night in the office. You get good at the oddest things. I'm also a dab hand at making a bed out of a swivel chair and a desk.' He laughed. 'It's all in the angle.'

Daisy smiled. 'I remember Hugh saying that. I was always amazed at how he could make a bed out of anything. He honestly could sleep standing up.'

'Yep, if you're tired enough, you'll find a way.'

Daisy realised for the first time in a long time she was talking about Hugh without a wrenching at her heart. Maybe the pain was beginning to soften, lessen. She had been told countless times it would but it was hard to believe in the midst of raw grief.

James had read her mind. 'I'm the same, Daisy, I feel the same.'

'How did you know…' Her voice trailed off. 'What I was thinking.'

'Because…' He paused. 'When you think about Hugh you get a beautiful shine in your eyes and I could tell they weren't filled with the same hurt.' He took her hand. 'Because it's getting a bit easier, isn't it?'

She nodded. 'Yes, slowly. Thanks to you, to Tom and Lisa. You've dragged me kicking and screaming through hell and I actually feel like there might be light at the end of the tunnel.'

James looked at her over his mug and nodded. 'Yes,' he said, holding her gaze. 'I think there is too.'

'But I'll never forget him, you know.' Her tone was defensive. 'I won't stop loving him either.'

'Of course not.' James lowered his gaze and stared into the remnants of his cocoa. 'Just do what makes you happy, Daisy, that's all that really matters.'

That heavy, almost charged, atmosphere had once again descended on the room and Daisy was suddenly highly aware that James still hand her hand in his. He followed her eyes and squeezed her hand gently before releasing it.

'Anyway,' he said eventually, 'I should probably try and get some sleep. You too.'

'Yes.' She felt as if in a dream, like everything had taken on a surreal quality. 'Yes, I need sleep too.'

She got up, pulled the tie on her dressing gown even tighter – though it couldn't get much tighter without her asphyxiating herself – and shuffled awkwardly from the kitchen, Snoopy on the left following Snoopy on the right.

Once she was curled up in bed, she thought about the strange events of the last couple of hours. She wasn't sure her heart could take much more emotion or, for that matter, testosterone. Daisy Ronaldson, she thought to herself, maybe there's life in the old dog yet. Then revisiting the subject of dogs she thought of Annabelle, and the quiet and beautiful calm was quickly replaced by a feeling of vulnerability. If she had known how her world would have been rocked by the arrival of her bed and breakfast guests, would she have agreed to the whole venture?

Her mind turned to Alistair and with a smile on her face, she realised, yes, it was quite exciting to never know who was about to turn up on your doorstep. She heard James quietly padding to his room opposite and then a creak from the bedroom next door: Alistair's room. She was sandwiched between two gorgeous men and she couldn't say fairer than that.

Chapter 11

Daisy moved about the kitchen in the morning with a skip in her step. She had been up since 5 a.m. trying to perfect the poached egg.

'How frigging hard can it be?' she muttered aloud as she dispensed of another hard yolk into the bin. She remembered an episode of Chris Evans' breakfast show about poached eggs. They had even interviewed Delia Smith and she had suggested putting cling film over the pan, or was it cling film over the eggs? And were they cooked yet or still raw? Where was Delia when she was needed? A bead of sweat rolled down the side of Daisy's face and she moaned with frustration. She remembered her conversation with Annabelle about her ovaries and clunked the slotted spoon into the pan.

He had said that he just wanted coffee and toast, though she wasn't even good at that. Luckily Tom was a dab hand at the coffee machine Hugh had bought. To Daisy it looked like an unidentified flying object but Hugh had described it as 'a thing of beauty'. How something that was essentially plastic and had lit up buttons with a long silver nozzle could be a thing of beauty, she had no idea.

Three hours later Alistair came down the stairs, by which point there were no eggs left and the coffee machine was complaining of a blockage.

He looked beautiful. *Beautiful.* The man had had incredibly little beauty sleep for such a god.

She pushed her hair back and retied her ponytail. She had put on the sexiest jeans she owned – admittedly they were a little tight around the middle but she had chosen a low cut black lace top in a bid to move attention away from the bulge and more towards the chest.

'Alistair,' she said, in as husky a voice as she could manage, though it hadn't come out quite as intended and instead sounded like a cat with a trapped fur ball. She tried again, more normal this time. 'Alistair, did you sleep well? I'm afraid we're out of eggs. What would you like for breakfast?'

He smiled broadly at her. 'Just coffee and toast. Us Scots don't need anything in particular.'

She blushed ever so slightly and glanced up at James who had just come into the kitchen.

'Well, even more embarrassingly the coffee machine has decided to have a paddy this morning but James will make you some in the percolator.'

James put down a couple of plates – eggs untouched – and looked up at her with the strangest look. Eventually he nodded and silently went about making coffee. Why was he being so awkward with their guest? She started to chatter nervously to make up for the dreadful silence.

'So, do you come from the Highlands or the Lowlands?'

She popped two slices of fresh farmhouse bread in the toaster.

Alistair laughed. 'Glasgow.'

'Right,' she giggled awkwardly, not knowing if that answered her question. She picked up her now cold cup of tea and took a deep gulp.

'Next you'll be asking me,' he said in what could only be

described as a beautiful and perfect lilt, 'if I wear underwear under my kilt!'

A snort of embarrassment built in her throat and she spluttered her tea over her aforementioned black top. 'Oh. Oh my.'

Alistair handed her a tea towel off the side, apologising profusely. 'Gosh, I'm so sorry. I didn't mean to…'

Their fingers brushed as the tea towel was passed between them and she felt a jolt of electricity. Their eye contact lingered, Daisy's eyes on his lips, as his tongue wandered the outline of his mouth seemingly in slow motion.

A loud clunk to her left alarmed her and shook her back to the now. James had placed, no, *slammed* down Alistair's coffee causing it to spill all over the farmhouse table. Wordlessly he left the kitchen and Daisy could only apologise.

'I'm not sure what's got into him,' she said, her hand rubbing the base of her neck. Was it really only eight-thirty in the morning? She felt like she had been up for hours and for no reason whatsoever as they had run out of eggs and the eggs she had cooked turned out to be as edible as a dog's breakfast. A tad cruelly, she thought to herself that that couldn't be true as Annabelle hadn't touched it either. Although, frankly, Annabelle could have James, she did not want to associate herself with someone who was quite so rude. She recognised this might have been a bit rich coming from her after the last few days but it was James who had disciplined her and told her to be nice to the paying guests. Well, he should have been taking a leaf out of his own book.

'Listen, I'm so sorry.' She passed her hand over her forehead, letting it rest there. 'We are normally much more, um, professional than this.' *Well, she wasn't sure that was strictly true either.*

'Ach.' He smiled kindly. 'You weren't expecting another guest so I totally understand. I really appreciate you letting me stay and I'm pretty sure I should be on my way now. So, if I could just pay the bill.'

She wanted to shout, '*No, have it free! On me! We're all a complete bunch of imbeciles and quite frankly someone so beautiful as yourself should never have to pay for anything.'*

Instead she chose, 'Of course. But we will not be charging you for breakfast obviously.'

'Oh no, you charge me whatever you need to.' He started to walk from the kitchen and Daisy walked as sexily as she could behind him, though highly aware of the now cold material of her top clinging to her bosom and the way her belt was digging into her muffin top. Once she had figured out how to use the credit card machine – Tom had tried to teach her but she could never remember which button came first and, so far, had taken one thousand pounds out of Tom's account when she had meant to type in ten – and had offered Alistair a complimentary chocolate about a million times, she decided she really had better let the poor man go. He had started to shift his weight from side to side in a bid to make a move.

'Well, listen, thanks so much for knocking on my door this morning.' Had she actually just said that aloud? 'It's not often we get Braveheart land up on the doorstep.' *Daisy, be quiet, you're making it worse.*

'Well,' Alistair said, picking up his small overnight bag sat by the door, 'I'll be passing this way on my return journey to Glasgow if you're around.'

It was his turn to look embarrassed.

'I mean I know it's your guesthouse, but I meant if you haven't gone away.'

She almost laughed. Going away would have suggested a life. 'No,' she said with the most certainty she had felt about anything for a while. 'I will most definitely be here. I have no plans.' She paused. 'Ever.'

He smiled. 'Perhaps you'd like to have supper with me, say on Friday. Have you got a spare room for Friday?'

She already knew they did but she was so overwhelmed with excitement, she dived head first into the book, pretending to study it hard. She could hear Tom's voice: *play it cool, Daisy. No, that doesn't mean turn Ice Queen, it means aloof.*

'Um, we are very booked up.' She looked up to register Alistair's disappointment. 'No, nothing.'

What was she going on about? Maybe she was deploying Ice Queen again.

'Oh no,' she continued, putting her hand dramatically to her forehead. 'What am I talking about? That's the following year.'

Why couldn't she have said week? Year? Great. Less Ice Queen or aloof, more lacking any form of intelligence.

'Great,' Alistair said, clearly bemused. 'Can I book?'

She momentarily looked up to the ceiling, waiting for some sign of approval from Hugh but instead she noticed the paintwork on the ceiling roses was flaking and there were cobwebs she couldn't reach.

'Of course,' she said after a long pause. 'That's great. All booked in.' She squiggled his name in the book but her hand was shaking so much, she could barely make out what she had put. It looked a lot like the word 'sex'. She quickly slammed the book shut. Freud would have a field day with her.

'Great.' Alistair put his hand out to shake hers but then they both went in for a hug at the same time which resulted in tangled limbs and their lips being dangerously close to one another's.

Lisa bounded down the stairs, Barbara in her arms. As she caught sight of Daisy and Alistair performing some strange interpretative dance routine, she stopped suddenly.

'Oh.' She looked at them, looked at the ceiling and back at them. 'Oh.'

Daisy managed to disentangle herself. 'Nothing to see here.'

'Right.' Alistair picked up his bag again. 'Great stay. Thanks so much. I look forward to my next stay.'

'Our pleasure. You are always welcome at my guesthouse. Always.'

He turned on his heel and walked stiffly outside. It wasn't until she saw him get in his car – a very smart sports car no less – that she dared breathe. It was only then that she realised how much she had failed to flirt. Why was she so unable to be sexy?

'Lisa,' she murmured eventually, glancing up the stairs at her friend who was stood, unmoving, a huge grin on her face. 'Why am I so clumsy?'

'Because you're Daisy Ronaldson,' Lisa offered, rather unhelpfully.

'Great.' Daisy looked in earnest at her friend. 'Can you teach me to be sexy by Friday?'

'Friday?'

'Yes, Alistair wants to take me out to dinner and last time I went out to a restaurant I managed to flick my martini olive in Hugh's business partner's eye.'

'You don't even drink martinis.'

'No,' Daisy admitted. 'That was my first mistake.' She pulled a face. 'Vile.'

Lisa made her way down the stairs towards Daisy and took her face in her hands. 'Daisy, you don't need to change for anyone. Any man worth his weight in gold is one that thinks you're beautiful for your clumsiness and lack of sexiness.'

'Thanks, Lisa,' Daisy narrowed her eyes, 'I knew I could rely on you.' She felt a familiar pang. 'And that man was Hugh and Hugh is dead.'

Lisa's face fell. 'Sorry, I didn't mean it like that.'

'No, I know.' Daisy nodded, brushing away tears. 'It is true though, I move as gracefully as a new born gelding.'

'You're not that graceful, Daisy,' Tom said, laughing behind her. Lisa shot him a look and Daisy stared hard at Lisa and Tom in turn.

'So glad we had this conversation, *friends*.'

'Come on.' Lisa took Daisy's hand. 'Tom and I are going to give you a master class in embracing your sexiness.'

Tom whooped with glee. 'I've been waiting to get my hands

on you, Daisy.' Daisy allowed herself to be led up to the top floor where Lisa and Tom had decamped. She hadn't been up here since they moved in and she was shocked to find that they really had made themselves at home. Clothes hung from every nook and cranny, empty wine bottles were strewn across the floor and the beds were unmade and fusty. It took her back twenty years to their university digs. Though she wondered, looking at her friends, was the environment conducive to dating? She couldn't imagine Bob (and Barbara) relaxing up here with Lisa in her quite frankly stinky room.

As if reading her mind, Lisa said, 'We go to Bob's room.'

Daisy raised her brows.

'You're not my mother,' Lisa pointed out.

'No, but it is my house.' She looked around her again at the bottles, the clothes, the mess. This is where she had thought she might make a children's nursery. She had imagined blue or pink bunting along the walls, a white cot and her mother's old wooden nursing chair. Then she looked at Lisa and Tom, their faces crestfallen at her ridiculous parental stance. 'But,' she smiled, 'I actually like what you've done to the place. It's very...' She searched for the right word. 'Deconstructed shabby chic...'

They exchanged looks with each other and fell about laughing. Daisy gripped her stomach in a bid to stop but she had gone. She felt a wonderful lightness again, her mind taking her back to their university house. The way they had looked out for each other on drunken nights, over break-ups and, of course, somehow dragged each other through their exams by the skin of their teeth. Particularly, her French; the nights Tom and Lisa had stayed up with her pretending to be examiners and listening to her garble on in some language entirely unintelligible to not only the English, but the French too. She had basically invented her own lingo. Hadn't that deserved some merit?

'OK, you two,' Daisy said. 'Make me into a sex goddess.'

'OK,' Tom said excitedly. 'I've been *dying* for this moment, darling. To get my smooth mitts on you.' He eyed her now tea-stained black cleavage top. 'Darling, that looks cheap.'

'Tom,' Lisa warned. 'It does not. It's sexy.'

'Oh, sorry is cheap bad?' Tom asked innocently. 'Because I love cheap.' He looked so apologetic. 'Gosh, I really did think cheap was a compliment.'

Lisa scowled at him but Daisy grinned. This was why she loved them.

'OK, so where are you going for supper?' Lisa asked, sitting Daisy on her unmade bed. 'Location is very important for dress code.'

'I don't know.' Daisy shrugged. 'He just mentioned it now as he was leaving.'

'OK.' Tom nodded seriously. 'We need an in-betweener.'

'A what?' Daisy said.

'An in-betweener.' He looked at her like she had the IQ of a gnat. 'An outfit that can see you through any occasion.'

'Does that exist?' Daisy wasn't sure about that. 'I mean a members' club is a bit different to a local around here.'

Lisa rummaged around under her bed and brought out a duffel bag. 'This is where this beauty comes in. We put the basics on you and then wherever you end up, you restyle.'

Daisy looked at them incredulously. 'I can't carry a sodding gym bag into a restaurant, go to the loo and come out a different person. I'm not Mrs Doubtfire.'

'Darling,' Tom said soothingly, 'it'll just be the essentials. You know things like a different pair of shoes, a pair of tights, a pashmina, jewellery, make-up…' He raised a brow. 'Knickers.'

Daisy stared at him. 'You know what, let's chuck in the sink and the filing cabinet.'

Tom shook his head. 'No need to be silly now.'

'Yoo-hoo!' came a very familiar voice from downstairs. 'Am I allowed to come up to the servants' headquarters?'

Annabelle.

Daisy braced herself and manufactured a smile for the annoyingly trim blonde lightly tripping up the stairs, no hint of being at all out of breath. Daisy could barely climb one level without wishing she was a mountaineer.

'Hello, you lovely people,' she drawled through her nose. 'So the brood are heading out on an adventure to a funfair.' She pulled a face. 'Can't bear things like that. You know? Full of…' Her voice trailed off.

'Rides?' Tom gave her.

'No, you know…'

'Music?' That was Lisa.

'No.' She looked at them all like they were complete morons. 'People.'

Daisy snorted. 'People?'

'Yes, bloody people.' She shook her head. 'God.' As if ridding herself of a bad dream, she visibly shuddered and then smiled. 'So I'm going to Cirencester.'

'Um, Cirencester has people too. It's a market town,' Daisy said.

'Oh come on, it's not *people*, it's *types*.'

'Types?' Lisa said.

'Yes, types. I do not like types.'

'Don't you think you are a type?' Daisy enquired. 'I mean surely we are all types.'

Annabelle laughed. 'God, no. I am not a type. I am me.' She laughed loudly. 'Bloody marvellous.'

Daisy bit back her comment.

'And James is downstairs. What a love, he's making the troops sandwiches and ginger ale. I mean he's just a delight, isn't he?' She looked pointedly at Daisy. 'Then, this really is above and beyond, he's taking me to Cirencester. I mean frankly he deserves a knighthood or something, you know? Such a gentleman.'

Daisy thought about James in the kitchen preparing food for the masses then thought of him holding hands with Annabelle in some chic coffee shop. 'He definitely deserves something,' Daisy said drily. 'A brain transplant for one.'

'So what are you lovely two people and person—' Annabelle looked at Daisy '—gossiping about up here?'

'Nothing,' Daisy started to say but as quickly Tom had blurted it out.

'Oh, our Daisy has been asked on a date by that fine Scottish man.'

Annabelle's face twisted with resentment. 'What, that Alistair chap? Gosh, those Scottish are very charitable, aren't they?'

'Meaning?' Daisy spat out, her heart pumping harder and harder.

'Oh just meaning what a nice gesture to take a widow out for dinner, I guess he doesn't plan on paying for his room or something.' She fell about at her own joke despite the tumbleweed silence from her audience. 'Anyway lovely peeps… must dash, need to ensure Agamemnon hasn't killed his sister yet. They're fighting over who goes to the posher school.' She sighed. 'I've told them a million times before, they are both at equally good schools and does it really matter as long as you're not having to mix with riffraff?' Annabelle smiled at her now stunned audience but hadn't registered the silence. 'So you're getting ready for a date, Daisy.' She eyed the duffel bag in Daisy's hand. 'Are you going to a gym? Word of advice, only lose weight for a man if he gives you enough incentive. You know…' And Daisy watched her desperately search for the right words. 'You know, for example, when I met my husband he said that I was carrying an extfa pound or two and I said fine.' She licked her lips. 'I said fine, you want to play that game…' She gestured to them like she was about to deliver a suffragette speech worthy of Millicent Fawcett. 'I will lose some weight for you but only, and I mean this, if you buy me a Balenciaga bag for every month I'm with you and, on occasion, a Fendi too.'

'Oh,' Lisa eventually managed. 'That's very… um, noble of you.'

'Yes,' Annabelle agreed. 'I thought so too.' She waved at them and then bounced out of the room.

Daisy looked at her retreating figure and turned to her friends, 'Right, make me sexy. Make me invincible.'

Chapter 12

The days passed slowly but eventually Friday came and Project Daisy went into full action. She had been made to drink some strange green juice instead of meals for the last three days and had tried on so much spandex she feared her internal organs might have been crushed repeatedly. Tom and Lisa had insisted they visit actual shops and try actual dresses on which required Daisy, once again, getting up enough courage for those dreaded changing rooms. She had finally given into a pair of wide black trousers and a corset top that was definitely worthy of an 18-rating.

'How do I make this subtle if we just end up in the local pub?' she had asked incredulously.

'Oh, darling.' Tom had shaken his head. 'This outfit is positively staid. I said you should have gone with the red bodycon dress.'

Daisy looked at him in disbelief. 'Two things, Tom, my body doesn't do bodycon. That would be like happily stepping out of the house in cling film. And secondly, there is nothing staid about this.' She indicated her bosom threatening to explode from the boned constraints of an Ann Summers corset. 'This is meant for the bedroom,' she pointed out.

'Well, kill two birds with one stone, you won't have to carry a bedroom outfit in your bag.'

Daisy looked hard at him but it was pointless as Lisa rammed two cucumber slices over her eyes forcing her to close her eyelids fast before she lost her sight in a vegetable accident.

'We need to depuff your eyes and I'll put some of this lavender mask on your face to help get rid of your blotchiness.'

'Good one, Lisa,' Tom said as he rubbed fake tan into her legs.

'God, I'm feeling so confident now, thanks to you both.' She lifted the cucumber slices to find Lisa and Tom smiling broadly at her.

'You are so welcome,' Lisa squealed, hugging her tight, oblivious to Daisy's sarcasm.

It was 3 p.m. and Daisy couldn't help but wonder if she had set herself up for a fall. She had barely exchanged a few words with the fly by night Scotsman, what if he didn't turn up? He had no reason to. Just because she had written his name into the book, he wasn't obliged to stay at her guesthouse. What if he turned up and no longer wanted to take her out for dinner and she was stood there dressed up to the nines in her toothpaste tube corset? She gasped aloud now, what if… *What if* he hadn't invited her out to dinner at all? His Scottish accent was very strong, he might have been asking her for a good place to pick up some Cotswold produce…

Her mind spun with the possibilities as she allowed Tom and Lisa to continue to manipulate her into a sex goddess. She was waxed, shaved, and tweezed into oblivion and then Lisa grabbed her make-up and they set to. Daisy didn't want to ruin their fun but her heart hammered as she waited for the results. She thought of those women on live daytime television that asked for a makeover and had the big 'reveal' in front of the likes of Holly and Philip. She always tried to pick out the wobbly lip, the tears of disappointment but she hadn't once yet seen anything of the sort. She was beginning to think if she was on the programme and Lisa and Tom were her makeover artists, as opposed to professionals, she may be the first guest to turn on the waterworks.

Lisa had nipped downstairs to make cups of tea before the big reveal. Minutes later, she came bounding up the stairs like an excitable puppy.

'He's here,' she squealed. 'I've shown him to his room and he was asking if you're around and I said that you were getting ready for your date tonight.'

Daisy rose quickly from Lisa's bed. 'You said what? It's not a date, it's dinner, if it's even that. It might not be happening.' Daisy paced, mortified. 'Poor man, oh God.'

Lisa looked baffled. 'What are you going on about?'

'Well, what did he say now that you've confirmed how cheap I am?'

Tom smiled. 'Remember, cheap is good.'

'He said he was glad and could I ask you if you could meet him in the drawing room at seven.' Lisa narrowed her eyes. 'So, there you go, Little Miss It Might Not be Happening.'

Daisy's heart thumped.

'And,' Lisa added conspiratorially, 'he looks bloody fine. Oh my God, if I wasn't taken…'

'Why? Am I overdressed? Is he wearing a tuxedo?' Daisy asked, panicking.

'No, but he is wearing the most beautiful jacket and shirt. The man is beautiful.'

Daisy blushed as excitement stirred in the pit of her stomach.

'I'm nervous and excited,' Daisy babbled, 'and feeling guilty all at once.'

'Don't feel guilty,' Tom said. 'You are living your life. You are living the life you deserve to live.'

'But I'm past it,' Daisy moaned. 'I'm as Annabelle described, "a widow".'

'A widow spider.' Tom held his hands up. 'Deadly sexy.'

Lisa nodded. 'It's true, look at yourself.' She had lugged over her full-length mirror.

Daisy caught sight of herself, fully expecting to be horrified after hours of primping and preening. But, instead, she was taken aback by what an amazing job they had done with frumpy Daisy.

'Wow,' she gasped. 'Is that really me?'

They had dressed her in the aforementioned black trousers and a black corset top. Her hair had been swept back in a sophisticated chignon. Lisa had made her face glow with the most incredible bronze on her cheeks and edible rose lips. Her arms and negligee looked smooth and iridescent.

'You two should go into beauty…'

They grinned and high-fived each other. Coming up behind her, they each put an arm around Daisy's waist and looked at her in the mirror.

'You're a gorgeous woman, it's not hard when the starting product is this great.'

She blushed ever so slightly and felt tears spring to her eyes. It was moments like this that she cherished, just being with those people who understood her.

Tom looked at his watch. 'You need to go downstairs, my princess.'

Lisa solemnly handed her the duffel bag and Daisy took it dutifully, trying to hide her dismay. Such a beautiful outfit shouldn't be accompanied by an oversized sports bag… but then Lisa backed up towards the bed and brought out a beautiful black clutch with diamante detailing.

'We bought you this,' Lisa said. 'Though it was fun to wind you up, we do want you to speak to us again.'

Daisy took it from Lisa as if it were a Faberge egg. It was a thing of beauty, so feminine and classy.

She felt the tears again and, unable to speak, they both gave her a big hug and sent her on her way down the stairs.

'Remember,' Tom said as she left the room, 'it's what Hugh would have wanted.'

She nodded, excited and nervous for the night ahead.

Chapter 13

She headed downstairs, her heart beating loudly in her ears. It had been a long time since she had felt first date nerves. In fact, when she thought about it, she hadn't felt them since meeting Hugh. Over twenty years. That was a long time and she was out of practice. As she rounded the stairs to go down to the entrance hall, she was momentarily taken aback and gasped inwardly. Alistair was dressed every bit as beautifully as Lisa had suggested. He looked up at her as she descended the stairs and smiled so gently she thought her heart might break.

'My goodness, you look amazing.' He smiled. 'Beautiful.'

She managed to get to the bottom of the stairs without tripping up and for a fleeting moment she felt as if she was in her own Hollywood movie. Then just as she reached the bottom stair her shoe caught in one leg of the wide black trousers and she landed face first at Alistair's feet.

'Oh, Daisy, are you OK?' He was kneeling down now and looking into her eyes with such compassion, it only served to make her feel even more foolish. This would be a romantic story if he was in this position because he was proposing or because together they were saving an injured animal. But no, she had fallen at the last fence and now needed to get up and save face.

She begrudgingly took his extended hand and rather ungracefully got to her feet.

She caught his searching gaze. 'Are you OK? You took quite a tumble there.'

'Yes, fine, right as rain.' She smiled despite the throbbing in her right ankle. 'That was me playing it cool, didn't want to come over too keen.' She flashed a wry smile.

'You did very well,' he offered kindly. 'I've booked us a table at the local pub.'

'Lovely,' she said, and meant it. She wasn't over or underdressed. Once again, her fabulous friends had been right.

'Table's booked for eight but I thought we could all have drinks first.'

Daisy was just about to ask who *all* were but then she thought she must have imagined it. Why would a man turn up on her doorstep at 2 a.m., stay in her house and then ask her out to dinner if there were more than the two of them involved? No, she said to herself, with a small shake of her head, she must have imagined it.

They walked out to his car, a Maserati no less, and he opened the passenger door for her. It was a windy night, but luckily no rain or she really might have started to look like something the cat had dragged in. She stepped into the car with as much grace as she could muster, clutch in one hand and her now billowing trousers clenched in her other. She realised she still felt nervous but put it down to the length of time she had been away from the dating-scene. But then Daisy being Daisy, her mind went into overdrive.

What if it wasn't a date and she had got herself all dolled up for some sort of lost in translation business meeting? Maybe he was interested in buying a share in her guesthouse? What was she talking about? Shares. She didn't even know what a share was. No matter how many times Hugh had explained to her that it was the way in which a company's capital was distributed, she couldn't help but feeling it sounded a bit childish. She imagined men in suits sitting around a table, projector overhead, musing about their 'shares'. But in her imagination the screen showed sweets or a chocolate cake cut into pieces. In fact, she was pretty sure that the business world liked to think they were very important but surely even with a company that sold pharmaceutical products, it didn't get much more complicated than playing shop at nursery? That was the one thing Hugh and Daisy had argued about. Her inability to take the business world and money seriously and, in the end, she had decided to just keep her thoughts to herself. Hugh felt he was changing the world one penny at a time, and that was fine.

They drove to the pub in silence. Her mind was whirring with conversational topics but none of them seemed right as a way to break the silence with such an incredibly dashing man. If he turned around now and told her that he not only was the CEO of one of those 'big companies' but also a model for Burberry underwear, well frankly she wouldn't have batted an eyelid. By the pale light of the car's dashboard, Daisy admired his chiselled jawline and impeccably shaped nose. How could a nose be impeccably shaped, she thought incredulously.

Eventually the car stopped in a pub car park and Daisy tore her eyes away from his profile in order to read the pub sign. It said *The Randy Duck* which ordinarily would have been her cue for uproarious laughter and Tom's worryingly realistic impersonation of a highly-sexed bird. But, now, all she felt was doom.

'Are you OK?' Alistair asked. 'I'll come around and open your door.'

She nodded, mute.

The thing is The Randy Duck was not just a pub, nor was it a one-Michelin-star pub. It was a *three*-Michelin-star pub. Ordinarily, she would have been super excited at the prospect of a tasting menu as long as her leg but, but – and this was a huge but...

She had been barred from this pub only two Christmases ago.

She ashamedly didn't want to admit it wasn't even when she was a young whippersnapper with not a clue about common courtesies and etiquette. It had been a festive drinks party. She may or may not have had one too many mulled wines before deciding she was the world's sexiest pole dancer (the pole was a medieval pillar) and the absolutely beautiful Christmas garland above the fireplace was her feather boa. In the space of what was apparently fifteen minutes, though it had felt much shorter to Daisy, she managed to drag the garland down and across the tables, tea lights setting fire to her 'boa' as she went and the vicar's wife who was trying to, it turned out, stamp out the blaze taking hold of the foliage, was mistaken by Daisy as a woman wanting to join in and soon Daisy was gyrating up against Glenda to the banging tune of 'Ding Dong Merrily on High'.

These images flashed back through her memory and it was only with the cool rush of air around her ankles as Alistair opened her door that she realised how *utterly mortifying* the whole situation was.

There was only one thing for it. She would have to pretend she was someone else. Surely anyone who had seen her in the last year or so would think of her as the woman who owned a big house but dressed like she had just finished mucking out the horses? Even though she didn't even own a horse. Yes, she thought with renewed relief, she could survive this. Was she Mrs Ronaldson? No. She was Miss Esmerelda from the south of Gloucestershire, thank you very much for asking.

As they entered the first set of doors to the pub, they were stuck in that strange limbo land she liked to think was called 'the landlord's test'. Daisy had decided years ago that if the visitor could make it through both doors without injury or making a complete fool of themselves, then they probably weren't completely inebriated and could be allowed in.

Alistair looked at her now with such intensity she had forgotten what it was like to have a man undress her with his eyes.

'You know, you really are beautiful.' His lips came towards hers and she gave her now very dry mouth from nerves a quick swish of saliva.

She closed her eyes, ready and then felt his lips land on her cheek. Her cheek? She snapped her eyes open, entirely mortified. She glanced at his bemused look and as he pulled open the second door, she rather hesitantly stepped inside.

A gathering – actually there were about twenty people, which Daisy classed as a crowd – turned around and on seeing Alistair shouted, 'Alistair! Happy birthday!'

Daisy fixed an extraordinarily big grin to her face even though her mind was taking some moments to compute. Men and women alike flocked to Alistair to give him a hug or kiss on his cheek. Daisy found herself being shoved this way and that, not one person, as yet, having introduced themselves. But then, why should they? She didn't know who they were so why should they care who she was? Or maybe (here went the mind again) she wasn't there and it was all a dream?

A man who could have been Alistair's twin brother playfully punched her on the arm as if to reassure her she was actually there, in The Randy Duck surrounded by strangers.

'Hello,' he said warmly. 'You must be Ali's love. We've heard so much about you and been dying to meet you.' He extended his hand. 'I'm Rabi, his twin brother.'

'Um, lovely to meet you,' she murmured. 'I'm Daisy.' Was she meant to be Daisy? Maybe Alistair had named her Susannah or something foreign. 'How long have you known about me then?' she dared to ask.

'Only a week or so, the dog,' Rabi said in hushed tones. 'But he says you've been living together for months and reading between the lines…' He started humming 'Chapel of Love'.

'Oh,' Daisy tried not to look too taken aback but was actually desperate to turn around and throttle the man stood behind her – her 'boyfriend'.

And she would have if she hadn't made eye contact with the pub manager William. Their eyes locked and she knew, just knew, that Esmerelda was a no-go. Even with the makeover, he had her sussed. William moved from behind the bar and made a beeline for her.

'Mrs Ronaldson,' he started. 'I'm afraid that…'

Alistair came up at this point and said, 'Have you met my girlfriend?' Alistair clamped his arm around her waist and for a split second she genuinely didn't know who she was anymore.

She looked angrily at Alistair and then weighed it up in her mind. Better that William, for now, thought she was someone else. She transformed her angry stare to one of pure joy.

'Darling' she purred. 'Would you get me a drink?'

'Your usual?' Alistair said confidently, not batting an eyelid.

'Yes, you know me so well. Never change.' She smiled sweetly at Alistair, though inside her stomach churning with anger.

She watched him saunter off to the bar and she very much got the impression that Alistair was not only enjoying himself but may have actually *convinced* himself they were a couple.

Now, alone with William, she turned to him, her eyes challenging.

'Well,' he eventually stammered, 'I hope you have a lovely evening, Miss…?'

'My name is Esmerelda Cartwright but you can call me Esmerelda.' She held out her hand, desperately stifling the laughter threatening to bubble up inside her.

He took her hand and they exchanged a fleeting look where she could tell he was momentarily wavering but she charmed him back with a sexy smile and he said, 'Enjoy your party, Miss Cartwright.'

'Thank you.' William left her to it as she watched her 'boyfriend' approach with a glass of fizz in hand.

She took it and through gritted teeth, said, 'What the hell is going on here?'

He looked at her in a dreamy way, but then clearly her hard stare made him get a grip on reality. 'Well, you see, it's a long story but basically…' She just watched him, incredulous. 'I come from the Edinburgh Set.'

'The Edinburgh Set?' she repeated.

He nodded, took a sip of fizz. 'Yes, a bit like in these counties, you know they are the families who have grown up with one another, done pony club together, been to each other's christenings, weddings and funerals.' He was on a roll now and Daisy watched him barely catch a breath. 'They hunt and ski… and every other sport that requires a certain amount of money… you know?' He barely registered her nod. 'I've never really fit in. My brother—' he gestured at the throng of people '—he fits in just fine. Me? I've always felt like a fish out of water.' Alistair pinched his blazer. 'These are just clothes, they just make you look like you belong, but I don't *feel* like I belong. Do you understand that?'

Daisy nodded. She had spent the first years of her life with cattle and the odd school friend who had been coerced into 'a fun day of milking cows and feeding lambs' (often never to be seen again) but had ended up living in a manor house which frankly she could never have afforded the entrance fee to once upon a time. So, yes, she understood.

'Yes,' she said, 'I get it. Totally get it, but this is ridiculous.' She clenched her jaw. 'In fact, I'm going to tell everyone what a complete liar you are.' She turned away from him, only to come face to face with another of his friends.

'Oh, you two lovebirds. Ali, you are a sly horse.' A woman with extraordinarily pearly big teeth grinned at her. She put her long arm around Daisy. Her equally long legs never stopped shuffling for longer than a nanosecond. Daisy decided she looked like an overexcited filly waiting to exit the gates at Aintree.

'Hello Samantha.' Alistair came over all shy. 'How are you?'

'I'm fine, my darling,' Samantha replied, a very slight Scottish accent coming through. 'But you kept this one quiet.'

'Well, you know me…' Alistair grinned, looking almost hopeful. 'Full of surprises.'

Samantha turned to Daisy. 'I've known Ali since we were like practically in the womb.' She guffawed, flicking her perfectly straight (and long, of course) brunette hair to the other side before flicking it right back to the original side. 'People always said we would get married but, here he is, still unmarried and seeing you, sweetie.' As if seeing Daisy for the first time, Samantha appraised Daisy. 'I mean we really couldn't be more different, could we? I'm thin, you're…' Daisy held her breath. 'Curvy and quiet.'

'Um, I think you'll find you have no idea…' The woman didn't even know her. Anyway, Daisy thought, anyone would be quiet around Samantha, because it was futile trying to get a word in edgeways.

'How long have you known each other?' Samantha interrupted.

Daisy went to answer, 'Only a wee—'

'Aye,' Alistair interrupted. 'A wee while. It was just love at first sight.'

'And where did you meet?' Samantha raised an overly groomed (and if possible, long) eyebrow.

'He turned up at my door—'.

'At her Dordogne villa,' Alistair said. 'Daisy has a whole portfolio of property, don't you, darling?'

Daisy was speechless, completely and utterly speechless. Alistair was on a roll. She almost didn't want to stop him. What else could he come up with?

'And your main residence?' Samantha clicked her hand at some poor unsuspecting waitress who had been given the job of refilling.

'Gloucestershire, just up the road.' Samantha barely nodded her acknowledgement at the teenage waitress. Daisy thanked the girl. 'It was my husband—'

Alistair dived in again. 'It was your love of husbandry that brought you to the idyllic Cotswolds, wasn't it, darling Daisy?' The man was now visibly sweating, his upper lip and forehead glistening.

'Oh lovely,' Samantha purred. 'Crops or animals?'

'Um…' Daisy stopped. This was her moment to completely drop Alistair in the cowpat but she met his gaze and seeing acute desperation and loneliness, she decided to help him out.

'Crops,' she said with assured confidence. She thought about the herb trays on the kitchen sill and her prized tomato plants in the summer; enough to feed two people on the Atkins diet. She had never understood how anyone became self-sufficient. She had always thought she could live off the land as long as she could reach a Waitrose by car.

'Marvellous. Been a hard winter, hasn't it? Roger was saying the delayed spring has played havoc on crops.'

Daisy thought about the parsley and chives on her kitchen windowsill; she supposed the chives were yellowing ever so slightly. 'Yes, very tough.'

Samantha gave them an affectionate group hug, though frankly her long arms could have accommodated many more. 'Well, you two are adorable.'

With that, she lolloped off and Alistair turned to Daisy. 'Thank you. I mean really, thank you.'

His eyes filled with such sincerity, Daisy was taken aback. Her anger started to dissipate and she saw a very lonely, confused man stood in front of her.

'I've been asked to make a speech…' He paused. 'Do you mind? I don't have to…'

Daisy couldn't believe what she was about to do. 'No, go ahead.'

Alistair flashed her a sincere smile and took a cocktail stirrer off the side of the bar and tapped the side of the glass. A sea of eyes turned to face him, still chattering but the odd person let out a whoop and Samantha told them all to quiet down.

Alistair looked desperately unsure of himself. 'Thanks so much guys for coming today… I know it was all a bit short notice…'

'You're telling me, I only got the invite yesterday!' A petite redhead at the back heckled, causing a ripple of laughter and murmurs of agreement.

'I know, I know…' Alistair put his hands up in mock surrender. 'It's just I didn't know when Daisy and I'd be back in the area and I know you lot have never left the sweet surroundings of Cirencester.'

'Once an Agricultural University student, that's it. You stay, forever.' This man, who Daisy put at Alistair's age, then winked at Rabi. 'Just you wait, you won't be going back to Scotland, trust me.'

'We can't both do that to Father,' Rabi joked back, patting Alistair on the arm. 'He'll have a heart attack. Mother's never forgiven Alistair for moving down the road to Glasgow, let alone a different country!'

Daisy watched Alistair look over at Samantha, momentarily sorrowful. Samantha, however, grinned back, seemingly unaware of some much deeper conflict he was fighting.

'Yeah, so, thank you for coming tonight at such short notice but I also just want to say a few words about my dear Daisy.'

Daisy stood watching him, deep in thought. Her mind had gone back to a day over twenty years ago, when Hugh had been making a similar speech to their family and friends. It made her eyes water as she remembered, a lump building in her throat.

'Aw, look, she's getting tearful,' someone whispered at the front.

'My dear Daisy, we haven't known each other for very long…' She glanced at him through a haze of tears. There was the understatement of the century. 'But the happiness you have brought to me during the past…' He fished for the next word. She almost said 'few days' but stayed quiet. '…the past while, has been amazing. You are very special and I think it's pretty obvious to anyone here today why I've had to fight other men off!'

There were a few murmurs of agreement which Daisy drunk

up the remainder of her champagne, then chose to ignore the same redhead who had hollered earlier and now turned to her friend and said in a stage whisper, 'She doesn't look his type, to be honest. Too matronly.'

Daisy shot her a look. *I'll give you matronly*, Daisy thought, before telling herself not to worry, the redhead was jealous because she looked no older than a schoolchild.

Filled with a sudden confidence, she stepped towards Alistair and kissed him on the lips. No one looked more surprised than he did but then even more alarmingly Alistair responded with his tongue. Daisy quickly withdrew and gathered herself as his friends wolf-whistled and applauded.

'Thank you everyone for coming, it means so much to both of us.' She spoke so genuinely she nearly nominated herself for an Oscar.

Redhead piped up again. 'Where are her friends though?' Again, another conveniently loud stage whisper. 'I mean, maybe she's a bit of a loner.'

Or maybe I didn't even know I was at my boyfriend's birthday party until I walked into this pub, you yappy little red thing…

'Cheers, everyone.' She held up her croakingly empty glass.

'To Ali,' they cheered.

At which point Daisy, so caught up in the moment, was startled to feel a very firm hand on her left arm and, noticing that Alistair had use of both of his, she guessed it might be redhead or the filly Samantha.

Turned out it was neither. She was face to face with William the landlord.

'I thought you weren't Esmerelda…' His face had coloured up like a beetroot and he whispered heatedly. 'I thought I discussed this with you and your husband. I can't have who think it's alright to dance exotically and try and burn down my *Michelin-starred* pub.' He narrowed his eyes. 'And what would your husband say if he knew you were pretending to be someone else?'

She looked at his hand searing her skin and shot him a warning look. He dutifully dropped his hand but he was so angry he was practically frothing at the mouth.

'Why, are you going to tell him?' Daisy challenged, her heart pounding.

'I may just do that. You're clearly cavorting and playing around.'

'Is that right?'

'Yes,' William nodded. 'That is right and I've always held the Ronaldson family in high regard so I feel it's his right to know.'

'Well, good luck with that.' Her eyes brimmed with tears.

William's confidence clearly ebbed. 'What do you mean?'

'You going to phone up to the castle in the sky?' Daisy glared at him. 'He's dead. My husband is dead.' Spittle flew from her lips. 'So unless you're psychic…'

William paled, his previously burning cheeks of rage disappearing, as if with an on and off button.

Daisy realised only then that the whole room had fallen silent and it was, of course, the bundle of redheaded joy who announced, 'Oh my God, she's been married before.'

Daisy looked at Alistair, tears streaming down her face, then pushed past him and his friends out the pub door. Once outside, she gulped in huge breaths of cool air. The sound of the double doors opening and closing behind her spurred her to move forward. She didn't want to talk to anybody, she didn't want to have to explain that all she wanted was her real husband to hold her tight and whisper her in her ear that it was all going to be alright.

She could hear his voice singing in her head, a tune he used to sing quietly to her even when he thought she was asleep as he stroked her hair.

'Daisy, Daisy give me your answer do…' She could almost feel his breath on her neck and closed her eyes. 'I'm half crazy all for the love of you. It won't be a stylish marriage, I can't afford a carriage…'

'Daisy?' Alistair's voice broke the moment. 'Daisy? I'm so sorry, I'm sorry. I should never have…'

She wanted answers but she also wanted to go home and lie on Hugh's sofa, and wrap herself up in his tartan throw.

'Just take me home,' she said quietly. 'You can explain tomorrow. I just want to go.'

Chapter 14

They didn't speak on the journey back home. Alistair went to explain but Daisy put her hand up. She had had enough for one night, maybe for one lifetime.

Wordlessly, she allowed Alistair to open the front door and they both walked inside. Not quite the 'happy couple' of an hour earlier. On the stairs outside their neighbouring bedrooms, she looked up and said, 'Goodnight.'

'Goodnight, Daisy.' He paused. 'And I am truly sorry. Please let me talk to you tomorrow.'

She nodded. 'I'm going to Hugh's study for a bit.' She indicated the room on the other side of his bedroom. 'It's where I go when I need to think.'

'Of course.' He stood aside to let her through. 'And thank you for tonight, for being such a sport about it all.'

Despite the emotion, she smiled. 'What were you going to say when we were no longer an item?'

He shrugged. 'I hadn't got that far.'

'No,' she agreed. 'The whole thing is quite bizarre. I'm sure you've got a perfectly good explanation.' She watched him hang his head and she offered, 'But I know that one day you will find someone who is perfectly suited to you and you'll be very happy.'

'Try telling my mother and father that.'

Daisy shook her head. 'I hope you don't mind me saying but you don't look like you're young enough to be caring what your parents think anymore.'

He looked sheepish. 'I know. I'm forty-five, I should have got over it by now. But they've always had this hold over me. Especially my father.' He cleared his throat. 'They spend their lives asking me when I'm going to meet someone nice, get married, join the set to go skiing and so on.'

'Surely, by now, you've met that person?'

'No, I've met the people my parents think suit me.'

'Ah yes,' Daisy thought of her own mother but how in her case her mother felt she had married above her station. 'Parents have a funny idea of who we should end up with.'

Alistair stared off into the middle distance. 'I met this girl, a long time ago. We were both studying at the Royal Agricultural University in Cirencester.' He glanced at Daisy. 'I told my parents and, of course, they were thrilled because she studied at the college, back in the days when your parents needed to have a certain amount of money to send you there. From the outset I knew that any woman I met must be educated and *the right sort*. Only, I knew in my heart, I should never have put this girl through what I did. Clare, her name was. She came from just outside London, her mother worked in the admin department for some big company and her father was a postman. She got a scholarship to the college because she was bright, bloody clever actually.' He paused, as if remembering was in fact too painful. 'Anyway, I didn't tell my parents anything about her, maybe in the vague and naïve hope they would see how beautiful she was. How beautiful her spirit was and how she made me so happy.'

Daisy, now captivated, leant up against the door to the study. 'Then what happened?'

'So we were both twenty and I invited her to my parents' house up in Edinburgh for a long May bank holiday weekend.' He sighed.

'From the moment my parents looked at Clare, I could tell they had made their minds up.'

'Why?' Daisy asked, although her own experience of introducing Hugh to her mother flashed through her mind.

'Clare had a London accent, she wore ripped jeans, had a piercing in her tongue and would occasionally drop an F-bomb.'

Daisy laughed loudly then put her hand over her mouth as she realised everyone else was trying to sleep.

'But that's what made her who she was.' Alistair smiled. 'She was beautiful, honestly, to look at as well as her spirit. She was the light of my life.'

His words clung to Daisy like a familiarly haunting rhetoric. Hugh, she had often said, had been the light of her life.

'Well, then you need to find her.'

'Ach,' he said, 'she's probably married and then why should she put up with the snobbery of my parents and friends?'

'You know what?' she said, tiredness making her eyes close. 'I say bugger everyone else. Do your parents have to live with her? They may not even like each other. Your parents, I mean.' She chuckled quietly. 'My parents looked like the perfect, hardworking married couple who ran a successful farm. My dad died of a heart attack when I was young. But I can tell you now, *that* marriage was far from perfect. Dad used to say to me, "If that woman goes on at me anymore, I'll get the vet out and bloody put her down".'

Alistair laughed, then looked embarrassed. 'Sorry, maybe it wasn't meant to be funny.'

Daisy laughed at his expression. 'Oh yes, it was funny and so ironic that he went first.'

She stifled a yawn and he apologised. 'God, sorry, you go to bed.'

'I'll go in here first but we can chat more tomorrow?' She smiled. 'You know I should be furious with you for what you put me through this evening…'

He nodded.

'But in a bizarre sort of way, it's the most fun I've had since Hugh died. Anyway, as you gathered, the landlord is a jumped up hunting type. Unless your name begins with Lord or Lady, you're nothing.'

After a moment's silence, he said, 'Goodnight,' and opened and closed his bedroom door. Daisy let herself into the study and flicked the small desk lamp on before settling onto the sofa.

'Hugh, are you there?'

She imagined him turning over from the depths of sleep.

'Sorry, darling, didn't mean to wake you.' She stroked the arm of the leather sofa with her hand as she spoke. 'Hugh, I don't know if you saw what happened tonight.' She smiled. 'I should be so angry but I imagine you laughing, saying "these things could only happen to you"…' She chuckled. 'You'd say, "You're just like Bridget Jones" and tonight it felt like it. I mean I went to my own boyfriend's party even though I know nothing about him or a relationship…' She grew serious and frowned. 'But the thing is, Hugh, I thought it was a date, and I feel guilty for even contemplating another man, let alone a date.' She shrugged her shoulders and looked around her. 'I mean everyone keeps telling me it's what you would've wanted, that you would've wanted me to be happy. But I'm not sure if there is a man who could make me happy and do I really need that?' She sighed. 'I know I'm babbling but I'm confused, Hugh, why can't you come back and then I wouldn't even think about other men?'

The desk lamp flickered – another brown out – and she smiled. 'I knew you were here.' Then being so tired and wanting to be near Hugh, she kicked off her shoes and dragged the tartan throw over her body and lay down, nestling into the slowly warming leather. She wanted to escape to dreams and sleep and, within seconds, she had dozed off.

A couple of hours later, Daisy woke with a start. She tried to figure out where she was, why she was lying on Hugh's sofa and then the evening's events flooded back. She turned over and tried to settle back into sleep but then realised she could hear voices. They were outside the door, whispering in a loud, drunken manner. She got up and padded quietly towards the door and listened. It was Annabelle and James. Daisy looked groggily at the clock on Hugh's desk. It was 1 a.m.

'I think you're fabulous…' Annabelle purred and Daisy rolled her eyes. 'You're like my James Bond…' She fell about laughing. 'Get it? Because your name is James.'

Daisy prayed James wouldn't react but he did: he laughed. Then there was some more whispering she couldn't hear.

'Oh, James…' Annabelle's husky voice. 'Kiss me again.'

Again, Daisy thought, alarm bells ringing. Then she had strong words with herself: *Daisy Ronaldson, it is none of your business what James does and nor should you care.*

Then why did it feel as if her heart was being twisted?

'Annabelle, come on, let's go to bed…'

Daisy couldn't take anymore and pulled the study door open with more force than she had intended and catapulted out of the door.

'Oh!' Annabelle shouted. 'What on earth?'

'Sorry,' Daisy mumbled, daring not look at James's face. 'I fell asleep in the study and—' she pointed at her room '—I'm just on my way to bed now.' She paused. 'Like you two are… on your way back to your bedrooms.' She watched them exchange looks and she offered, 'Or bedroom?'

James smiled. 'Yep, I should be going to bed.'

'Oh, oh,' Annabelle said, shooting Daisy a look. 'You're not going to let *her* ruin our fun, are you?'

'I am tired,' James admitted. 'It was a fun night, though, thank you.'

'Where did you go?' Daisy berated herself for showing so much interest.

'We,' Annabelle was quick to offer, 'went out to a simply marvellous cheese and wine tasting event in Cirencester.'

'Oh, that sounds nice.' Daisy tried desperately to hide the overwhelming desire to slap Annabelle across the face.

'Yes, I came to ask you if you wanted to go. It was an event for hotels and guesthouses in the area.' He paused. 'A chance to meet local suppliers.' He looked at her intently under his thick eyelashes. 'But you had gone out.'

'With that Scottish man,' Annabelle was keen to confirm.

'Yes, we went out…' Daisy stopped. 'And…' How could she explain she had unknowingly attended her own 'boyfriend's' birthday party?

'Dinner?' James asked, his voice had a slight tremble in it but Daisy put it down to laughter. James was probably laughing at the idea that Daisy Ronaldson would have been taken on a date.

'No, not dinner, much more interesting than that.'

'Oh,' cooed Annabelle. 'Do tell.' She flashed James a sexy smile. 'We were only talking earlier about when and how you might, you know, move on…'

'Well, I don't think we did actually talk about that, Annabelle,' James said, his voice full of warning.

'You were saying how it would be good to see Daisy move on.' Annabelle fluttered her eyelashes. 'Didn't you?'

'No,' James said firmly. 'I said that I want to see Daisy happy.'

Annabelle frowned; she didn't like being told off. 'Well, same thing.'

'Not really.' James shook his head, his jaw visibly tightening.

Daisy looked hard at both of them. 'Maybe you two should concentrate on your own lives instead of prying into everyone else's, particularly mine.' She looked at James. 'I thought you were different. I thought…' Her voice faded. What had she thought? She didn't really know because it was her heart that was thinking, not her head. Maybe James had felt compelled to carry out Hugh's wishes as his friend lay dying but actually he would have preferred to stay in London.

'In fact,' Daisy said quickly, 'you two are well suited, aren't you? Both have houses in London, both have as much tact and sensitivity as Trump.' Annabelle stood with her mouth open and James shifted under her stare. 'Actually, why don't you both just sod off back to London? No offence, Annabelle, we're so grateful you and your family love this house and have agreed to pay a higher rate but I will happily refund two nights' worth and James…' She felt disappointed tears cascading down her cheeks. 'I thought that you were here, you know, because Hugh and you had agreed mutually but I see now that Hugh just made you feel guilty. You don't want to be here at all.' She started to turn but James put out his hand and gently held her shoulder.

'Please, Daisy,' he whispered. 'That is not true. I want to be here more than anything in the world.' He glanced at Annabelle who was not about to budge. 'Can we talk tomorrow?'

'Well, you'll have to form an orderly queue.' She wiped her nose and eyes with the back of her hand.

'Oh?' James asked.

'Yes, I have to speak to my good friend Alistair first thing.'

'The Scottish man?' Annabelle had perked up. 'He's attractive, isn't he?' You could practically see the oestrogen emanating from Annabelle's pores. Daisy thought that if she had been a dog she would have had her spayed. 'Did your date not go to plan?'

'What? Our date?' Daisy looked at James and Annabelle in turn. 'No, our date was a great success. Which is *exactly* why I have to speak to him tomorrow.' She smiled sweetly at them both. 'We've agreed to go on another date together.'

'What?' Annabelle shrieked. 'Another one?'

'Shhh…' Daisy warned, holding her finger up to her lips, she didn't want Alistair to come out and clarify that it was all make-believe.

'Wow, and to think James was worried about your lack of a love life.' She winked at James.

James's face hardened and he remained silent.

'Have you two...' Annabelle tilted her head coyly to the side. '...you know?'

'No,' Daisy said honestly. 'We're so in love that we're happy to wait until the time is right.'

Annabelle laughed; she was having far too much fun. 'Isn't the time always right? Imagine holding back like that. You must have amazing self-discipline, Daisy.'

'Yes, Annabelle, imagine that...'

Annabelle looked blankly at her. 'Imagine that.'

'If you'll excuse me I'm going to bed now.' James glanced at Annabelle. 'My bed.'

'Oh.' Annabelle looked disappointed and Daisy wanted to shout with glee. It had worked: her interruption had stopped them from sleeping together.

Only, she realised, it hadn't entirely worked. She had now told people about a relationship with Alistair that didn't actually exist. She realised she was quickly convincing herself about their relationship even though Alistair was due to check out tomorrow and return to his friends and family, and, at some point she presumed, to tell them it was over. But if Alistair was that lonely and she wanted companionship, wouldn't it make sense that he moved into the guesthouse. He could still have his own room but conversation and sex on tap could be a good thing, couldn't it?

Daisy put her hand to her forehead as she watched James open and close his door and Annabelle forlornly head back up the stairs in the direction of her own bed and husband. What had she just done?

As she went back into the study to turn the lamp off, it flickered again and she looked at it. 'I know, I'm an idiot, Hugh, a complete idiot. You see you've left me and I've gone mad. Quite mad.'

She flicked the switch, felt her way out of the room and to the light of the landing and her bedroom. As she nestled under the sheets, she realised Alistair lay asleep on the other side of the wall to her. Little did he know what she had just said… Though, she thought, maybe all was fair. He had coerced her into a relationship and now he could have a taste of his own medicine.

Chapter 15

She must have fell into a deep sleep because she thought it still the middle of the night when Lisa pounced on her.

'Wakey-wakey!' Lisa sat on Daisy's weary legs. 'You slacker.'

Daisy looked at the clock. 9 a.m. 'Holy crap, breakfast!'

'It's alright, sleepyhead. Tom whipped up pancakes and has fed the masses.' Lisa grinned. 'How many children do Annabelle and her friend actually have? They must have been going at it like rabbits.'

'Yeah, well,' Daisy said, a sour taste filling her mouth. 'She can't wait to get into bed with James. Or maybe she has, maybe my plan was all too late.'

'Plan?' Lisa arched a brow. 'And is this because you're madly in love with James?'

'Am not!' Daisy threw a pillow at her friend's head.

'Yeah, and does the Pope kiss tarmac?' Lisa cocked her head to one side. 'Actually James is in a right piss this morning and there's been no sign of Annabelle.'

'I saw them last night. Annabelle probably has a raging hangover and James is probably still reeling from my news…'

'News?' Lisa leaned in, intrigued.

'Alistair and I are going on a second date.'

Lisa released a raucous laugh. 'Well, that's brilliant!'

'James clearly doesn't think so.'

'OK, not being funny, but what's it to do with him? It's good to see you getting out. Anyway, a date doesn't equal marriage.' She sniggered. 'Because if it does, Bob and I are married, have had a million children, reached our Golden anniversary and probably about to snuff it.'

Daisy filled Lisa in on last night's events.

'I think that Ali and I would make good companions.'

Lisa's turn to throw the pillow at Daisy. 'Companions?' She rolled her eyes. 'You can meet people at village clubs if you want, you don't need to date a complete stranger, who ordinarily lives at the other end of the country, to make a *point*.'

'Listen,' Daisy said seriously, 'he opened up to me last night…'

'Yeah, I should bloody think so, after lying to everyone about who you are!'

Daisy had to release a nervous laugh despite the gnawing in her stomach. 'No, I mean later on he opened up too, and I can relate to him. Like I totally get what he's been up against.'

Lisa stood. 'I think you're mad. If you want to date him because you like him, then that's great. But for the sake of companionship?'

Daisy pouted. 'Bit rich coming from Miss Dive-into-the-first-guest's-pants.'

Lisa stared, mouth open. 'You cannot compare my relationship to yours!' She paused. 'I'm not trying to make another man jealous!'

'What on earth do you mean?' Daisy's voice grew louder

'James, it's so clear you adore him so don't compare me to you, Daisy Ronaldson. Your relationship is ludicrous, mine is love.' Lisa turned on her heels. 'I'm going out.'

'Lisa, don't be like this. Let's not argue over stupid men.' She smiled at Lisa as she turned back. 'I shouldn't have said what I did. You're right mine is ridiculous and I will put a stop to it before it gets out of—'

'O. M. G.' hollered Tom up the stairs. 'You are kidding me!' Tom's footsteps could be heard bounding up the stairs and then Daisy's door burst open. 'You've got a second date!' He ran over to her and hugged her tight. 'You do not waste time, my love.'

Lisa gave her one last look and left as Tom sat and asked if he could be the bridesmaid at their inevitable wedding.

'Well, the thing is, Tom,' she started to say when James barged his way in with a tray of toast, orange juice and coffee with a flower in a small vase. He barely glanced at her, but slammed the tray down on the bedside table, orange juice sloshing over the side of the glass.

'Breakfast,' he said gruffly, pointing at the tray.

'Um, thanks, James,' she said. 'That's really kind of you.'

'Not my idea, it was Annabelle's.' His face remained stony. 'Hence the flower.'

'Oh, well, thank you.' Daisy tried to catch his eye but he wasn't giving her anything.

'Annabelle and I are going out to lunch,' he said and Daisy felt that familiar lurching in her stomach. 'So I'm going to go and book somewhere now.'

'Oh, well…' Daisy didn't manage to finish her sentence once again as there was a brief, polite knock at the door. 'At least someone around here has manners.'

Alistair appeared around the side of the door. 'Good morning, Daisy,' he said, a formality to his voice. He looked at Tom and then let his eyes rest on Daisy. 'I hear we are going on a second date.'

Daisy nearly snorted with now excruciatingly nervous laughter. The ridiculousness of the situation was like being in a very vivid, Nineties happy pill state of mind. If a doctor had appeared over her bed and said, 'Don't worry, Mrs Ronaldson, you're tripping out. Or as we would describe it officially, you're experiencing a transient mind state.'

'Yes, we are.' She nodded and then suddenly feeling very self-conscious, pulled the duvet up over her gaping nightdress. 'Would everyone mind just giving me some time to get changed and then I'll come see you, Ali. Is that OK?'

'Of course, it's just I don't actually, you know, expect you to—'

She broke him off mid-sentence, just as he had done to her last night. 'Yes, I know, you don't want it to sound so serious when you've only asked me on a second date, it's just that—'

'He's got you summed up pretty well.' Tom grinned. 'Daisy doesn't know how to do casual.'

'Do too.' She pouted.

'Have you ever had a fling?' Tom pushed. 'Have you ever just snogged someone because you could?'

'Well, not that I can remember,' admitted Daisy, 'but at university I was either clubbing and high as a kite, then soon after university I was married.' She narrowed her eyes. 'We haven't all led the same liberal existence as you, my friend.'

Tom kissed Daisy on the cheeks. 'Aw shucks, thanks babe.' He grabbed Alistair's hand. 'Let's leave the beast to become the beauty.' Alistair followed like an obedient puppy, looking somewhat dazed.

This time Daisy shot the pillow at Tom as she fell about laughing.

'I'll come and find you,' she said more gently to Alistair. 'Give me half an hour.'

It was a gloriously sunny day and she opened the shutters to her room wide, allowing the warmth of the sun to sink into her skin. She looked out the window at Annabelle's children playing hide and seek and James showing one of the girls a rosebud about to bloom. She ran herself a bath with oil she used only on special occasions. Then once bathed, she put on a hint of blusher and lip tint and chose the most flattering pale blue dress she owned.

It had a tie-waist that she hoped made her look womanly, and not like a ribbon keeping a Christmas cracker's goodies in place.

With one final glance in the mirror, she decided she didn't look a day over sixty, and as she stepped from her room she took a deep cleansing breath.

She found Alistair sat in the drawing room looking undeniably anxious.

'Daisy,' he breathed heavily as he rose from his chair. 'Can we talk? Please.' He wrung his hands. 'I'm a bit confused.'

'What? As about confused as I was when I thought I was going on a supper date and instead found myself in the middle of your birthday party?'

He hung his head. 'I know, I truly am so sorry.' He looked up at her. 'Is this why you're doing this? To get back at me?'

Daisy shook her head and took his hand, inviting him to sit next to her. 'Well, I was thinking that maybe us dating one another wouldn't be such a bad idea.'

He furrowed his brows. 'Why?'

'Well, I know it sounds daft, but you are under a certain amount of pressure to find the right woman and I clearly can't be all bad or, trust me, Hugh wouldn't have touched me with a barge pole.'

Alistair smiled at this.

'And I do get lonely, even though I'm surrounded by my friends now, it's still not quite the same as *being* with someone. So,' she paused, 'we could be companions.'

'Why do we need to date to be companions?' He looked confused and Daisy had to admit his point was valid.

'Well, I guess we don't, but if you want people to stop piling pressure on you to find *the one* and I want people to stop waiting for me to move on… it might just work.'

She watched his face soften and then he chuckled. 'Well, it would save me the bother of now having to announce our relationship as over.' He smiled. 'Not sure why I did it… I think that if you had been the one to supposedly break it off, I thought people would feel sorry for me. In actual fact, I'm pretty sure they'd let me be for a few weeks and then the matchmaking would start all over again.'

She pushed her hand through her hair, suddenly feeling somewhat self-conscious. 'I mean we don't have to share a bedroom or anything like that…'

Alistair blushed. 'Not that it wouldn't be nice to sometimes…'

'Oh, absolutely,' Daisy agreed, wishing she could keep that desperate tone out of her voice whenever she talked about sex. Sex nowadays was like a foreign language. She was pretty sure she needed to go back to school to learn the basics. Sex with Hugh, well… whilst she had loved him dearly, he had never been one for anything spontaneous. Their lovemaking took on a rigid routine of its own. She had never imagined she would end up marrying someone who had to carefully place his trousers in the trouser press and line his shoes up before any action took place.

'I mean, look, we're in our forties. This could be a good thing for people of our age.' She noticed Alistair visibly flinch.

'I don't consider that to be old. Do you actually feel any different to how you did when you were in your twenties?'

She heard people stamping past the door to the drawing room and she wanted to tell them all to mind their own business. There was the sound of suppressed laughter too but she tried to ignore whatever was happening on the other side of the door.

She considered this. 'No, I suppose not.' She laughed. 'Though my bed looks more and more inviting and not for sex… and parts of my body have started hurting that I didn't even know I had.' She smiled. 'And I've started complaining about the youth.'

He joined in her laughter. 'Well, I guess I can understand all of those.' He held up his hands. 'No wait, one more…'

'Go on…' Daisy grinned.

'Someone invited me to Glastonbury last year and the thought of camping and those loos filled me with horror.' He pushed his hand through his hair. 'So I stayed in a four star hotel up the road. It took me that long to get to the site I missed most of the acts but I slept bloody well.'

'You see,' she said, 'we're a match made in heaven. Frankly, I think you were brave to actually even go to Glastonbury.'

'No, it was fun,' he admitted. 'But yeah, probably even more fun when you're twenty-something.'

'Anyway, listen, I don't know about you but I don't want to be alone for the rest of my life.'

His face grew serious. 'No, I often think how much that scares me, being alone for the rest of my life. It's not to say I don't like my own company or love my friends' company for that matter but it would be nice to have someone to share a bottle of wine with in the evening.'

Daisy took his hand. 'Look, maybe it was meant to be.' She smiled.

His face lit up. 'Yes, maybe I'm not such an idiot after all.'

'Oh no, you're still that and I will never let you forget what you did but it's oddly romantic.'

'Right, shall we go and join everyone?' He stood, his hand still in hers. 'Well, I mean the two people in the world who don't already know.'

'Your friends knew before I did.' She chuckled. 'Let's go.'

They walked out hand in hand towards the garden where there appeared to be a hive of activity. As they walked out, Daisy was taken aback to find a lot of familiar stood on her lawn, as well as Lisa and Bob, Tom and the Dream Team and a scattering of others she didn't recognise.

'Here they are!' Tom hollered and whooped. 'The happy couple!'

Daisy was confused and through gritted teeth, asked, 'What's going on?'

'I've thrown you a dating party.'

'Is that an actual thing?'

Tom put his arm around her shoulders. 'It's all the rage in London.'

Daisy was once again ensconced in a party where she had no idea how she came to be one of the guests of honour.

Alistair grew increasingly confident in his role as her boyfriend and his face shone with happiness and pride. Daisy felt her stomach flip with guilt; why couldn't she embrace the situation like he had? She knew it was her idea after all.

Tom ensured the Saturday brunch party flowed seamlessly and the Dream Team, it turned out, were a dab hand at creating canapés from scraps in the fridge. Between them they kept wine from Hugh's ever depleting cellar flowing and everyone appeared to be having a jolly time. In a brief moment of quiet, Daisy decided to slip back indoors and have some time alone. She looked at Alistair and wondered what his hobbies were and what sort of music he was into…

Once inside the quiet of the house, she escaped upstairs to Hugh's study. She noticed the door was slightly ajar and gently pushed it open. James was sat in the big leather armchair opposite the sofa, the same chair he had always sat in when he had stayed over and he and Hugh had talked for hours into the night. Daisy had often left them to put the world to rights and gone to bed.

'James,' she said, her voice tinged with irritation. 'I thought we all agreed that no one was to come in here.'

He nodded, clearly armed for this. 'I know, I know.'

'Then why are you here?'

He took a deep breath. 'Because I think you're making a huge mistake and I don't think Hugh would have been happy.'

Daisy shut the door behind her, her hand momentarily resting on the oak panels. 'Please don't say that, James.' Her eyes welled with suppressed tears. 'Please.'

'Well, you know it's true.'

She turned on him, anger bubbling up inside her. 'No, I don't know it's true, James. You kept giving me letters from Hugh, telling me he wanted me to be happy. He wanted me to find love again.'

James laughed sardonically. 'And you're happy? You don't even know him.'

'You make it sound like we've agreed to get married!' She paused. 'And I know he's a kind and gentle man who is lonely.'

James stood, shaking his head in disbelief. 'Can you hear yourself, Daisy? It's utterly ridiculous... the whole thing. He was a guest for one night and, as far as I know, you two didn't…'

'How do you know?' she challenged, even though he was quite right.

'OK, fine, let's say you did.' His face clouded with anger. 'But still, one week later, you two are infatuated? He hasn't even been here for the week.' He clenched his jaw. 'It's just…' He searched for the word. 'It is just desperate.'

Daisy took a few steps closer to him. 'Desperate?' A sob escaped her lips. 'Desperate? That's what you think of me?' She wiped her eyes with the back of her hand. 'I thought Hugh asked for you to look out for me.' She stepped closer again, his face inches from her own. 'To protect me. Not make me feel like crap.'

He brought his face closer to hers, his breath juddering. 'Exactly, Daisy, I'm trying to protect you.'

'Are you? Or are you letting your own perceived ideas of how life should go blur your vision? Because—' her eyes met his glistening eyes, filled with emotion '—all I'm seeing is a man who refuses to let his dead best friend's wife get on with her life. I am pretty sure that Hugh would tell you to back off if he could hear you now.'

'No, he wouldn't,' he said, with such confidence, Daisy was momentarily taken aback.

'How can you be so sure?'

'Because…' he started, his lips now unbearably close to her own. 'Because…'

She found herself leaning in, her eyes closing and then as his lips brushed hers, she heard Alistair's voice on the stairs, calling out to her.

'Daisy, are you up here?'

Daisy jolted back to the now, her eyes still locked on James.

'Sorry, I shouldn't have…' James started. 'I just can't help the way I feel…'

She wiped her lips with back of her hand. 'I don't know what's going on, James,' she said quietly. 'But you can't stop me from moving on, from being happy.'

He looked at her, motionless. 'Daisy…'

'No, I have to go.' She walked fast to the door, her back to James. 'Please can you go too? This is not a place for you to come and sit.'

He didn't say anything, just walked wordlessly up behind her and she stood aside, not meeting his gaze.

'Daisy, I…' He put his hand gently on her shoulder.

'Please, don't.' Tears blurred her vision and she resisted every fibre of her being telling her to turn around and collapse into his firm hold.

'I just don't think you need to date a man you don't know.' He lowered his voice. 'You've got all of us… you've got me.'

The lump in her throat meant she was unable to speak and he continued.

'I just think it's a bit out of the blue, a bit out of character.' He paused. 'It was only a couple of weeks ago you read your card from Hugh on your anniversary and you seemed…'

She turned now, their faces once again inches from each other. 'What is this, James? I thought Hugh asked you to look out for me, to ensure I was happy? It seems you want to dictate to me what I can and can't do.'

He clenched his jaw. 'But I think you're doing it to make me…' He stopped abruptly. 'You don't know him. You don't need this or him.' James's voice grew louder.

'No, James.' She felt her anger boiling over now. How dare he tell her what was right and wrong. 'I am dating him because he makes me feel happy.'

She could hear Alistair still calling out for her and then muffled voices in the hall. They would all be looking for her soon; after all, thanks to Tom, she was guest of honour at a dating party. Or was she not allowed to be happy?

James gave her one last pleading look but her eyes continued to flash with anger, and he nodded silently and opened the door. 'I'm going back to London.'

Her heart started to hammer in her ears. 'Why? Don't you want to stay and run the guesthouse?'

'I can help you from London. I don't really need to be here.' She noticed the tremble in his voice. 'You've got my number, ring me anytime.'

'James, is it Annabelle? Are you going to be with Annabelle?'

James looked at her. 'Annabelle is married.'

Daisy shook her head and replied bitterly, 'It hasn't stopped her mauling you.'

James shook his head in disbelief. 'God, Daisy, can you hear yourself? You just don't get it, do you?'

Daisy, affronted, fiddled nervously with the button on her dress. 'Get what?'

'Well,' James said, emotion choking his words, 'if I have to explain it then I must be wrong. It's a feeling. Not something you can describe.' He gave her a small smile. 'Bye, Daisy.'

Daisy stood stock-still, her stomach churning, and heard James's footsteps on the stairs and then the opening and closing of his bedroom door. She wiped away the tears falling down her cheeks with her hand and realised she must look a sight. She headed to the bathroom, splashed cool water on her face and waited for her red-rimmed eyes to calm.

She opened the bathroom door and waited, listening. She didn't want to bump into James and as she snuck towards the landing, she collided with him as he came quietly around the corner.

'Oh.' Her cheeks flushed. She noted his bag and he held it up wordlessly as if to confirm he really was leaving. Then he walked fast down the stairs and he was gone.

Alistair appeared on the stairs below and smiled. 'Hello.' His eyes filled with concern. 'You OK? Have you been crying?'

She forced a smile. 'No, not at all. Hay fever starting early this year,' she lied. 'There you go, now you know one more thing about me, I'm the least sexy woman ever in the spring and early summer.' She paused. 'Unless you like women who sound like they're wearing a clothes peg on their nose and have no control of their mucus.'

Alistair climbed the stairs to where she stood and gave her a big, slightly awkward hug as he wrapped his long limbs around her. But she was grateful nonetheless.

'Come on; let me get you a drink. Looks like you need one.'

She wasn't going to argue. She allowed him to take her hand and guide her down the stairs and back outside to the growing throng of people.

Tom ran up to her. 'I put it out on Facebook and everyone in the area we know is coming to celebrate.'

She smiled. 'Well, better keep the wine flowing.' A very chiselled member (she knew this didn't narrow it down – they were all tanned and angular) of the Dream Team offered her a glass of white wine and a plate of canapés. She recognised some cheese she thought had gone way past its best before date and vegetables cut into stars and hearts. 'You lot are amazing.' She smiled at him gratefully. 'I mean honestly amazing… sorry, remind me if we've met?'

He shook his head, flashing his pearly white. 'I'm new to the Dream Team.' He paused. 'My name's Alvin.'

'Lovely to meet you, Alvin.' Tom came up to them. He exchanged a shy smile with Alvin and Daisy looked knowingly at her friend; that was his smitten look. A petite woman with a dark smooth bob and a tattoo on her wrist stood next to Tom and smiled tentatively at them before her eyes came to rest on Alistair's.

Daisy glanced at Alistair who had visibly paled.

'Clare,' he managed quietly. 'What are you doing here? I mean I haven't seen you since…'

'Your mum told me I was uncouth?' She gave a wry smile.

Daisy stuck out her hand to shake Clare's but Clare barely acknowledged her. The air was thick with heavy tension and Daisy, despite 'dating' Alistair, felt like she was intruding and stepped away, motioning for Alvin and Tom to do the same.

She watched Alistair and Clare as Tom chatted away to her about Alvin's bottom. They hadn't even touched each other yet, but Daisy wasn't stupid, they didn't need to. The way they looked at each other was enough to tell her everything. It made her heart sad because she realised it was the way James had looked at her in Hugh's study.

Chapter 16

The party continued all day and into the small hours. Daisy continually checked her phone for any messages from James. Tom found out halfway through the evening that Alvin not only could play guitar but he carried his guitar with him everywhere. After Bob and Tom had set up halogen heaters throughout the garden and the Dream Team had hung tea light lanterns from the trees, Alistair's friends cajoled him into asking her to dance. She could sense his reticence and she saw the fleeting look he gave Clare. They held each other as Alvin strummed Eric Clapton's 'Wonderful Tonight'.

Alistair's body remained tense against hers and she looked furtively at her bag, wondering if James had messaged yet, though she knew, in her heart, he wouldn't.

She spotted Tom sat on the floor next to Alvin's feet – both of them now barefoot, despite the cooling temperatures. Tom was staring up at Alvin as if he were the most beautiful specimen he had ever laid eyes on. Alvin tapped the rhythm of the songs with his right foot but every now and then fondled Tom's leg with his left foot.

Lisa and Bob were slow dancing under the oak tree and Lisa looked as if she had arrived in heaven. Maybe that was why Daisy was panicking; she recognised her support network were, quite rightly, moving their own lives forward. As Alvin moved seamlessly into the next song, she clung more closely to Alistair who looked down at her with a soft look of surprise.

'You OK?'

She nodded. 'Just wondering if we really are mad.'

He smiled and held her more closely. Daisy allowed herself to relax into it the music and Alistair's body. 'Yeah, we are,' he admitted.

'That's *the* Clare, isn't it?' She kept her voice neutral.

He nodded. 'Yes, she lives locally. Heard I was in the area.'

'Is she married?' Daisy asked tentatively.

'She was,' Alistair mumbled into her hair. 'Her husband died five years ago, before they could have children.'

Daisy stopped moving to the music and held him at arm's length. 'You love her still, don't you?'

'Of course,' Alistair said softly.

'Then go to her.'

He shook his head. 'I can't put her through my parents' interrogation again.'

'Alistair…' She knew she sounded like a teacher. 'You are forty-five, not fifteen, and if you love her, you love her. You can't deny yourself your feelings.' She paused, moving closer to him as the lawn filled with couple and non-couples moving to 'La Bamba'. They were jostled this way and that.

'Does Clare love you still?'

'She hasn't said.' He looked down. 'She just keeps reminding me of how appalling my parents were to her.'

'Shows she cares.' Daisy gave him an encouraging nod. 'Go and talk to her. Life's too short.' A lump grew in her throat. She thought about Hugh, his life cut short in its prime.

Alistair smiled gratefully and headed in the direction of his long-lost girlfriend. Daisy fought her way out of the bobbing mass of people.

Tom grabbed her ankle as she walked past. 'You alright, babe?' he shouted up at her.

'Great,' she forced a grin. 'Thanks for putting on such an amazing party!'

He smiled at her, his eyes barely leaving Alvin's. 'Least we could do, doll. You deserve to be happy after everything you've gone through.'

She smiled and bent down, planting a kiss on his head. Daisy noted his hair had thinned even more of late. Tom dreaded balding, used every pro-growth shampoo on the market, but she supposed they were all growing older and you could only fight so much.

She headed inside to find Lisa and Bob talking heatedly in the entrance hall.

'You guys OK?' Daisy asked, trying to judge the situation.

'Yes, we're OK, thanks hunny,' said Bob, clutching Barbara who was trying to wriggle out of his grasp.

'No, actually, we're not.' Lisa shot him a look. 'We both think you're acting weird.'

Daisy gave a shallow laugh. 'Oh good, more people out to judge me.'

'I also,' Lisa said, her eyes shining bright with emotion, 'have known you for over twenty years and I know you are not *genuinely* happy. You are pretending to have fallen head over heels in love with a bloody Scotsman because you're panicking about being alone…'

Daisy narrowed her eyes, realising the truth really did hurt.

'And he's panicking,' Lisa went on. 'Because you're both of a certain age…'

'A certain age!' Daisy shrieked. 'Priceless. Lisa, do I need to remind you we are the same age. What exactly happens at *our* age and moreover since when can you not date and have fun?' As she spoke, she saw something glint in the overhead light. She gasped. 'You're engaged!'

Lisa blushed. 'Yes. You've been so busy with all this stuff, I didn't tell you.'

'Oh, Lisa,' Daisy rushed towards Lisa and hugged her close, and despite the slow response Lisa then clung onto her friend. 'That is so amazing.' She stood back to admire the ring. 'That's a beauty, Bob.'

He grinned and Daisy kissed Lisa on the cheek, then Bob and, of course, Barbara's furry muzzle.

'Listen, both of you, I am an adult and I would appreciate it if you could treat me like one,' Daisy said evenly. 'I don't think that's too much to ask, is it?'

Lisa pulled a face. She was being as stubborn as ever, Daisy thought, but then she smiled. 'We could buy some wedding magazines like we used to talk about!'

Daisy smiled. Lisa's moods could change as quickly as clouds passing over the sun. 'What a beautiful idea.' She hugged her friend again and ruffled Barbara's silky ruff.

'I'm just going to go upstairs for a bit.' Daisy smiled at the three of them and treaded softly up the stairs to Hugh's study. She didn't know why but she felt like she needed to talk out the situation with him.

Once she had shut herself in the safety of Hugh's study, she sat on his sofa once again and looked up.

'Hugh, I don't really know if I'm coming to ask your permission or what really but I imagine, by now, you've got wind of the fact that I'm technically dating this guy. His name's Alistair…' She paused, furrowing her brows. 'Actually, I can't remember his last name. He's from Edinburgh but went to an agricultural college down here.' She shrugged. 'I mean I didn't even know I was dating him, he kind of just surprised me with it.' She chuckled. 'To say the least. But then it gets more complicated because you see, his old flame, Clare, turned up today. I can tell they're madly in love and who am I to stand in the way of that, even though it was Alistair who set this whole thing in motion…'

She smoothed the leather with her hand. 'I miss you, Hugh, but I can talk about and to you without crying. I don't know if that makes me a bad person?' She shook her head. 'I really hope not. All your cards and letters that you gave to James to give me said you wanted me to be happy, find love again.' She squinted at the ceiling, deep in thought. 'How do you know if it's the right person? I mean Alistair seems nice but he doesn't love me and I don't love him. We could be each other's companions…' She fisted her hand and gently hit the sofa's armrest. 'Can't you give me a sign of what I should do? You were always Mr Sensible and now you've left me to make my own decisions.' She closed her eyes, enjoying the moment's peace. She could hear people still chattering downstairs even though by now it was dark. The lanterns hung like fireflies from the trees.

She decided she might pen her thoughts. Hugh had always said the best way to sort through your feelings was to write them out. She got up and went to sit at the desk, opening the first small drawer where she knew Hugh kept a pile of overly priced, smart and stiff paper. He had insisted that even the paper used to send a letter said a lot about a person's standards. She thought about her own mother and father who quite often hadn't any paper at all to hand so messages were sent on the back of the local pub's cardboard drink mats or old vet bills.

She took a sheet and apologised. 'Sorry, Hugh. Probably not what I should use it for.' She took out Hugh's favourite pen; he hadn't allowed anyone else to use it because the nib could get bent the wrong way. 'Again, sorry.'

She started her list of pros and cons of dating Alistair.

Pros:

Good looking (beautiful, in fact)

Great dress sense

Impeccable manners (apart from the lies)

Someone to talk to (I know nothing about him so there should be loads)

Sex (presuming he's not gay and doesn't have a medical condition. Though imagine Tom's radar would have picked up on this)

'Sorry, Hugh,' she mumbled again, blushing despite herself. 'I know you hate people being so open about it.'

Comes from a good family (well, he says he does)

Both share a hate of camping

She nodded, pleased with her efforts.

Cons:

He's ridiculously good looking (making me feel even more unsexy and ungainly)

Great dress sense (highlighting how nice it must be to be slim and fit into anything therefore making me feel even worse)

He makes stuff up (compulsive liar???)

Someone to talk to (though nothing mind-blowing or scintillating has been talked about so far)

He might be rubbish in bed (or gay)

His 'good family' might think they're above me

If he hates camping, what else does he hate? He might hate open-air opera (which I love) or eating. Oh no, what if he hates food??

Talked for the grand sum total of…

Daisy thought about it, adding up the figures in her head. She knew maths wasn't her forte but, surely, that couldn't be right.

'Daisy, be honest with yourself,' she said aloud.

Talked for the grand sum total of… six hours.

Oh, fiddlesticks. Not looking good. Maybe Lisa had a point. She sighed deeply and put down Hugh's pen noting that the nib definitely sat at a different angle now. 'Sorry.' She knew Hugh kept spare nibs somewhere 'just in case some moron tried to use my pen'. Well, turned out she was the moron. She could just make them out at the back of the drawer but it was such a narrow space that she could barely fit her hand in the slot, let alone wiggle her fingers. When she felt something small, pointy and metal, she pinched it with two fingers and shuffled it forward.

When she had finally managed to retrieve her now very squished hand from the drawer, she looked at the nib, only to find it wasn't a nib, but a key. A very small key. For a second, she was confused and about to dive back in to get the nibs, when she remembered the metal box under the desk.

Her heart pulsed in her throat. She wasn't sure why she was nervous; it was just a gut feeling that she wasn't about to find some utility bills and a card she had written to him on his birthday years ago. She knew, because Hugh wasn't that sort of person. By now, the bills would have been filed in an exact order – probably colour coded – in the filing cabinet and she knew that even his sentimental box with cards etc. had a system. No, if Hugh had taken the time and effort to buy a metal box – a lockable metal box – there was a reason.

She knelt down and, hand shaking, put the key into the lock. It fit perfectly. With bated breath, she pulled the door open and there appeared to be nothing inside. Then, on closer inspection, there were two envelopes.

She pulled them out slowly, almost as if they might combust in her hand. Did she want to know what was inside them? On the one hand, she thought, they might be nothing to do with her. Her mind started to whirr with possibilities: what if it was addressed to another woman, what if it was a photo of a child he had with another woman…

'Stop it,' she whispered, gathering her dress up and sitting back on the chair. 'Just look.'

She flipped the envelopes over and with a mixture of relief and dread was pleased to see her name on the front.

The first envelope had a Post-it stuck to the front and it read, 'James, for Daisy's birthday.' Her birthday wasn't for another few months but she ripped it open anyway.

It read:

Dearest Daisy, by now I imagine you will have moved on and I'm glad of it. If you haven't, please do, please remember how important your happiness is to me. I wasn't a barrel of laughs when I was alive, so imagine putting up with this for the rest of your life?

Daisy laughed, and realised she was crying, despite telling Hugh she was over that.

I love you Daisy, darling. This is the last card I will send you because I hope by now James has explained his feelings for you and I can see, I have always been able to see, truth be told, that he loves you. He loves you truly and deeply, like I do. He is a good man. The best. In my heart, I know you love him too, and that's good. That's as it should be.

Love always, yours,

Hugh xxx

She sobbed, tears of happiness but also despair. She had pushed James away. Why had she pushed him away? Maybe because she knew she loved him.

'Please don't let that be the last I hear from you, my darling Hugh,' she said, her voice shaking. 'It can't be the last.'

She plucked the envelope from underneath which again had been colour coded with a red Post-it note that read, 'James, only when time is right. And thank you.'

Daisy didn't like the sound of those words... *when the time is right*... for what? If he was about to announce he was married to another woman, there probably wasn't a great time for that. Or if he was questioning his sexuality, she thought, that was probably best kept a secret at this point. There was a time and place for honesty, and when you were six feet under, it probably wasn't it.

She slid her finger under the sealed flap and ripped it open. There was a letter to her and a formal letter from a place called the Live Well Clinic. She had no idea what it was and decided it was best to read his letter first. Since spending years nursing Hugh, she now found anything that could remind her of the trauma too much to bear. She knew that with illness came watching the person you love diminish before your eyes: their corporeality and spirituality evaporating. And, for the moment, she preferred to avoid any reminders of that time.

She started to read, her eyes unable to compute what was in front of her. She could hear Hugh's voice, louder and clearer than ever before since his death.

My dearest Daisy, I have a confession...

The word *confession* set alarm bells ringing and she almost didn't want to read on but, short of burning the letter, she knew she would read on and find out the truth.

Years ago, when you started talking about wanting children, I knew I didn't but I couldn't bring myself to tell you.

She gasped, and her hand flew to her mouth.

I had a vasectomy. I am so sorry, Daisy, please understand that I thought children would ruin us, would ruin the routine we had together. However, as you will see from the certificate with this letter, I did freeze my sperm. You know what I'm like, I'm never without a plan.

Daisy could hear her own heart thumping in her head. He had lied to her for all these years? She had thought she was unable to have children; she had done what every woman did and absorbed the guilt when it turned out, she might well be able to have children. Only now it was too late, or it was becoming too late. She was a biological time bomb.

Anyway, when I found out I had cancer; it was as if life slowed down to make me appreciate everything more. I never took you for granted but the way you looked after me until I came here, to the hospice, was amazing. Thank you for letting me die with dignity. It was then I realised I was leaving you behind in the house and because of my selfish act, and particularly never having told you, you wouldn't have children to look after you.

I confided in James many months ago and we spoke. I told him I knew that he was in love with you. He didn't seem surprised I knew. I asked him to look out for you because I am pretty sure you feel the same about him.

Daisy grabbed a tissue from the leather holder on Hugh's desk and dabbed at her eyes and nose, almost pointlessly as the tears continued to stream.

We agreed he would look out for you and during this first couple of years I wanted you to know how much I need you to find happiness. I have been selfish once before, and I now, from the bottom of my heart, want you to find happiness. Seeing as I'm a boring old fart, I hope you'll be happier. If you do love James, love him, and let him love you. Have children, Daisy, if it's not too late, because you would make the most wonderful mother. Maybe that was why I was so selfish. Maybe you looked after me so well in our married life, I didn't want to share that with children. But now, I can see how truly selfish that attitude is. I don't know if you will use the sperm or not, and if you do I hope they take after you. But I will be looking down at you from the stars above, tell them to look out for me. If you don't use the sperm, that's fine too. I just thought it only right I share my unspeakable lie with you. Love you always, Hugh.

She slammed the letter and the card down angrily. The certificate sat on her lap, searing her thighs. Her eyes swam as she read legal signatures, her name, Hugh's name. This was possibly her ticket to having children should she choose. Only, it felt like she would be creating a little person without love, without Hugh's parental input and there was something quite strange about that. Then the fact that James knew all this: did he really love her? Or was he purely an extension of Hugh's betrayal?

She stood, grabbed everything she had found and strode meaningfully towards the door.

Alistair stood on the other side, his face sweaty and ashen. 'I don't know how to tell you this, Daisy, but I think I made a huge mistake…'

She would have laughed if it hadn't been for the tide of anger swelling up inside her.

'You want to break it off?' She patted his arm. 'That's fine.'

Relief passed across his features, and the colour rushed back to his cheeks.

'Anyway,' she continued, 'I have to go to London.' Daisy walked down the stairs and grabbed her coat and keys off the side.

By the light of the hall, Alistair was now able to see her tear-stained face properly. 'God, are you OK?'

She looked down at the papers in her hand. 'Yes… no. I don't know.' She drew a deep breath and tried to calm her jangled nerves. 'I need to speak to James. I need answers.'

Alistair smiled. 'Ah, James.' He chuckled. 'Yeah, he spoke to me before he left.'

'Really?' Daisy was surprised. 'Only he didn't seem to like you much. No offense.'

'Exactly,' Alistair agreed. 'He told me that if I do anything to hurt you, he would find me and break me.' He paused, deadpan. 'So he seems like a nice chap.'

The car keys slipped from her hand to the floor as she laughed. 'I think it's called *being protective*.'

'Something like that.' Alistair bent down and handed her keys back to her. 'Go and find him. He loves you.'

Daisy nodded. 'You go and find Clare, she loves you too.'

They held each other's gaze in a companionable silence before Daisy turned on her heels and headed out to the car. She tried ringing James as he hadn't responded to any of her messages and when it went to voicemail, she put the key in the ignition and started up. If he was going to ignore her, she had no choice but to go looking for him without any prior warning.

Chapter 17

As she drove away from the peace of the Gloucestershire countryside, down the M4 to London, she found herself getting increasingly aggravated. She had no idea how people lived like this day in, day out: the constant noise, traffic and sheer numbers of people. Maybe it had been growing up on a farm but she was a country girl through and through. Hugh had worked in London and had often complained of the commute back home, but she insisted she would have been so unhappy living in the city. He bought a flat in Docklands and she had only ever been to it once after the theatre. In fact, she had been to James's apartment in Marylebone more times, purely because she found that part of London enjoyable and the living space was light and airy. She didn't feel trapped like she had in Hugh's sixteenth-floor flat where the view was of other high-rise buildings.

In Marylebone, James had a small courtyard garden and the front of the house looked out over the main high street, the baker being directly opposite. So when she had come to London and because, quite often, James had been invited to join them by Hugh, she made all sorts of excuses to stay at James's. Hugh would always begrudgingly leave her there, stating he wanted to be able to get into work early the next day and as his flat was only a stone's throw away from the office, he would have to leave her. When she thought about it now, why had Hugh been so accepting of the time she spent with James? It was as if the last few hours had lifted the curtains on the fog of her marriage. Maybe it hadn't been as harmonious as she had thought; maybe Hugh had already given into her love for James, and his for her. There were so many questions circling her mind she didn't know where to begin unravelling the truth and her past.

She drove the route to James's house as if she had only been there yesterday. In actual fact, Hugh had been so ill in his last months they wouldn't have been able to make it to London. She parked up on a road a couple of minutes from his apartment that she knew required no permits and at this time on a Saturday was a free for all.

She pulled her coat tight around her and walked the two-minute journey to the familiar steps of his apartment building. She saw the glow of a lamp and her heart lifted. She thought of the way James had kissed her only this morning, the way, she realised now, she had fought the urge to kiss him back. She wanted him to hold her, tell her everything was going to be OK, that they were meant to be.

She tried the buzzer again and when no one came to the door, she retrieved the key James had given her to his apartment. It felt a bit wrong to be letting herself in after what had happened that morning and the atmosphere between them after the kiss, but she decided he could have been in the shower, and not have heard the door. She slipped the key into the lock and pushed the heavy front door open. The Victorian entrance hall table was filled with post for the three apartments. She picked up James's couple of letters and turned to his front door. Using the other key, she jiggled it in the lock and pushed it open. Wary she didn't want to scare him, she called out, 'James, it's me… Daisy. Are you in? Sorry, I hope you don't mind me letting myself in. I need to talk to you urgently about something.'

She turned to close the door and as she looked back around, she screamed in shock. There in front of her was a woman, but not any old woman: Annabelle. Annabelle was wearing only a towel and her face was flushed.

'Annabelle!' Daisy squealed, anger, frustration and hurt building fast inside her. 'What on earth are you doing here?' She knew it was a silly question: what she was doing in James's apartment, flushed and almost naked didn't really need explaining.

She could tell Annabelle had – not surprisingly – had a few drinks. She was slurring her words, and her towel kept slipping downwards forcing Daisy to look the other way.

'Hello, darling,' she said, lurching herself at Daisy. 'How good to see you.'

'I should be going, sorry, I shouldn't have let myself in,' Daisy blundered, making a fast get away. Realising she was still carrying James's post, she turned back to find Annabelle now completely starkers, giggling like a schoolgirl.

'Gosh, I'm so sorry, Daisy, flashing my bits at you... I can't seem to keep my towel in place. The naughty thing wants to run away.' She leant up against the hall wall, and then slid inelegantly down it until she was sat on the floor. 'What brings you to this part of the world? I thought you hated London, that's what James said anyway.'

'Oh, he did, did he?' Daisy smarted. 'Anything else you two have discussed?'

'Well, he never stops talking about you which is annoying.' She pulled a face, hiccupping at the same time. 'But I told him you need to lose a few pounds and lighten up.'

'And he said?' Daisy snapped, wondering why the hell she had come this far to be told by a drunken Chihuahua that she needed to lose weight and lighten up. She was pretty sure she was getting a sense of déjà vu. If she wasn't mistaken, Annabelle had delivered a few home truths after the dog comment debacle too.

'Not much actually,' she admitted.

When Daisy realised she was getting no further, she made a move to go. 'Well, I think there's no love lost here, Annabelle. So I'll leave you and James to…' She gestured towards the bedroom, wondering how long he was going to hide in there for. 'To do whatever it is you do.'

'James has gone.' Annabelle smiled crookedly, her eyes glistening. 'But I'm sure he'll be back soon.'

Daisy imagined him nipping out for a post-sex takeaway. That was what she imagined happened when you had hungry sex. Well, the clue was in the title… you got *hungry*. She had never had it so she wouldn't know. Sex with Hugh had been such a rigid, formal affair that quite often she thought that in the time it took him to fold up his trousers and align his shoes, she could have whipped together a risotto and an Eton Mess. Once, she remembered, she had actually brought a can of Mr Whippy to bed along with strawberries dipped in chocolate. Her thought process had been that if the excitement wasn't already there, bring the excitement to the situation. Only it backfired.

Hugh firstly told her off because they would get cream and chocolate on the bed sheets and once he had got over that (she reminded him that she did the laundry), he then sat upright in bed, pillow in his back reading the *Financial Times* and chowing down on her erotic cream and fruit. Not quite the sexy evening in she had intended.

Realising she had become entirely absorbed in her daydream and was in rapid danger of James walking back in with a Chinese, she opened the door and turned to Annabelle. 'Drink some water, or have a coffee.'

Annabelle started to cry much to Daisy's horror. She couldn't bear drunken tears. Never had been able to tolerate it. Even when she was alone, she just ended up in a slanging match with herself in the mirror as if she was, in fact, two people.

'Daisy, get a grip!' she would shout and then the real her would cry pitifully into her sleeve, the smell of cheap student vodka emanating from her pores.

'Why are you crying, Annabelle?' She almost felt sorry for her and it took every ounce of willpower to not pull the towel back around her. Even though, truth be told, she was incredibly jealous of her petite frame and slim figure.

'Because everyone leaves me.' Annabelle hung her head, large tears dropping into her lap. 'Well, I mean obviously I left him…'

'You left who?'

Annabelle looked at her as though she had just crawled out from under a rock. 'My husband, who do you think?'

Daisy didn't want to say that she had no idea how they had remained together even this long but she imagined the way Annabelle had conducted herself at the guesthouse had been enough for him to snap.

'So you left him?'

'Yes, I left him because the man doesn't even know what a downward dog is and if I have to tell him, one more bloody time, that I like Tattinger, not Bolly, I will literally tear my eyes out.'

Daisy smiled falsely at Annabelle's first world problems. Next she wouldn't be able to understand why her husband bought non-organic guacamole.

'And,' as if reading her mind, 'if he buys another tub of sodding non-organic salsa, I won't know what to do with myself.' She frowned. 'I mean who eats food that's not organic. Well, I mean, I know the poor do but anyone else?'

'I think you'll find that most people do, Annabelle.' She couldn't believe she was even having this conversation with her. 'I mean, I do.'

'Do you think that's why you might be carrying a few extra pounds?'

'No,' Daisy replied stiffly, 'that's because I like food.'

'Oh.' Annabelle was clearly trying to get her head around this concept. 'I don't.'

'Well, that must be fun.' Daisy rolled her eyes. 'So you've left your husband and he's currently looking after the children…'

'No, silly.' Annabelle now attempted to stand. 'The nannies are looking after the children. You don't think I'd let him loose to run the house, that would be like leaving my children with a complete stranger.'

Daisy went to say something but bit her tongue. 'Quite right.'

'Anyway, so I left him and James said I could come here.'

'I bet he did.' Daisy gave her a hard stare. 'Men, they're all the same.'

'Oh no, James is not like any other man I've met. He is genuine and kind-hearted. He listens to me talk about all sorts of things. Like we had a great conversation about St Tropez only yesterday and do you know, James too, loves those olives in that salty stuff, and not oil.'

'Brine?'

'No, it's like salty water.'

'Yes,' Daisy nodded. 'Brine.'

'Are you OK?' Annabelle peered at her. 'Are you sneezing?'

'Never mind.' Daisy turned once again to the door, keen to get out of the way before a flushed James pranced through the door with sushi rolls for one. Or olives. In brine. For two. 'Listen, I'm so glad you two have all this stuff in common.' When she thought about it they perhaps did know one or two things more about each other than she and Alistair had, but that point aside, either James had reached new levels of shallowness or she didn't know him either. She didn't know Alistair. Fact. She thought she had known everything about Hugh. Wrong. She wanted to believe she knew James. Maybe she was completely out of touch with reality. She didn't have a problem with conversations about St Tropez (Daisy thought that was in France, but she wasn't sure) or olives in brine for that matter, but she and Jams had talked about love in the past, had talked about what life was all about, about the universe. But maybe he was happier when talking about antipasti and the rich living it up in France.

'Well, listen, Annabelle, sorry to hear it's not all going that well for you but maybe you should head home to your husband if you're that distressed.'

Annabelle laughed raucously. 'Yeah, so he can bring home yet another secretary he's hired "to show her the ropes"?' Daisy watched Annabelle's face crumple with pain and her heart softened towards her.

'Oh.'

Annabelle's mobile bleeped on the side and Daisy passed it to her but not before she noticed it was a text from James. Her heart sank.

'Here.' She passed Annabelle the phone.

Annabelle opened up the message and grinned. 'Oh, he's on his way.'

Daisy knew she had to leave and quickly. 'OK, well, I'm off.'

'So are you going on another date with that Scotsman?' Annabelle rose now and wrapped the towel around herself, fluffing her hair in the hall mirror. She pinched her cheeks and licked her finger in a bid to remove the mascara that had run down her face. Annoyingly, she looked transformed again. When she was inebriated and had been crying for England, there was no way of getting away from the fact she looked like an intoxicated panda.

'Yes, I'm dating Alistair,' she lied; she was getting as good as Ali.

'Wow, you two really hit it off, didn't you?'

'Not really,' Daisy said. 'It's what happens when you're in love. You just act on emotion.' She smiled. 'Bit like you and James.'

Annabelle smiled at Daisy in the reflection of the mirror. 'Yes, we are a match made in heaven, aren't we? And now that you're with Alistair, James and I can get on with our plans.'

Daisy's head reeled. 'Plans?'

'Well, we talked about travelling together and so on.'

'Right.' Daisy was tempted to slap her but she was interrupted by the sound of keys in the door and then, before she had managed to debate another escape route, there stood James. He looked at Annabelle in her towel and Daisy, who was frozen to the spot. He smiled softly at Daisy.

'I… I…' she stammered. 'I came to…' She looked desperately around her and spotted his post on the side. 'To bring your post in.'

Her mind was a panic, a blur. Post? What was she bleating on about?

'Thanks,' he said with a gentle smile. 'You really didn't need to come all this way for that.'

'Well, you know me.' Her voice sounded overly cheery. 'Always willing to help out where I can.'

Annabelle sidled up to James and linked her arm through his. 'Daisy was just telling me how she is definitely dating that man. The Scottish one.'

James's face clouded over. 'Right.' James's voice grew stiff. 'Thanks for picking up the post. You didn't need to.'

'Well, I was in the area…' She let out an empty laugh.

'Thanks for popping by.' Annabelle was practically pushing her out the door. 'Don't forget to send an invite to your wedding.' She guffawed loudly at her own wit.

And before Daisy had had a chance to explain her lies, the door was shut in her face.

'Charming,' she muttered, tears falling down her cheeks.

She got in her car, looked at her phone – there were about twenty missed calls from Tom and Lisa – and then once more at James's bay window. She just caught a glimpse of Annabelle laughing hysterically.

'Oh Hugh, you idiot,' she said to thin air, as she angrily changed gears. 'First you tell me James loves me and then you tell me we could possibly have had children all those years ago.' She pulled up in ensnarled traffic and hit the steering wheel. 'I have no idea what to think anymore.' She choked back more tears. 'And it was your stupid sodding idea to have this guesthouse. I did it for you and all that's happened is Annabelle arrived in our lives and a man called Alistair.' She shook her head. 'Well, that's worked out really well.'

Her phone rang and she put Tom on speakerphone.

'Hey,' she said, manoeuvring her way onto the M4.

'Daisy! We've been so worried about you. Why haven't you been answering?' Daisy could hear Lisa and Bob in the background firing questions at Tom to ask her. 'We spoke to Ali, and he said you'd gone off really upset to London to find James…' Tom barely drew breath. 'Then I find him necking some other woman called Clare… What on earth is going on?'

'It's a long story,' she said and then smiling, 'but I may have the chance to get pregnant.'

'OK, Daisy Ronaldson, get your sweet ass back home now. We need deeeeetails…'

She cut the call and joined the fast lane. Daisy desperately wanted to get back to the safety of her friends and the guesthouse.

Chapter 18

She breathed a deep sigh of relief as she drove up to the house. It had never looked so inviting. Tom came to the front door and as she made her way up over the stones, he was already asking about a million questions.

'So, wait, you're not seeing Alistair? Is that why you are so cool about him kissing another woman? And why did you go and see James?'

'Whoa, slow down.' She took off her coat and slipped off her shoes, dropped her car keys into the basket. 'One step at a time.'

She walked through to the kitchen to find Alvin and his guitar, Lisa, Bob and Barbara. Tom pulled up a chair next to Alvin and then five sets of eyes were on her, waiting.

'What?' she said, knowing full well they wanted every detail but she needed to calm down first, 'Glass of wine, please?'

Bob was already up and pouring her a glass of Chablis. She imagined Hugh's cellar must be pretty empty by now.

She filled in her audience on everything including Annabelle sitting in James's entrance hall half naked and her thoughts on hungry sex. They all knew different amounts of what had gone on but none of them knew what she was about to pull out of the bag now.

'So, you know I went to London for answers. Not only about James and how he feels about me but this too.' She pulled the certificate from the Live Well Clinic and placed it in the middle of the table.

Tom grabbed it and his eyes widened, Lisa moved behind him and she gasped, even Bob, Barbara and Alvin joined them and from their faces Daisy could tell that they understood the significance of that piece of paper.

She then left Hugh's letter on the table and they all read in silence with the occasional 'bloody hell', 'oh my' and 'unbelievable'.

After a few minutes, they all returned to their chairs and looked at her.

'So?' Lisa said. 'What are you going to do?'

'I'm going to book a consultation at the clinic and see what they say.' She shrugged, her eyes glassing over with tears. 'I've always wanted children, as you know, but maybe it's too late. The doctor described me as geriatric and now I'm *even* older.' She paused. 'Would you guys come with me? All of you?' She glanced at Barbara. 'You too, darling, if they'll let you in.'

'We'd be honoured,' drawled Bob. 'And we can hide Barbara in a bag. Done it many times before.'

The others nodded and Tom and Lisa jumped up to give her an all-consuming hug. She felt so grateful in that moment for her beautiful friends. 'I love you guys.'

They planted sloppy kisses on her cheeks.

'And we love you,' Tom said, Lisa nodding her agreement.

'I was also wondering,' Lisa said, almost shyly, 'if you'd consider being my maid of honour.'

Daisy grinned. 'Um, let me think… yes!' she squealed. 'As long as you don't put me in some shapeless apricot dress just to make yourself look good.' She gestured the length of her body. 'Because there's no need to make this even worse.'

Lisa laughed. 'You silly mare.' She hugged Daisy again. 'I'm so glad. I thought after what I said to you, you might never forgive me.'

'Lisa, how many times have we fallen out and bounced back. That's the beauty of friendship over love.' She glanced at Bob. 'No offence.'

'None taken, ma'am.'

She nodded defiantly. 'OK, I'll ring the clinic tomorrow.'

She had a restless night's sleep debating whether or not she could in fact be a mother. Did she have the energy to chase a toddler? How on earth did anyone go about weaning a baby? Potty training looked like a little person's version of Tough Mudder. And then, could she really do this without a man? Without Hugh.

She rang at 8 a.m. on the dot and a very efficient secretary answered.

'Good morning. The Live Well Clinic, London. How may I help you?'

'Um,' Daisy hesitated despite having rehearsed her opening gambit all night. 'Well, you see, my husband.' She paused. 'Well, actually, he's dead now.'

'Oh, right,' the woman said. 'I am sorry to hear that.'

'Well, it was a long time coming…'

Silence.

'No, that makes it sound like I did him in.' Daisy laughed self-consciously. 'He died of natural causes, well, cancer and I'm not sure how natural that is…'

Silence.

'Are you still there?'

'Yes, I'm here? Can I help you in some way?'

'Yes, I just found a certificate from your clinic with legal signatures which says he, my dead husband, froze his sperm years ago and I'd like to use them.' She was rambling. 'I mean, not all of them. Well, you know as many as it takes for it to work.'

'Well, you're best placed to talk to our consultant who can talk through your individual case.' Daisy could hear her tapping on her computer. 'Can I get your last name and a reference number?'

'Ronaldson.' Then she reeled off a number in the corner of the certificate. 'Crikey, if that's in numerical order that's a lot of the little swimmers in your bank.'

The lady laughed. 'It isn't in order but we certainly are kept busy.'

After Daisy had agreed that she could make a now cancelled slot that afternoon, she put the phone down and hit her forehead. Why did she always feel the need to talk through silence and dig herself hole after hole?

Daisy messaged Tom and Lisa, despite them being at the bottom of the garden, and they both texted back with smiley faces and she heard shouting and whooping. Tom also sent an image of a fish with the words, 'they don't have a sperm emoji on my phone so this will have to do.'

After a frantic five-hour car journey that felt like a university road trip to London, she was sandwiched between Lisa and Tom in a sterile clinic with not a hint of 'baby' about the waiting room. She supposed they had to be sensitive to people's feelings. Bob held Lisa's hand, Barbara's head poked out of a duffel bag and Tom, thinking he was being subtle, kept brushing fingers with Alvin.

After ten minutes or so, a man in his sixties wearing a very sharp suit came out to greet her. 'Mrs Ronaldson?' He peered over his spectacles.

'Yes.' She stood, wiping her clammy hand on her skirt before she shook his firm grasp.

'Hi, I'm Dr Neilson. Do follow me.' The consultant moved towards a hall and turned back to ask Daisy something. 'And how…' His eyes surveyed her entourage. 'Sorry, I think it's best if I talk to Mrs Ronaldson alone, initially at least.'

Daisy turned and gave them the nod and the gang trooped back to the waiting room.

As she was invited to sit in the chair opposite the doctor, she apologised for her friends. 'I was nervous, you see. So I asked for their support.'

Dr Neilson laughed. 'Don't worry, I've had all sorts in this clinic. Had one family who arrived with the Jeremy Kyle television crew.' He smiled gently. 'I totally get the need for support. It's a hard decision and as I'm going to explain to you, I believe in total honesty, and there is no certainty the procedure will work.'

'No,' Daisy said quietly, nibbling her lower lip, 'but I had thought there was no chance of me having a child at all and now there is a small one.' She pushed down the lump in her throat. 'I'll take that chance.'

'And you've clearly got a good support network around you.' He put down his specs. 'Do you mind me asking if you're in a relationship?'

She felt a nervous giggle flutter up into her throat. 'Um, no.'

'And have you received grief counselling?'

'No.' She shook her head adamantly. 'Why would I want to talk about it with a stranger?'

'Because depending on how you've dealt with your husband's death, sometimes it's good to talk through the mixture of emotions that come with grief.' He smiled kindly. 'It's not a bad thing or a criticism.'

'No, I know.' She realised she was getting defensive. 'But I've dealt with it by talking to Hugh. That was my husband. I go to his study and I'm sure he can hear me.'

The doctor raised a brow.

'I'm not nuts,' she said resolutely. 'It's just that's how I cope. Believing he can see and hear what I do.'

Dr Neilson nodded.

'And James, that's Hugh's best friend, has been amazing, though he's moved back to London now.'

'And you're OK with that?'

'Well, I miss him but I'm fine really.' She looked at his desk. 'Yes, fine.'

'Well, as you are older, this of course reduces chances of success but it's by no means impossible.' He jotted something down in her notes. 'Now there is a lot of paperwork, and of course legally we have to verify various aspects but should this all run without a hitch, I am more than happy to act as your consultant.' He smiled. 'If you wish to go ahead?'

'Yes, yes please.' She couldn't stem the flow of tears.

He offered her a tissue. 'I know, it's such an emotional time and, in your case, even more so I imagine.'

'You're so kind,' she sniffed loudly. 'Can you stop being so kind, it makes me cry?'

He chuckled. 'Well, I'd be pretty rubbish at my job if I didn't care.'

She gratefully accepted another tissue.

'So I'm going to have to get quite personal in regards to your cycle and I need you to keep a diary because every month we actually only have twenty-four hours when we can inseminate vaginally.' He nodded. 'On the other hand, and I would suggest this as it's better for your age group, we could go down the IVF route.'

'Which means?'

'Your eggs are surgically removed, injected with semen in a laboratory and the embryo is reinstated back in your womb in the hope that it grows and develops.'

'It sounds…' She tried to find the word. 'Intrusive.'

'Yes, I have heard other women say this… I can tell you that we have performed this procedure countless times. You are in safe hands with us.'

Daisy nodded. 'I just know I couldn't not know… does that make sense?'

'Yes, of course.' The doctor put down his spectacles. 'I always say that I cannot answer the emotional side, only you can do that but we can provide you with first class care.'

'Yes, thank you.' She was sure of her decision. 'I know that I want to do this. I couldn't live with myself for not trying, and I've always wanted children.' Her eyes blurred with tears. 'Always.'

He nodded. 'Well, firstly we will put you on a drug to encourage your body to develop multiple eggs and then a synthetic hormone to prevent them from being released too early.'

'Crikey,' Daisy nodded, what she was about to undertake dawning on her.

'Then you'll have to visit us here every few days so that we can check your blood hormone levels and use ultrasound to monitor your ovaries.'

She pulled a face.

He looked at her. 'I know it sounds very clinical but it's my job to give you a full idea of what you can expect. You have to remember why you want to undertake the procedure.'

'Yes,' she said resolutely.

After he had explained about the trigger shot, the gathering of the eggs and fertilisation, she felt exhausted but despite the information overload her confidence in her decision hadn't wavered.

In fact, as the crew drove back to Gloucestershire in two cars, she excitedly told her passengers of Tom and Alvin about what the consultant had told her.

Tom blew a low wolf whistle. 'Makes you feel sorry for cattle now, doesn't it?'

'Huh?' Daisy looked at him in the rear-view mirror; she had already spotted him holding Alvin's hand. 'Cattle?'

'Yeah, darling, you know,' Tom chuckled. 'Intensive farming and all that when they inseminate the cows.'

Daisy smiled. She thought about her mother and father who had always refused to go down that route, believing instead in nature taking its course. If she was now being compared to a heifer, she was grateful for science and the chance to have a child but, yes, maybe he had a point – if it was a regular occurrence and you were stuck in a field with a load of other heifers.

'Just wait until I tell my mother,' she said as she pulled off the motorway. 'That is going to go down like a lump of lead. Not only did she believe Hugh came from a different class to me, she would never ever think having a child without him around would be a good idea.'

'Well, when you compare it to farming, she might be alright about it,' Alvin offered unhelpfully.

'You clearly haven't met my mother.'

They drove the remainder of the journey in silence, Daisy musing over what the future might hold and Tom whispering in Alvin's ear and making him giggle like a little schoolboy. Daisy could not remember seeing Tom this smitten with anyone since that older gentleman at university. If she remembered rightly his name had been Alfred and he had adored Tom, treated Tom like a king. He was a fine-looking man, with impeccable dress sense and they shared a love of leopard print and interior design. They were a match made in heaven despite the twenty-five-year age gap. But, then, one day, Tom was in town with Alfred when a woman appeared out of nowhere demanding to know why they were holding hands. Alfred introduced Tom to his wife and that was the last Tom ever saw of Alfred. It took him a good few months to get over that relationship, and she had always believed that he had never fully given his heart away again. Plenty of flings, but nothing serious. She caught sight of them again in the rear-view mirror. Perhaps until now.

She drove through the gates of the house and lo and behold, as if her mother had some incredible psychic power, she was sat in the front garden. Daisy tried to judge her mood as she got out of the car. It was impossible as her mother always scowled, even when she was happy, it was the natural lie of her features. Today, tomake matters worse, she was wearing sunglasses. It was like playing Russian roulette, only with a quick-tongued mother instead of a gun. Actually, as she approached, she was thinking a gun might be the easier option.

'Hello, Mum,' she said with forced cheeriness.

Her troops, including Lisa, Bob and Barbara who drove up and parked behind Daisy's car, all filed into the house giving her mother the odd hello and wave.

'Where have you all been? On some jolly on a Monday? Don't you know Mondays are for working?'

'Yes, but we haven't got anybody staying tonight,' she said smoothly, 'other than those on a permanent board basis like Bob and possibly Alvin.'

'Who's Alvin?'

'Tom's new man.' Daisy tried to catch a glimpse of her mother's eyes behind her reflective sunglasses.

'Well, it's not natural.'

'What?'

'Being gay.'

Daisy rolled her eyes and sighed deeply. 'I'm not going through this again. It's as natural as being a heterosexual.'

'Daisy,' her mother warned.

'No, I'm sick of hearing your incredibly ignorant views on my friends, Mother.' Irritation swelled insider her. 'Or my now dead husband. Dad was never this closed-minded, so what happened to you?'

Her mother's mouth twitched and she knew she had hurt her. She hadn't meant to get so personal but she was fed up of being pushed.

Then, unbelievably, Daisy saw a tear roll down her mother's cheek, under her sunglasses and towards her now non-scowling, but trembling, lips.

'Oh, Mum.' Daisy winced with guilt. 'I am sorry.' She went to hug her mother, who ordinarily stiffened like a plywood board, but much to her amazement crumpled against Daisy's frame. Daisy clung to her tightly and stroked her hair, disbelieving that this was the same woman who moments ago had looked as stony as the small Cupid fountain off to her left.

'Mum, has something happened?' Daisy looked at her, and then gently pushed her mother's sunglasses up onto her head, revealing red-rimmed, puffy eyes.

'The farm, I have to sell the farm.' Her mother broke down in floods of tears and Daisy stood back, shocked.

'What do you mean you have to sell the farm?'

'We've been doing badly for years.' She sighed. 'Well, it's been doing badly since your father died, really. I just never wanted to admit to myself or anyone.'

'Oh God, Mum.' She shook her head. 'Why didn't you tell me and Hugh, we could have helped you out?'

'Because I've got pride, Daisy.'

'And you know what they say, pride comes before a fall.' Daisy heard herself and realised the mother-daughter roles had reversed.

'Well, I've had it valued and actually as the farm is running at a loss, it is easier to declare bankruptcy.'

'Oh, Mum, I'm sure there must be a way.'

Her mother sighed. 'In a way, I guess I'm relieved because I'm tired.'

Daisy understood this. Working the farm was a job that demanded attention every hour of every day. This was why she had had no social life until she went to university – because she spent all waking minutes helping her parents on the farm.

'What's that?' Her eagle-eyed mother had caught sight of the Live Well Clinic folder in her hands. 'Is that where you've been?' She looked up quickly. 'You're not ill, are you? You're as stubborn as me then when it comes to big secrets.'

'No,' she assured her mother. 'I am not ill. Quite the opposite, in fact.' She took her mother around the shoulders and said, 'Let's go inside for a cup of tea and I'll explain.'

Five minutes later, with two steaming cups of tea in front of her, Daisy announced, 'I'm having Hugh's baby. Or, at least, that's the plan.'

Her mother howled with something resembling hysteria and disbelief. Then she stilled. 'Daisy, I know you've not taken it very well but he's gone.' Her mother pursed her lips. 'He's not coming back.'

Daisy realised she hadn't broached the subject in the best manner possible. She showed her mother the certificate and Hugh's letter.

'You can't seriously be thinking about doing this.' She took an indignant slurp of her tea.

'Yes, why not?'

'Because then you'll be a single mother to a dead man's child.'

Daisy's eyes widened. 'Sheesh, don't hold back, Mum. Would hate for you to not get your message across.' She stood. 'Why do you do this? I'm in my forties, for God's sake, you can't dictate to me for the rest of your life.'

'So you trooped across to London with your groupies and signed up to have a dead man's baby.'

'Shit, Mum.' Daisy sobbed. 'Just go away. I felt for you when you told me the farm has gone bankrupt, but you've done it again; you've managed to make me feel worthless. You know, I think it's best you just go home.'

Her mother didn't move, her hands gripping her mug until her knuckles whitened. 'I always wanted a grandchild.'

Daisy looked at her. 'What did you just say?'

Her mother put down her mug. 'I said that I always wanted a grandchild. I was suspicious when Hugh refused to get himself checked out.'

'Really?' Daisy sat again. 'I never even thought about it, I just became so involved in the marriage and the house, I guess I didn't allow myself to think about anything like that.'

'I've always thought you'd be a good mother,' she said quietly.

'You have? Mum, don't want to alarm you but you may have just paid me a compliment.'

Her mother smiled softly. 'Imagine that, Daisy, maybe I'm not such a horrid old woman after all.' She cleared her throat. 'I know I haven't always been openly supportive of you…'

'That's one way of putting it.'

'I think when Dad died, I just withdrew into myself. It's only since the farm has been declared bankrupt that I've realised how tired I am of pretending that I'm coping.' She wiped a tear from her cheek and swallowed hard. 'I never got over Dad's death. When Hugh died, it brought back all the same emotions again, and I know I said things to you that I shouldn't have said about your marriage, but I couldn't stand to see you hurting the way you did.' She sipped her tea. 'I knew that feeling of grief all too well.'

'So why didn't you say something or hug me or anything….'

'Because I was trying to keep a lid on it all.'

Daisy took her mother's free hand and massaged it between her own. 'Well, I want to try and have a child. In a way, I think I am allowing Hugh to live on.'

'You can't think like that.' Her mother shook her head. 'Because if the IVF doesn't work you may take it even more badly.'

'Yes, true but above all I'm doing it because I want to be a mother. This might be my only chance.'

Her mother sniffed. 'Then, you must do it. You have my support.'

'Mum, come and stay here with us, you can't be alone at a time like this.'

'Oh, I don't know if you want an old lady hanging around all you young folk…'

Daisy laughed. 'We've got a combined age of a million and

we'd love you to help with the day-to-day accounting. You're good with figures.'

'Clearly not that good, I let the farm go bust.' She pulled a face.

'That's not down to your accounting, that's down to farming being one of the most competitive and hardest industries.'

'Anyway,' her mother said, 'don't you have that James fella looking after your books?'

She thought of James's face as she had left his London apartment on Saturday night. 'No, I think he's found himself someone else.'

'Someone else?' Her mother arched a brow.

'Hmm?' Daisy had lost herself in a world of reverie.

'You just said "someone else".'

'No, I didn't.' Daisy grew defensive.

'Yes, you did.' Her mother was not one to miss a trick.

'Oh, well, I meant to say something else.'

'Daisy Ronaldson, I think you're not being entirely honest with me.' She put down her tea and took her daughter's hands in her own. 'Come on, tell me about this James fella… tell me what he's gone and done.'

For the first time in forty years, Daisy cried on her mother's shoulder and told her everything.

Chapter 19

Tom insisted on moving Daisy's mother, with the help of the Dream Team, into the guesthouse. Daisy didn't want to warn him off because he would take it the wrong way but waited back at the house for news of the next civil war.

Nursing a cup of chamomile tea (part of her new cleansing diet readying her body for motherhood), she tried to forget that she was drinking herbs and no caffeine. She stood ready by the door and phone to help ease relations should it be necessary. Only two hours later, she watched Tom's car chug up the drive followed by the Dream Team's van.

Daisy held her breath as Tom climbed out and then nearly choked on her herbal concoction when he rounded the car to open the door for her mother, who got out laughing and looking freer than she had in years.

'Well, this world is not short of miracles,' she muttered to herself, before she put her mug down and went to see if she could help with any unloading.

'Oh, Daisy, Tom has had me in stitches.' Her mother grinned. 'Honestly, I was dreading the move as you know but he has made me feel so much better about it all.'

Daisy turned her back on her mother and mouthed to Tom 'thank you' who looked tickled pink at the compliment.

The Dream Team, once again half-dressed and not an ounce of fat between them, started to unload the van of boxes, and the odd familiar Seventies-style lamp she had grown up with. It had been agreed that her mother would stay in the annex at the bottom of the garden because the number of spare rooms in the guesthouse was ironically dwindling due to the more permanent arrivals. Plus, her mother would appreciate the space having lived on her own for years.

'Honestly, this is so lovely of you, Daisy,' her mother started, her eyes glassing over with tears. 'I really mean that.'

Daisy's heart swelled. 'Mum.' She hugged her close.

Daisy led her to the annex where she had made the bed up in crisp white linen and filled vases with her mother's favourite flowers: peonies. She had even lit a cinnamon smelling candle.

'Oh my,' her mother said. 'I'm not sure I can sleep in here… it's too clean, too white.'

'Oh.' Daisy's face fell. 'I thought…'

'No, I mean it's amazing, I'm not sure I deserve such luxury.'

Daisy looked at it and didn't see luxury, just a nice atmosphere and surely every woman deserved that? She realised now that her mother had really scrimped and saved living in the farmhouse and probably, when she had married Hugh, it had only served to emphasise how tough her own lifestyle was.

'Mum, you deserve this and more, and you deserve to be happy and not worry.'

'I'm seventy-five,' she said. 'I thought I'd spend the rest of my life talking to cattle and eating soup for one.'

Tom bounced in with a fraying Ottoman covered in a rust-coloured velour – oh, the memories came flooding back – and placed it next to other boxes. Daisy remembered she had pretended that Ottoman had been her horse and carriage to take her to the ball or she had imagined that she owned a medal-winning horse… She smiled broadly at her mother. 'I am so glad you're here. This feels so right.'

That night, Tom cooked all the guests, who were now friends and family, a huge pan of paella with large, fresh prawns and a beautiful velvety Tiramisu for after.

'Tom,' her mother said, her face glowing with happiness and wine, 'you are full of surprises. What a fine chef you are!'

Tom grinned. 'Thank you.' Alvin squeezed his hand.

The only thing missing for Daisy was a glass of wine but she sipped her water, telling herself it was all in the name of motherhood.

Over supper, they devised a plan and timetable for Daisy's IVF as she would have to go to London every three to four days to check all was developing as it should. They were all determined to help and although Daisy sort of wished she could go through the process in private, she did appreciate her friends and family rallying around.

'I mean I suppose it would be easier to stay in London, Daisy,' said her mother. 'Can you think of anyone you could stay with?'

'Well, I mean I would have stayed at James's, but he's got Annabelle staying there and…' She paused. 'It's all too awkward now.'

'You could just text him and find out.'

'No,' said Daisy firmly. 'I will not look desperate.'

'OK,' Tom agreed. 'You don't have to, I will. I'm very good at looking desperate.' Before Daisy could argue, he already had his phone out and read his message aloud as he typed. 'Hey Sexy…'

Daisy rolled her eyes.

'How's life? How's your divine body?' he continued and Daisy felt her mother shift uncomfortably next to her. He looked up and on seeing Jenny's disapproving face, blushed. 'Sorry… but he is a beauty.'

'Have you got a spare room by any chance?' He held his phone up and dramatically pressed SEND. 'There, he'll think he's in with a chance with me…' Tom winked as Daisy winced.

Seconds later, Tom's phone beeped.

'See, I told you he wants me badly.' He grinned at his audience. 'I've already explained to Alvin that James is as straight as a ruler.' Then opening the message, he read aloud: '"Hey Tom, nice to hear from you."' Tom winked. 'You see, he loves me…' Tom kept reading. 'Of course, come and stay. No, Annabelle and I have gone away for a bit so flat is all yours. Daisy has a key. Any news?'

Tom's fingers flew over his phone. 'I'll say, no news except Daisy trying to get a bun in the oven.'

'Tom!' Daisy shrieked in horror, grabbing the phone. 'Don't you dare…'

Then she saw he had only been pretending to write.

Tom laughed. 'I wouldn't do that. I'll just say that Daisy and I fancied some time in London.' He smiled at Alvin. 'Which I would.'

Alvin lived in Bethnal Green.

He took the phone back and sent the message, Daisy checking he was true to his word.

'Gone on holiday with Annabelle, huh.' She smiled, tried to pretend her guts weren't churning at the very thought. 'Well, there you go, sounds as if that'll be the next wedding…'

Silence fell over the table as they searched for some comforting words. Finally Lisa spoke, 'Well, you can do so much better than him, anyway. I mean what does it say about a man who gets involved with one of our guests?'

Bob just looked at her and realising what she said, she flushed. 'Oh, you know what I mean…'

They burst into uncontrollable laughter and spent the remainder of the evening debating whether they could set up a guesthouse that specialised in matchmaking.

Chapter 20

Daisy and Tom spent the next three weeks in James's apartment and managed to make themselves very much at home. Daisy visited the clinic every three days to have her hormone levels checked and have ultrasound scans of her ovaries taken. She spent her days reading books on parenting and generally scaring herself senseless whilst supping chamomile and trying to perform some sort of mindfulness yoga. According to the glowing, skinny woman with a small bump, it was bending herself in various directions and drinking herbal tea that meant she got pregnant. Daisy thought she made it sound like Immaculate Conception but she was willing to try anything (except give up chocolate). She wondered how on earth a small human being could bring such chaos to one person's life but she knew she wanted that chaos. She did however have a near heart attack when she tried to figure out car seats and child safety locks.

Her mother, probably wisely, suggested she didn't do the research and spend every waking hour in Mothercare but Daisy couldn't help it. She was now addicted to the notion of motherhood.

Today was the day the clinic was due to plant the embryos; she was simultaneously excited and sick with nerves. She had been awake since 3 a.m. praying that they would take and she could start a new chapter in her life. She felt as if Hugh would become a part of her life again.

She rose early, looking around James's room; her safe haven for the last few weeks. His love of art was apparent; every inch of wall space was taken up with black and white photography, modern acrylics and even some practice sketches by artists. The furniture had clean, modern lines and Daisy adored lying in bed in the morning, a gentle shaft of light from the sun filtering through the slats in the shutter. This morning, she lay back and smiled happily. She knew, of course, that her age wasn't on her side, that the whole process could fail and she didn't know how many times she could put herself through the emotional roller-coaster of IVF but, at least, there was a glimmer of hope when once she had entirely given up on the thought of children.

She caught sight of her alarm clock. It was 6.30 a.m. She rose and made herself a pot of decaffeinated tea. Daisy didn't know if it was just her imagination but did the tea taste like fish? She Googled it on her favourite expecting mothers' site, Mothers' World, and discovered, no, it wasn't just her, Susienumber3ontheway and NauseousZoe agreed with her. A thread on IVF caught her eye in which SingleAgainTara wanted to know if it was right to bring a child into the world knowing there was no father figure around. She had put that humdinger of a question out there at 3.30 a.m.; no doubt, she was suffering the same insomnia and worries as Daisy. NauseousZoe, who appeared to comment on every thread all day and all night, suggested it was immoral. Daisy immediately took a dislike to NauseousZoe (even if they did agree about the tea) but then MotherEarth72 said that it was fine because every child was a blessing and who needed men anyway? Daisy nodded as she slurped her cod-tasting brew.

'Quite right,' she muttered aloud.

She was in the middle of reading women's thoughts on the

length of men's parts correlating with the size of the baby at birth when Tom walked into the kitchen in his cropped denim shorts and a tight white vest.

'Good thing you've got a good body,' Daisy said. 'Otherwise that would be enough to send my fish tea up the wrong way.'

Tom grinned and pushed his bottom out. 'Just like Kylie.'

'Only the hairy version,' Daisy mused.

'You ready for today?' He sat and nursed a glass of water.

'As ready as I'll ever be.'

He nodded. 'Well, look, you've got this far… you're doing well.'

At the sound of a key in the door, Daisy nearly dropped her mug, and slammed the top of her computer down on the raging debate about men's genitalia.

'Who's that?' She suddenly felt like an intruder in the house, and sat bolt upright. She knew she looked a mess so if James appeared she would probably die of mortification before she had even had the chance to have eggs implanted.

Tom, the worst guard dog on planet Earth, stood behind Daisy. 'I don't know, doll, but if it's James I haven't done my ablutions yet.'

'That makes two of us,' Daisy said drily and together they waited instead of searching out their visitor.

Moments later, Annabelle appeared in the kitchen doorway, her cheek a marbled effect of purples and reds.

'Good God.' Daisy stood straight away and rushed to Annabelle's side. She was pale and trembling.

'Who did this to you?' Daisy demanded to know. 'Did James…'

Annabelle sniffled and allowed herself to be ushered to a kitchen chair by Tom. 'No, not James. Why would it have been James?'

'Well, you've been on holiday with him for the last three weeks or so, haven't you?' Daisy furrowed her brows. 'Haven't you?'

'No.' Annabelle accepted a tissue from Tom. 'I never went away with James. He has gone out to his place in the south of France and he left me here.' She shook her head, a tear trickling over her lip line. 'I thought I would go back to my husband, try and make things work, but from the moment I got back it went wrong.'

'Oh, Annabelle,' Daisy breathed, sitting next to her with Tom on the other side. 'Tell us.'

'Well, I walked back in on him and Petra, our nanny, halfway up the stairs. She was…' Annabelle couldn't find the words and Daisy shushed her.

'You don't need to explain to us, we understand.'

Annabelle choked back another sob. 'I mean what was more galling is I always thought he didn't like women with curves and she is a proper woman. You know what I mean?'

'Yes,' Daisy said. 'I know very well.'

'Yes, exactly, like you… the sort my mother called good child-bearing… oh shit, sorry.'

Daisy's sympathy began to wane but the more she looked at the welt on her cheek, the more she knew that even Annabelle deserved to be treated better than this.

'Go on…' Daisy encouraged, pushing away the images of her as an oversized St Bernard sat next to Annabelle, the Chihuahua.

'Well, he actually fired Petra and I thought he might respect me but how wrong I was…' She took a deep breath. 'He doesn't respect me at all, he then met up with her in hotels and has even asked her to marry him.'

'What?' shrieked Tom. 'That's poly whatsit!'

'Polygamy.' Annabelle nodded. 'Yes. Anyway, I just went to the hotel where I found out he was staying for a—' she did quote marks in the air '—business trip. Well, even the staff at the desk tried to stop me. He probably paid them to stop me if I turned up but I was determined.' She snorted bitterly. 'It was easy actually to get past them, I just pretended to be room service.'

'What did you see?'

Annabelle shuddered. 'I saw him, Petra and another of our

old nannies laying on the bed smoking some sort of joints, completely out of their brains.' She shook her head. 'In fact, my husband was so out of his brains, it took him a good minute to realise I was stood over him. When he did, he panicked and pushed me out of the way to get to the bathroom to hide. I tumbled into the table and…' She indicated her face. 'And here's the result.'

'And this all just happened?' Daisy asked.

Annabelle nodded. 'Just now.' She took a long laboured breath. 'I was so shaken I didn't know where to go and I knew I had a key to James's apartment so it seemed the obvious place to sort my head out a bit...' She paused. 'But I didn't expect to find either of you here. I was kind of hoping James would be here.'

Daisy narrowed her eyes. 'Why isn't James here with you? Or why aren't you there with James?' She frowned. 'Last time I saw you, you seemed very much in love.'

Annabelle's lower lip trembled. 'What? When you came here and I was sat out there…' She pointed to the hall.

'Yes,' Daisy nodded. 'Wearing a towel. I think James had popped out for a takeaway or something.'

'Oh yes,' Annabelle blushed ever so slightly. 'I remember now. I might have had a glass of wine before I spoke to you…'

'A glass?' Daisy looked at her.

'OK, maybe more than one.' She held her hands up. 'Fine, I was plastered, is that what you want to hear?'

'No, Annabelle…'

'I was plastered, and after you left, he gave me a hard time about much I had drunk.'

'He gave you a hard time?' Not the post-sex cosy takeaway she had initially thought.

'Yes. And now he's at some tourism conference in France to try and get people to go to your little guesthouse.' Annabelle tried not to pull a face but Daisy caught her look of bitterness.

'What do you mean?' Daisy was confused. 'I thought he was

on holiday. Well, actually, I thought he was on holiday with you.'

Annabelle pouted. 'He's been at this bloody conference in France touting your bloody guesthouse. When he quite clearly could have been spending time with me and helping me through my difficult time.'

Daisy felt a lump in her throat and tried to push down the sudden tide of emotion. He had been away helping sell the guesthouse abroad. She couldn't believe it.

'But why didn't he tell me? Tell us?' Daisy pulled her dressing gown cord tighter around her waist. 'I don't understand.'

'He thinks you're dating Alistair, that the guesthouse was the last thing on your mind.'

Daisy remembered that she had in fact told Annabelle she was dating him.

'I'm not actually with Alistair, after all.'

Tom grinned. 'No, that man is long gone.'

'Oh,' Annabelle said, clearly befuddled.

'So you're not staying in London to be near Alistair when he does business down here?' She pushed her hand through her perfectly highlighted hair. Daisy mimicked her gesture and put her hand through her slightly greasy, with the odd grey coming through, bob.

'No.' Daisy shook her head.

'Then why are you here?'

'Because Daisy is going to have a baby,' Tom announced proudly. 'And she's asked me to be godfather.'

'Well—' Daisy shot Tom a hard look '—not quite.'

'A baby?' A smile toyed at the edges of Annabelle's mouth. 'Not being funny, darling, but don't you need a man for that?' She gasped. 'Unless Tom? Are you?'

'What? Going to have sex with Daisy?' He smiled broadly. 'Bloody hell, no. That's like doing it with your sister.'

'Then how?' Annabelle arched a brow. 'Are you in London scouting out a man?'

'She's having her eggs planted today.'

'Tom,' Daisy warned.

'Oh sorry!' Tom looked momentarily abashed; but only momentarily, he was actually loving the sensationalism.

'IVF!' Annabelle screeched. 'Wow. And the father? A random sperm donor?'

'No.' Tom dropped his voice to a conspiratorial whisper. 'Hugh. That's Daisy's dead husband.'

Daisy rolled her eyes. Tom: Mr Say It As It Is.

'Well, how come?' Annabelle face twisted with even more confusion. 'I mean, if he's dead…'

'He froze his sperm.' Tom left his mouth aghast to add to the effect, his eyes wide, checking he was creating the right amount of atmosphere.

'Um, I am right here,' Daisy reminded them both. 'Maybe just talk to me.'

Annabelle ignored Daisy and said, 'So Daisy will be a single mother?'

'Yes.' Tom nodded defiantly. 'Single.' He flipped his hand and said, 'There you go, better than an Eastenders boom-boom-titty-titty, don't you think?'

'Um guys, still in the room,' Daisy pointed out. She looked at the kitchen clock. 'Right, speaking of, I need to go and get ready.'

'When do you head home?' Annabelle asked.

'Tomorrow. It's just a waiting game after that.'

'Right, well James is due back in a couple of days.' Annabelle smirked. 'Shame you'll just miss each other.'

'Yes.' Daisy turned to head to the bedroom pushing down the need to rearrange the smirk on her face. 'I'm sure James will help you with your problems.'

Daisy looked back at Annabelle whose lips were trembling. 'No, he won't. He's bloody in love with you, isn't he?' She slumped in her chair, her chin dipped towards her chest. 'I actually knew you were no longer with Alistair. I saw it on Facebook and thought about telling James but I knew if he found that out he would go running back to the guesthouse.'

'What?' Daisy couldn't believe what she was hearing.

'He wanted to convince you to not be with Alistair.' She looked at Daisy and, for the first time, Daisy saw genuine sorrow. 'I tried to kiss him after you left that night a few weeks ago but he told me to leave, to go and sort out my marriage.' She lowered her eyes. 'The next morning, I did just that, like I told you.' She pointed to the bruising on her cheek. 'It didn't end well.'

'Why are you telling me this now?' Daisy wished she was having this conversation dressed and with make-up on. Instead she suddenly felt very naked, very vulnerable.

Annabelle let more tears flow down her cheeks. 'Because I have come to terms with the fact that I was using James as a way out of my marriage but…' She swallowed noticeably. Bbut he loves you.' She gave a small smile. 'He loves you so much. He never stops talking about you and the night you were here, when we thought you were dating Alistair, he sat in the sitting room drinking and crying.' She blew air through her mouth in a long, drawn out sigh. 'Honest to God, he was beside himself.'

Daisy's legs had gone weak. She leant against the kitchen door to steady herself. 'Hugh kept telling me in his letters and cards but I didn't believe him once I saw you here, in his apartment. I thought Hugh must've been mistaken.'

'Do you love him?' Annabelle asked quietly.

Tom had sat down, watching their conversation like a Shakespearean play.

Daisy's eyes welled up. 'I know that when your husband dies, people expect you to grieve for the longest time and to not love again. Or, at least, that's what I thought people wanted. Then I realised I had to do what I needed to do, that if my heart was falling for another man, maybe I couldn't control it. Maybe it was meant to be.

Then in his dying days, Hugh and James had talked. Hugh

had realised these deep emotions that ran between her and James and he could have ignored it. He could have died with that knowledge.

You know Hugh, in his letters and cards, made me realise how much I love James but I was not willing to admit my feelings. My own husband wanted me to love again.'

Annabelle rose from the chair and very tenderly took Daisy in her arms. 'You deserve to be happy, Daisy. I am a cow.' She snorted with a self-conscious laugh. 'I tried to get in the way of your happiness because I was unhappy in my own marriage.'

Daisy stroked her back. 'Well, we are all human. I have said some pretty awful things to you, too.'

Tom perked up. 'God, yeah, the Chihuahua conversation…'

'Thank you, Tom, for reminding us,' Daisy said drily. Then a thought occurred to her and she pulled away from Annabelle. 'What if James wouldn't love me if I was pregnant?'

'With Hugh's child.' Annabelle pulled a face.

'Exactly.'

'My advice,' said Tom, serious for the first time, 'would be not to let a man get in the way of what you want.'

'But it would be Hugh's, that could be strange for him.'

'Honey, that's what any man you meet will have to face but at the end of the day, it'll be your child and if they love you then they will love him or her.' Tom waved his hands in front of his eyes. 'God, making myself cry now.' He got up and took Daisy's hand. 'Come on, you never let a man stand in the way of anything. If he loves you, he accepts all of you.' He looked at Annabelle. 'Something I should have learnt a long time ago, sweeties.'

Two hours later, she was back in the clinic. Tom and Daisy felt so at home there now, they were on first-name terms with all the staff and even knew how the receptionist liked her coffee.

Dr Neilson came out to greet her, smiling broadly. He led her to his office, Tom by her side. 'Good news, I think we have two successful pre-embryos and I think, as advised before, it would be best to plant both of them because of your age and the risks.'

Daisy's hands had grown sweaty, she felt a bit faint. After three weeks of switching off to the monotony of constant check-ups, the time had come and she was nervous.

'Are you OK?' Dr Neilson asked as his eyes filled with concern.

'Yes,' Daisy assured him. 'Just realised how real it is.' She laughed softly. 'I know that must sound so silly.'

'Not at all.' He shook his head. 'It sounds very normal.'

Three hours later, they were heading back to James's apartment, and despite not having had any anaesthesia Daisy felt sleepy. She kept her hand on her tummy as if to protect what might be happening inside her.

Tom fussed and cared for her, not allowing her to lift a finger.

'What would you like to eat? Drink?' He bowed. 'Your wish is my command.'

She laughed. 'Oh, kind sir, I would give my right arm for fish and chips.'

'Fish and chips.' He nodded solemnly. 'A fine choice. I shall run to the chip shop straight away!'

Daisy laughed as he gathered his man-bag and coat. 'Thank you, fine sir.'

She lay back on the sofa, resting her eyes and heard the door open and shut. Moments later, she heard a key in the lock again.

'Did you forget something, Jeeves?' she said, her eyes still closed. When he didn't answer, she looked up, confused. She could have sworn she'd heard the door again. Then, suddenly, there he was. James. He stood in the doorway and smiled tentatively at her.

'I didn't know if you'd still be here.'

'Yes, sorry.' She sat upright, feeling oddly nervous. 'We've been here for the last three weeks. We'll obviously give you money for electricity, water and, oh, we have broken a couple of plates and glasses…' She pulled a face. 'Sorry.'

'Stop saying sorry,' James said softly. 'It's just nice to see you.' He cleared his throat. 'Have you managed to spend time with Alistair? And have some fun?'

She kneaded her skirt and dropped her gaze. 'I'm not dating Alistair.'

'What?' His face reflected confusion then pain before lighting up. 'You're not?'

'No, I never really was,' Daisy admitted. 'Well, I was but it was all a bit desperate really. As you might have said.' She thought of the evening with Alistair's friends in the pub. 'In fact, it was incredibly surreal.'

'Wow.' He pushed his hand through his hair, 'I've been…' He searched for the word. 'I've been so miserable, Daisy.'

She stood now, her heart racing. There was a huge part of her willing herself to run to him, for him to hold her. But she stayed where she was.

'Why did you tell everyone you were with him?'

'I was, for a few hours…' She gazed intently at him. 'When I came here, that night…'

'To collect my post?' He laughed.

'Yes.' She smiled. 'To collect your post, I came to tell you I wasn't and then I saw Annabelle and she made out that you two…'

He jerked his head back. 'That us two… what?'

'That you were, you know, together.'

He laughed sharply. 'Together? I have spent hours, days now, telling her to leave me alone and to sort out her own marriage.'

'Wow.' Daisy shook her head gently. 'I found the key, you know.'

He gave a small gasp. 'What, to the box in Hugh's office?'

'Yes.' She nodded. 'I found his last letter and I found the certificate from the clinic.'

'Oh, OK.' He nodded, trying to take that in.

'Were you going to show me those last two?'

He remained silent. 'Honest answer?'

She nodded, her stomach turning.

'Honest answer is when I heard you were with Alistair, I decided not to but then, later, when in France, I thought I should at least show you the letter.'

She moved a step closer to him. 'But you couldn't have shown me one without the other.'

He nodded, his tongue moving nervously around his teeth. 'I know, so you're right, in the end, I wasn't going to show you either.'

Daisy turned from him, a sob escaped her lips and her shoulders rose and fell as further sobs racked her body. 'You too?' She laughed bitterly. 'You, as well as Hugh, keep trying to dictate life. Life doesn't work like that, not if you love someone. If you love someone, you let them choose their own journey, you don't tell them which direction to take.' She moved herself so she faced him once again. 'Even if you think their choices might be wrong, people are put on this earth to make their own mistakes. But, then again, maybe nothing is a mistake.' She voluntarily moved her hand over her tummy, aware now of what was potentially happening inside of her.

'It's just that I love you, Daisy.'

She looked up. It was the first time he had used those three words. Her heart lifted but then she wondered if she wanted a man who, like Hugh, would perhaps obstruct her path to being a mother? She didn't know who she could trust anymore.

Tom's keys jiggled in the lock and he burst in.

'Madame, your fish and chips.' He walked into the sitting room, a white plastic bag with greasy paper goods steaming inside. On seeing James, he smiled. 'Oh hello, big boy.'

James smiled tersely at him. 'Hi, Tom.'

'Am I interrupting something?' Tom looked from one to the other and shuffled backward. 'You know what, I'm going to pop these in the oven to keep them warm. Let me know if you need anything.'

Daisy smiled gratefully at him. 'Thanks, Tom.'

James nodded as Tom pulled the door behind him.

'Daisy, I would never stop you having children, I guess I just always hoped you'd have them with me.'

She sniffled, wiped her running nose with back of her cardigan sleeve.

'I can't hear any more of this,' she said. She put her hands on either side of her face, closed her eyes momentarily, wishing to be somewhere else. 'It may be too late, anyway.'

'What on earth do you mean?' James looked at her intently and then realising what she was saying, his eyes widened. 'You mean…? Is that why you've been staying in London? You went to the clinic?'

A single tear ran down her cheek and she nodded. 'Yes, I had the embryos implanted today.'

James sat down hard on the Ottoman, put his head in his hands. 'So you may be pregnant with Hugh's child?'

'Yes,' she said simply.

He nodded, his face paler. 'OK, wow, OK.'

'You know I don't have to justify that to you. Hugh was my husband up until recently and I never divorced him, he died, James. He *died*. I had no choice in that matter and then I'm given the opportunity to not only have children but have the child of the man I married.' She clenched her jaw. 'Can you blame me?'

James shook his head. 'It's just that I love you, Daisy.' He stood, grabbed her hands and held them tight. 'I love you so much, it hurts me. Do you know that feeling?'

'Yes,' she nodded, more tears spilling over. 'I do because when I saw you flirting and spending time with Annabelle, something happened. I realised that I felt such deep feelings for you and I didn't know what to do.'

'And then Alistair…' James's words tailed off. 'Oh my goodness, what a mess.'

'Well, is it? I mean why is it such a mess?'

He kissed the tops of her hands. 'Because, just because.'

She withdrew her hands from his grip. 'You mean, because I now may be carrying part of Hugh again you can't love me? You couldn't love his child?'

James just looked at her and in the silence that sat between them, she had found her answer. James had wanted her as she was, as she had been, when she needed him in her grief.

'I think we should drive back tonight. We'll get out of your way.'

'No, Daisy, you don't need to do that.' He sighed deeply. 'I'm sorry, I'm just not thinking straight.'

'No, it's fine, I think you've made your feelings quite clear.' She moved towards the door to tell Tom they were leaving. 'I just want to wait now and see the results and I am hoping and praying I am pregnant, James. This child, if he or she happens, is a part of me.'

James went to say something but stopped himself and Daisy walked quickly to the kitchen to fetch Tom. Less than half an hour later, she was sat in the car, Tom rattling on trying to diffuse the mood, but her mind had wandered to a life when Hugh might have been alive and seen his son or daughter.

Chapter 21

Daisy knew she had to wait two weeks before she could even begin to think about taking a pregnancy test so she filled her days with helping the Dream Team do the rooms and breakfast, and tending to the garden. She felt extraordinarily calm and she wanted to keep stress to a minimum whilst she hoped her body produced a miracle. It didn't however remove the crazy sense of loneliness she felt. Her mind drifted constantly back to James and how happy he'd looked when he found out she wasn't getting married. Every time Daisy thought about the way he'd said, 'I love you' with such tenderness, she thought she might cry. She checked her phone constantly but no messages, nothing. Occasionally she went to write a message to him but she was lost for words, she didn't know what she wanted to say.

On the morning of the fourteenth day after her trip to London, she sat on the loo seat staring at a pack of highly sensitive ClearBlue and wondering if her life was about to change. She also knew that it might not have worked and that thought broke her heart. She reached for the box, put it back, thought about it again. Her hands were trembling and she was just about to unwrap the packet when there was a knock on her bedroom door.

She put the box down once again and walked back into the bedroom.

'Yep?' she called out.

Tom stuck his head around the door. 'Um, Daisy, he's downstairs, wants to see you.'

Her heart started to beat faster. 'Who?'

'Who do you think?' He smiled kindly. 'Mr Lover Boy.'

'James?'

'That'd be the one, unless you've got others hidden away.' He realised what he was saying and snorted. 'Actually, you might well have another Alistair somewhere for all we know!'

'Ha ha, very funny.' She looked in the wardrobe mirror and pulled a face. 'God, I look so tired and horrid.'

'No, you don't, silly. You look beautiful.'

'Can you tell him to come up here? But give me a couple of minutes?'

Tom nodded and left, as Daisy ran back to the bathroom to apply blusher, lip gloss and a squirt of her favourite perfume. Whoever said women should go au naturel clearly hadn't realised the power of make-up and scent. Moments later came another knock on the door. She gave herself one last look in the bathroom mirror; Daisy thought she looked like the same tired woman but now with overdone plum-stained cheeks.

'Just give up,' she said to herself trying to blend the colour into her cheeks. 'You look like a sad clown, face it.'

She opened her bedroom door and there he stood. His eyes lit up at the sight of her.

'Daisy.'

'Come in.' She stood back and as he moved passed her, the smell of his laundry detergent and cologne hit her and she felt the familiar tingling of attraction and such a deep love all mixed together. 'Sit wherever. By the window, if you like.'

He nodded and sat in the bay window seat, gazing outside. 'The garden is looking beautiful.'

'I've been working on it over the last couple of weeks.'

He nodded. 'You look good, the sun's brought out your freckles.' James smiled softly. 'I love your freckles.'

She smiled. 'Took me years to love them.'

'Always the way. If only we knew better when we were young.' His face momentarily saddened. 'I found these.' He withdrew an envelope and handed it to her.

She took them uncertainly and sat by his feet in the bay window. Carefully she opened the envelope and took out a bunch of photos. As she went through them, her eyes grew hazy with tears. There was photo after photo of her on holidays they had taken with James, on the day she had entered an art exhibition, from every single occasion that James had been a part of.

'There's no Hugh,' she realised aloud, and looked up.

'Oh, I have plenty photos of Hugh but I often took ones of just you. I got them all developed and would look at your beautiful face over the years.'

'Oh James.' She smiled through her tears. 'You know Hugh hated taking photos or having his photo taken. I never understood why but I think it was probably something to do with a fear of losing face. The lack of control over it.'

'Yes,' James agreed. 'I think that's right. I think the only photos I ever saw of you two alone were either at your wedding, the professional ones, or that one of him on that bridge in Amsterdam.'

'Yes, I took that one.' She smiled at the memory. 'It feels like a lifetime ago. He proposed to me that day.'

'Did you know straight away you wanted to marry him?'

'Yes and no,' Daisy answered honestly. 'I knew he was a decent man, the right sort of man but, when I think about it now, I was too young. I remember in the moment he asked me having all those thoughts but there you go…' She paused, and looked up from the photo. 'How come you never married?'

He shrugged, smiled shyly. 'Well, other than having always been madly in love with you, you mean?'

She smiled.

'Never met the right woman. I almost married this woman from Surrey in my early thirties, someone my parents had found for me but ironically enough she, Diane, called it off.' He laughed. 'I think she did us both a huge favour.'

'I never knew about that!'

'No, not something I wanted to broadcast to anyone.'

'Why have you come here, James?' Daisy searched his face and he grabbed her hand.

'I came here because I love you and I've wanted you for all these years, I'm not going to let the possibility of you carrying Hugh's child be a reason to stop me from trying.'

Daisy winced at his choice of words. 'If I do have Hugh's child, that child will be a part of me. If you cannot love my child, then really you cannot love me.'

She knew she should not have got her hopes up when she heard he had come back.

'In fact, I was about to take a test.'

'Oh.' James stood, her hand still in his. 'Do you want me to go?'

'You can stay if you want?'

'OK, I'll wait here.' He looked suddenly nervous, his gaze fleetingly caressing her body.

She nodded, let go of his hand and walked to the bathroom. Once again she took the box off the side and removed one of the sticks, wondering how something so small and plastic had the power to change a woman's life in an instant. She waited the two minutes, not daring to look at the test.

'Are you OK, Daisy?' James's voice filled with concern and nervousness all at once.

She picked up the stick, not looking at it and opened the door. 'You look for me.'

'What am I looking for?'

She kept her eyes on his. 'It says right next to the window.'

Daisy grew exasperated. 'Thank God men don't have to go through this stuff.'

'Alright, alright.' He peered more closely at the stick and said slowly, 'Well, um, I think, um…'

'James,' she warned.

'Well, I think, you are.'

'I am?' She flipped the stick around and sure enough, there were two very definite lines. 'I am!' She threw the stick onto the bed and hugged James tight, squealing with delight. After a minute or so, she held James in front of her by the shoulders. 'You haven't said anything.'

'I can't believe it.' He shook his head. 'Amazing.'

'But you also mean you can't love me now.'

He removed her hands from his shoulders and kissed them all over, and then very tenderly dropped butterfly kisses along her arm and down her front to her tummy.

'Hello,' he whispered, and when he looked up he was beaming. 'Daisy, I love you so much. Please let me be a part of your life.' He looked at her with such deep passion and intent. 'Both of your lives.'

'Really?' Her eyes welled with tears of joy. 'Really?'

'I came here today to tell you that if you are carrying Hugh's child, I want to be here for you and for them, boy or girl.'

James leant in towards Daisy and she immediately felt every inch of her body tingle with anticipation. Very gently, almost too gently as it belied the urgency she felt deep in her groin, he kissed her lips and then with greater passion, his tongue moved around her mouth. Their eyes locked in lust and love.

He pulled away and Daisy was alarmed at the abruptness of his gesture. She watched him gulp hard and Daisy recognised that look, the same look Hugh had given her all those years ago on that bridge in Amsterdam.

Then, as if her life had taken on a dream-like quality, he got down on one knee and took her hand. His own hand was trembling and from his left jacket pocket he withdrew a box, a velvet purple box.

'My darling Daisy, please will you do me the biggest honour and become my wife?'

She gasped, her head reeling with the suddenness of it all but then as she gazed down at the man in front of her, his mouth twitching with nerves and the look of abounding love in his eyes, she smiled and said, 'Yes.'

'Yes?' He looked up and she nodded quickly. Carefully, he slipped the most beautiful of rings on her finger: a rose gold ring with a simple diamond. She gasped at its beauty as he jumped to his feet.

'Yes!' She planted her lips on his once more and he responded with urgency, his hands moving from her shoulders and down the length of her body, skimming her curves until he came to rest on her hips. She felt her stomach somersault at his touch and then he gently started to lift her dress above her head. She slowly unbuttoned his shirt and as he kissed her passionately moving back towards the bed, removed his trousers. He lay on top of her, holding his muscular body above her; even the slightest touch of his skin sent shivers all over her skin. He kissed her hair, her face, down her neck and to the very tips of her toes. She thought she might have died and gone to heaven.

With every touch, the feeling of yearning inside her grew and grew. He kissed his way back up her body and moved to her mouth once more.

'I want you,' she breathed deeply.

He took off his underwear and then hers before he slipped himself inside her causing her to gasp with delight. She looked into his eyes and he searched hers with such intense want and love, she felt tears roll down her cheeks. He gently kissed them away.

'Shall we stop?' he asked quietly. 'Are you OK?'

She nodded. 'Don't stop. Please.'

As they moved against each other, it wasn't long before they reached the dizzying heights of making love and they lay entwined in each other's arms, a sheen of sweat covering them delicately like a cloth. Their breathing was deep and quick as they nestled into one another, Daisy's heart only just beginning to slow.

James leant across her and picked up the pregnancy test. He beamed. 'You are going to be the best mother. Hugh would be so proud of you.'

Daisy took his other hand and held it against her cheek. 'I love you, James.'

He smiled and rolled towards her to kiss her gently on the lips. 'And I have always loved you, Daisy and now, you, too, little Daisy.' He kissed her bare stomach and gently, ever so gently, they made love again.

Chapter 22

A year on and the guesthouse looked as glorious as ever. Only today the garden was laid out with row upon row of white folding chairs, at the very front of which stood a double arch of pale pink peonies. The trees rustled with white linen bunting flags and the dance floor and area for the band were all ready for the evening's festivities.

Daisy looked out at the garden from her bedroom and then down at the two little people she now loved more than she ever thought possible. They were happily swishing her long dangling diamante earrings with their small pudgy hands, the first sign of a proper smile from both of them, and not just the smile that came from relief from wind.

Her mother bustled in, knocking as she entered, wearing a sky-blue dress and jacket.

'You look beautiful, Mum,' Daisy remarked as her mother efficiently took the twins off her. 'Really beautiful.'

Her mum, never one to handle compliments well, brushed it aside. 'You mean, not bad, for someone who has spent her life amongst cow udders.'

Daisy laughed. 'Not quite what I was thinking.'

Her mother very ably jigged one twin on either hip. 'You need to get ready, darling girl.'

'I know, I know, I need someone to help me with the zip.'

'Let me pop these two down here and then we'll get you ready.'

The boys were gently popped on the bed, with cushions either side of them. 'Right, Oli and Jack, be good for Grandma Jenny.' She lost herself in looking at her grandchildren with such fondness; she had to shake her head to remind herself what she was doing. 'Ah yes, the dress.'

Daisy stared at her post-pregnancy body in the mirror: she had worried about her curves and cellulite before, but now she really knew the meaning of how hard it was to keep weight off and the everyday hunt for a remedy against the orange peel. But despite all that, she was more proud of her body than ever before.

'You look beautiful,' her mother said in the mirror's reflection as she stood behind her daughter. 'I know you're being self-critical, but I can't understand why. You are all women; you are what women are meant to look like. I'd do anything to have looked like you.'

'Mum, you don't have to just say that.'

She smiled. 'I'm not.' Very carefully she manoeuvred the dress over Daisy's head and let the weight of the fabric fall into position over her daughter's body. 'Oh wow, wow.'

Daisy looked at herself as her mother did the zip up. She did adore the dress. It had a gorgeous boat-shaped neck and long sleeves, the dress hugging her frame to her waist where it flared out slightly in a long A-line of ivory silk.

A small knock at the door caused her to look around. 'Come in.'

Lisa walked into the room and they simultaneously shrieked with delight. Lisa looked like an angel. She wore a very straight white dress with lace sleeves.

'Lisa!' Daisy wiped away tears. 'You look beautiful.'

'You look gorgeous.'

They held each other's hands, tears running freely down their faces.

'Oh, you two, come on…' interrupted Jenny. 'I've only just done your make-up. Here, sit on the edge of the bed and I'll touch it up.'

Lisa walked up to the bed and leant over the twins, cooing at them. 'Hello my gorgeous godchildren.' She smiled. 'They really are the spitting image of Hugh.'

'They really are,' Daisy agreed and came up to the other side of the bed to kiss her darling boys on their foreheads. They gurgled and blew bubbles in her direction. 'If they had come out reading the *Financial Times*, I wouldn't have been surprised.'

At first she had been shocked by how much they looked like Hugh, and then worried that James would have a change of heart.

But, in actual fact, James had looked down at them with such love and swore to them both to protect them forever more.

'They look just like Hugh,' he had said, crying. 'Just like him. I'm so glad. They're beautiful, darling girl.' He had leant over and kissed her so fondly on the lips she knew, just knew, everything would be OK.

Jenny righted their faces and Daisy had to admit, for a woman she had never associated with femininity, her mother was so skilled at hair and make-up. Perhaps Jenny had practised in secret. She certainly wasn't just the stalwart, boiler-suit, no-nonsense mother she had imagined. Daisy now planned to spend as much time as she could with her mother, to go some way to remedying their fractured relationship.

'Right, you two. Let's have a quick selfie,' Jenny said, bundling both women in towards her.

'How do you know what a selfie is?' Daisy asked, bemused.

'I'm not archaic, Daisy. I may appear to have been left behind but I do have a mobile.' She smiled. 'Which is good because I'm on a dating app for the over-seventies.'

Daisy grinned. 'And…?'

'There is one man.' Jenny flushed slightly.

'What's his name?'

'The Silver Surfer 36.'

'No, his real name.'

'Oh, Graham.' She smiled shyly. 'He's asked me to go to an art gallery and dinner in Cheltenham.'

'Oh, that's fabulous, Mum.'

'It sure is.' Lisa nodded vigorously.

'Listen to you, Lisa, it sure is… You sound as Texan as your man.'

'Howdy, partner,' she joked.

'Right, you two,' Jenny said looking out of the window. 'Most guests are here by the looks of it. Don't go near the window. Remember James and Bob can't see you.' She rushed to the door. 'I'll go and see if everyone's ready for the blushing brides.'

She hugged Daisy close and whispered in her ear, 'Dad would have been so proud. He was proud when you married Hugh and he'd be proud now.' Her eyes glistened. 'As am I.'

Jenny rushed from the room and could be heard talking to someone in the entrance hall. Shortly after, the youth orchestra started up, and Daisy and Lisa made their way to the bottom of the stairs holding hands. Jenny came back in from outside, colour high in her cheeks. She was to walk them both down the aisle and she couldn't have looked more proud or happy. As they stepped out onto the veranda there were gasps of delight and the odd low wolf-whistle. James and Bob stood at the front, their backs to the women even though it was obvious from their body language how much they wanted to turn around. Jenny linked arms with both women and giving them both an encouraging smile, walked slowly but assuredly down the aisle.

Daisy smiled at relations she hadn't seen in years, at friends, fellow villagers. The sun had come out to play and light glinted magically off the still, ever so slightly dewy grass. As they neared the men both started to turn. Bob's face lit up with a huge grin. Barbara's dog basket sat by his feet and it had been jazzed up with glitter and pom-poms, which Barbara had already mauled and spat out.

The twins had been placed in their double buggy at the front by James – and it had had a similar glitter treatment to Barbara's basket – and as Daisy approached, she bent down to kiss their chubby cheeks, before looking properly at James. She smiled. He looked dashing in his dark grey suit, tailored in London, and as he gazed at her through his soft eyes, he mouthed, 'You look beautiful.' His face glowed with pure happiness.

The village reverend stood in front of them and as people sat and took up their places, he began.

'I welcome you all to this the most special of weddings and most special of days. Today we are conducting two of everything which,' he said, smiling at the twins, 'seems most appropriate.'

The reverend led them through the ceremony and within minutes Lisa was married to Bob and hugging him ecstatically. The reverend turned to Daisy. 'And I believe Daisy has something she would like to read to us?'

She nodded and turned towards the congregation. Suddenly she wondered if this was such a good idea. James had given her the letter. A final letter – a final letter from Hugh.

'Many of you knew Hugh and whilst he, more than anybody else, would hate for this to turn into a sad occasion, I wanted to share his letter with you because it made me realise that there are many versions of love. Hugh knew that, he even recognised and encouraged the love that James and I have for one another. In his dying days, he didn't wish me to be alone or to never find love again. No.' She shook her head, the tears she feared springing to her eyes. 'Quite the opposite, he wanted this day to happen.' She smiled softly at James. 'In fact, you will like his letter because I think it shows what a selfless human being Hugh was.'

She cleared her throat, glanced briefly at the twins as if to check they were listening to their father's words. Their tiny hands and feet were flailing as they sat in the pushchair, their big round blue eyes on her.

'OK, here we go.' She took a deep breath and began.

Dearest Daisy,

I asked James to give you this letter on your wedding day. I know you'll read this and think, "what a pompous ass to think that he knew I was going to marry James." But please don't think that. As I have said before, your love for one another has always been apparent. I never doubted your love for me but when I became ill and I knew that I didn't have long, I wanted to know you were going to be OK. I knew that James would look out for you.

A tear made its way down her cheek but she ignored it.

James has always been my best friend and I know what a decent, genuine man he is and you, my darling, deserve that. You deserve happiness and love and to not be plagued by the boring old fart anymore.

She laughed despite herself and a ripple of laughter worked its way through the seated guests.

If you have children with James, wonderful. If you have children with me, also wonderful. I am looking down on you today and I'm so proud of you both. Keep me in your hearts as I keep you in mine.

All my love, Hugh.

Daisy could barely speak by the end but she managed to finish. She looked up and blew a kiss into the sky.

When she looked back at the guests she noticed so many women but men too were crying and smiling all at once. Daisy smiled at them. She knew what they were feeling because it was, without a doubt, the most joyously sad she had ever felt. James took her hand and as the ceremony continued, she felt a lightness that she hadn't felt for such a long time.

When James was asked to kiss the bride, Tom hollered out, 'Get a room!' and the Dream Team laughed, one of them shouting, 'They can't, they're all booked up!'

Daisy laughed as James kissed her deeply once more. As they were pronounced man and wife, Lisa and Bob came over and they had a group hug. Then Daisy walked over to the twins and undid their harnesses, plucking them easily out of the pushchair and popping one on each of her hips. The photographer asked for James to come into shot and he clicked away. Daisy knew that if she could have sent that photo to Hugh, he would have been delighted. The twins, as they scrunched their faces up against the May sunshine, looked suddenly so like their father, it took Daisy's breath away.

The rest of the day was spent drinking champagne and dancing to the live band. It was only when her feet really started to hurt that Daisy headed inside the house, removing her shoes as she went, grateful for the coolness of the flagstone floor on her tired, hot feet.

She walked quickly and quietly up to Hugh's study, grateful for a moment to herself to think. Daisy sat in the bay window and watched the comings and goings outside. She could see Tom and Alvin jiving – or their version of the jive, which didn't look totally unlike an amateur version of *Riverdance* – and then there was Lisa and Bob (and Barbara) giggling with one another under the large oak tree. Her mother had decided to phone Silver Surfer 36 and see if he wanted to come over for a drink and a shindig. When Graham had turned up in a beautifully cut suit and slicked back silver hair, she was sure her no-nonsense mother had gone as shy as she might have done around a rock star. They were now getting on famously well. Even Alistair was here, with Clare of course, and she was glad to see him looking so happy. He had told her on the phone that he'd taken Clare back to Edinburgh to re-meet his parents. Clare was a brave woman, Daisy had thought, but it turned out that with the years his parents had mellowed and were now very much involved in the wedding plans for next January.

Daisy had even invited Annabelle. Yes, she had had many a

sleepless night in which she wondered if James would refuse to marry her and go running off into the sunset with Annabelle on his arm, but she knew she had to let go of that. James had proven his commitment to her and, amazingly, it turned out Annabelle was an expert at wedding planning. She had somewhat relished the role of wedding planner, because as she had said, 'If I'm thinking about the colour of your meringue and if you might like a cheese board, well, that means I'm not then thinking about my husband shagging the ex-nanny or whichever poor woman he's got his mitts on.' Annabelle had smiled wickedly. 'I can assure you, dear Daisy, I will not only divorce that man but I will take him to the cleaners.'

And she had done just that which was why the pale pink dress she wore today screamed money and she had insisted on buying only the top champagne for her friend Daisy on her special day.

Daisy looked up at the ceiling. 'Hello darling, can you see them all? They're so happy, aren't they? As am I.' She nodded. 'I probably won't talk to you as much as I did but only because I have to concentrate on the twins and James now. But remember if I'm not talking to you, I'm thinking about you.' She glanced outside at her beautiful twin boys as Grandma Jenny swished them one at a time up into the air and back down causing a fit of gorgeous baby giggles. 'You'd be so proud of them, Hugh. They're just like you. They're perfect.'

She got up and ran her hand over the smooth green leather on his desk. 'Goodbye my love, I'll be back soon. Thanks to you I have a family, someone who loves me and a guesthouse.' She smiled. 'You may, at times, have been a boring old fart but let me tell you something; you were my boring old fart and, it turns out. a bloody lovely and insightful one at that.'

She walked to the study door and as she left the room, James met her on the landing.

'You okay?' he said gently, his eyes filled with concern. 'You're not unhappy, are you?'

'No,' she said with such certainty. 'I am the happiest woman alive.' She smiled. 'This isn't just a guesthouse, it's a family.'

James brought her into him and kissed her deeply and passionately as Daisy tried to capture the moment in her mind forever.

Acknowledgements

This book has been on quite a journey with me over the past year or so. There are many people I'd like to thank who not only contributed to the book but also gave me strength and encouragement when I needed it most.

Firstly, my editor Charlotte Mursell, who is truly amazing.

Everyone at HQ, who continue to do a brilliant job – thank you.

To Sinead, for her incredibly generous winning bid at the Authors for Grenfell Tower auction. Her sister Lisa McDermott provided the wonderful character name. Happy fortieth, Lisa.

All the gorgeous crowd at The Cutting Shed and, in particular, Russell, Jane and Kate.

To my scrummy Clifton friends – love you Em and Ros.

To Lory, for her generous spirit and for making nursery drop-off ridiculously fun.

To every single person who has helped me achieve a new life, you are all fab. Too many to mention! However, a special shout out to Maria, Toni, Nat, Abbie and Colin.

To my cousins, Katie and Lucy: you are the best.

My goddaughter Isabelle.

As always, my parents, who have been incredible. They have helped me move from pastures old to pastures new in the most loving and beautiful way.

My brother Ed and his wife, Nik, who are now living on the other side of the world. Miss you both.

To my gorgeous son Finn – you are the best T-Rex ever. Love you to the moon and back.

Willow, you are beautiful. Welcome.

And finally, a major part of the Dream Team: TJ. Thank you. Your friendship is extraordinary.

Dear Reader,

Thank you so much for taking the time to read this book – we hope you enjoyed it! If you did, we'd be so appreciative if you left a review.

Here at HQ Digital we are dedicated to publishing fiction that will keep you turning the pages into the early hours. We publish a variety of genres, from heartwarming romance, to thrilling crime and sweeping historical fiction.

To find out more about our books, enter competitions and discover exclusive content, please join our community of readers by following us at:

@HQDigitalUK

facebook.com/HQDigitalUK

Are you a budding writer? We're also looking for authors to join the HQ Digital family! Please submit your manuscript to:

HQDigital@harpercollins.co.uk.

Hope to hear from you soon!

ONE PLACE. MANY STORIES

Turn the page for an exclusive extract from *A Little Cottage in the Country*, another charming romantic comedy from Lottie Phillips…

Two Weeks Earlier…

Anna took a deep, cleansing breath as she knocked. The name on the door read 'Barry Smith, Editor-in-Chief'. The faint trace of Tipp-Ex, where Sheryl had crossed out Smith and written White at last year's Christmas party, still remained.

'Come in,' boomed the voice.

Anna opened the door, gripping the handle tightly as she tried to control her nerves.

Barry looked up briefly from his computer, a sheen of sweat glistening across his bulbous, bald head. 'This had better be good, Compton. I'm trying to make a meal out of the crap you lot give me, and you know what? I've said it before, I'll say it again, I don't know why I put up with it. I could fire the lot of you and start again.' He pinched the top of his nose and rubbed his eyes using his free hand, his spectacles jiggling up and down. 'Come in, Compton. Sit, for God's sake.'

Anna moved forward, closed the door behind her and smoothed her skirt. As she did, she caught sight of the remnants of her son's porridge near her behind. She grew hot under the collar and then realised she must also have got caught downwind of her daughter's milk tsunami. The smell of gone-off cheese started to permeate her nostrils and she tried to remained focused.

'Barry,' Anna started, taking a seat as requested, 'I'm leaving *The Post*.'

She had been hoping he might show even a vague sense of regret but, instead, he grinned.

'Leaving?'

Anna cleared her throat. 'Yes, that's right.'

'Going anywhere good?'

Anna clenched and unclenched her fists, kneading her skirt. 'Barry, I just said I'm leaving.'

Barry let out a bark of a laugh. 'What do you want me to do? Cry?'

'No,' Anna started. 'Oh, do you know what, you can stuff your job. I was going to ask for a reference, but frankly…' As Anna spoke, her head was buzzing with regret (she *needed* a reference, she had children, she was going to the great unknown). 'I don't need a sodding reference from you. I mean, who'll have heard of the *The Post* in Trumpsey Blazey?'

Barry chuckled. 'Ah, so you're making a break for the countryside, old gal.' He paused. 'I presume you've got a job, or have you…?' He grinned. 'No, Anna Compton cannot have found a new man – a millionaire?!'

Anna stood. 'I don't need to take this rubbish from you. I've found a beautiful home, the children are going to a wonderfully rated primary school and I…' She stammered. 'Will find another job with a *reputable* country paper.'

'You mean the *Hare and Hound Gazette*?' He laughed, his belly shaking unpleasantly as he did so. 'I know Tim, the big man behind that little number, and you won't get work with him.'

Anna stuck out her chin. 'Why ever not?' She bristled with anger.

'He only employs men.' Barry looked back at his screen, then said seriously and with no sense of irony, 'He's quite the chauvinist.' Barry returned his gaze to Anna and then to his screen, then back to Anna. Anna grew immediately worried. She could almost see his brain steaming and puffing with the energy of an idea.

'Well, I'll be off,' Anna said, turning on her heel before she got involved in whatever strange idea he was concocting. 'Good luck with the paper.'

As she pulled the door open, Barry spoke again. 'Compton, I've just had an idea.'

She turned slowly.

'You know what this paper needs? It needs fresh air, it needs something different, something fun, something rural, something idyllic.' He stood now, his podgy hands flying through the air. 'It needs to see a woman making the most of Blighty!'

'Barry?' Anna almost didn't dare ask.

'You clearly don't have a job, and you have children to think about, Anna.' He smiled, as though he really was the saviour. 'I'm offering you the chance to write a weekly column for the paper.' He drew his hand across the air in front of him. "Anna's Little Cottage in the Country", that's what we'll call it!' He moved inelegantly from around the desk and shuffled his excess weight towards Anna, who grimaced at the sight of her (ex) boss moving in on her, like a puffer fish. 'What do you say, Compton? Give us the lowdown on what it's like in the Wild West of Wiltshire?'

'Um, that's very, um…' she started, her mind whirring. 'Well, Barry, the thing is…'

'You need money? You want to keep your foot in the door as a successful journalist?'

'Successful journalist?' She reeled under the weight of such a compliment; one he had never, ever come close to giving before.

'Well, a…. you know… an OK one,' he clarified. Then, wagging his finger in front of her face, 'But you could become a wonder. You could personally help this paper survive with your take on rural life.'

'Really?' She wasn't convinced.

He looked at her intently. 'Yes, it'll be brilliant. Well…' He paused. 'You need to make it brilliant. Join in, make friends, get a loooovverrr…' He purred this last word in such a way, Anna had to turn away from the sudden gust of stale coffee emanating from his mouth.

'Barry, the thing is, I want a fresh start.' She was resolute.

'Yes, but the thing is, Compton, you can have a fresh start, but you have to think of your children. You need money.'

She turned towards the door again, took one step out.

'When do you leave?'

'Two weeks,' she said, her back to him.

'Excellent! Give me something juicy in two and a half.' He grinned. 'Actually, I might talk to Diane, see if she can't take some shots.' His mind was whirring and his upper lip glistened as he smacked his lips together. 'People will love to follow your story… I can see it now. City girl living the dream.'

With that, he started to close the door and she shuffled forward before he could catch her ankles with it.

'Good luck, Compton. Over and out,' he wheezed from the sudden exertion. 'I'll get Sheryl to ping you over the details.'

The door slammed behind her, totally befuddled by what had actually just happened. But then, she realised, he had a point. Anna shrugged. She supposed she did need money, and at least she wouldn't have to see Barry every day. She imagined herself happily typing her column in the pretty cottage garden, the birds tweeting and the twins making daisy chains under the dappled light of the apple tree.

'And so the next chapter begins,' she thought as she made her way to her desk to pack away her notebooks, pens, laptop and snowglobe.

Arriving in Trumpsey Blazey

Anna grinned as she sped towards the countryside, leaving London and her past firmly behind. She felt as if she was, in fact, stepping where no thirty-two-year-old divorcee with two young kids had ever been before (she allowed herself this slight exaggeration). She was unstoppable. She knew she was on the verge of something spectacular. She was totally in control and her heart lifted at the sign: *Welcome to Wiltshire*. Yes, she had made it. Goodbye Big Smoke, hello Country Glamour Queen, Domestic Goddess and Yummy Mummy Extraordinare.

She beamed as she pressed 'Play' on the stereo system – OK, she admitted, not quite stereo system: more like tape deck – of her 1989 Nissan Micra and started to sing (wail) along to the first track on her homemade mix tape.

'Born to be wiiiiiiillldddd….' She looked in the rear-view mirror and her smile quickly faded. 'Freddie, don't put a Smartie up Antonia's nose.' She glanced quickly at the road and turned in her seat, batting the air behind with her free hand in an attempt to stop her five-year-old son sticking a chocolate up his twin sister's nostril. 'Freddie, have you stuck the chocolate up her nose?' She looked at him.

Her son grinned back at her, his angelic face flashing a mischievous grin, and she forced herself to focus once again on the road. Oh bum, she thought, why now? Why today? She needed to pull over and somehow lever a Smartie from her daughter's nose without causing long-term damage. She imagined a repeat of the Blu-Tack-in-ear incident and, remembering the doctor's words, winced.

'Antonia will be OK, but this is not a rerun of *ER*, Ms Compton. It's best if you leave it to the professionals.'

'Mummy.' She glanced in the mirror at Freddie's chocolate-smeared face. 'Look.' He pointed.

She turned quickly in her seat. 'What are you talking about?'

'A horse.'

She flicked her eyes back to the road and let out a scream. 'Oh bugger!'

Slamming on the brakes, the car came to an abrupt halt as she narrowly avoided driving the Nissan Micra up the rear end of the animal. The rider turned and scowled, backing his horse up in an over-the-top dressage-like fashion and moving alongside her now-open window.

'You know, you could kill someone like that, yah?' He looked down at her, his eyes narrowing. 'That was awfully dangerous.'

Anna watched his mouth, trying to make out exactly what he was saying. It appeared he was speaking from the back of his throat and not actually using his lips. 'Pardon?'

He rolled his eyes. 'I mean, you need to be more careful. There's a hunt on, yah?'

'A hunt?' she repeated.

'Yah, you know, horses, dogs, a fox.' He scowled again.

'Oh, a hunt. Right.' While the man in the strange black riding hat and red jacket ranted, she took the opportunity of having come to a standstill to turn and look at Freddie again. 'Freddie, where's the chocolate?'

He smiled and held up his hand to reveal a green palm with rapidly melting chocolate stuck to it. Anna smiled with relief. 'Good boy. Just eat it.'

'What the...?' She jumped at the touch of something wet and slimy running up and down her forearm and swivelled in her seat, coming face to face with the horse happily nuzzling her steering wheel.

'You've made a friend,' the man on top of the horse said and smiled.

When he smiled, he didn't look quite so officious. She thought how he actually looked like a normal human being and less like a Stubbs painting brought to life.

'The name's Spencerville…' He paused. 'Horatio.' He held out his gloved hand and she shook it.

Anna snorted.

'What's so funny?' He raised an eyebrow.

'Nothing.' She laughed. 'Well, it's just funny to hear someone introduce themselves using their surname first.'

Clearly affronted, he hit the flank of his horse with his crop and started to trot. 'Well, there's nothing funny about driving at speed. Just be careful, yah? You could injure someone, yah?' He rode off down the road. Oddly, Anna couldn't see any other riders.

She revved her engine in annoyance. 'How dare he bloody tell me how to drive. Horatio…' she muttered. 'Who's even called bloody Horatio? Riding around like a Rear Admiral.'

'Mummy,' Antonia's voice came from the back.

'Yes?' she said, taking the turn towards Trumpsey Blazey.

'Why was that man dressed silly?'

Anna smiled.

'He looked like a plonk-ah,' Freddie said.

'Freddie, I've told you not to use that word.'

'S'OK, Mummy, I don't think you're a plonk-ah.'

'How kind.' She slowed the car as they approached Trumpsey Blazey: their new home. Tears filled her eyes at the sight of the Cotswold stone bridge crossing the infant Thames and the chocolate-box thatched cottages either side. This was all theirs to enjoy.

The news had come out of the blue. Anna had been battling

with the children over the merits of eating peas, in the kitchen, when she had received the letter from her dear aunt's solicitor: she was to inherit her Auntie Flo's country home. Auntie Florence was stepsister to her mother, Linda. There had been very few details, but the idea of moving from their tiny, mildew-covered, two-bed flat in London to the fresh country air was beyond exciting. It was her chance to give her children a better way of life. After all, she had failed at marriage with their father, Simon. She was, she hated to admit, lonely too. So very lonely, and when she thought about her aunt and remembered how very active her social life had been, she thought that, yes, she too could have that! This might be the way of making everything better. After all, she thought, in the midst of dreaming up freshly baked pies from her Aga, she had just received the dreaded news that her children would not be afforded the privilege of places at the best state school, but the one ten miles away that was deemed 'dire'. She had phoned Simon (the *ex*) to explain the situation. She had thought this would be an appropriate time for him to step up, show himself to be the man and father he should always have been.

'Simon, it's Anna.' She had breathed deeply into the receiver. 'The twins haven't been accepted at Royal Oak.'

'What?' he screeched and, for once, she knew they were on the same page. 'They're not going to…'

'Yes. Sully Oak.'

'Oh, Anna, blimey.'

She knew then, in that shared moment of grief, that they had failed their children. What she wasn't expecting was the next curveball.

'Can't you get more work? Surely, someone needs an article on…' She could hear his brain whirring, grasping at straws. 'On the micro-climate of Hammersmith.'

'Thanks, Simon.' She held back a sob. 'Thanks for making me feel even more shit.'

'Well, you know, if I had the money…' He was a cameraman for the Beeb.

Anna was about to argue, knowing full well he'd just sold his house and shacked up with some bird from the PR department, but she held back. She reminded herself that she had what she wanted: her children. Nothing mattered but them and he had threatened, not that long ago, to take her to court for access to his children. Anna wouldn't give him any room for manoeuvre. She had hung up.

After receiving the news from her aunt's solicitor, she had a good cry in the privacy of the loo (where she often escaped, glass of wine or Bailey's in hand, for a moment's peace).

She had adored her aunt. Flo had been a dear friend as well as surrogate sunt. The immense sadness that threatened to overwhelm her was tinged with a sense of hope. They could escape London and the poor state school. Within minutes, she was online checking out the Ofsted 'Outstanding' merits of Trumpsey Blazey Primary and reading about all the various clubs and village traditions they could be part of. There was even some giant pie-rolling competition. She chuckled at the thought of how much fun it all sounded.

Once Anna had had a quiet cry in the loo, she grabbed the twins' hands and they danced and danced around their poky kitchen until Anna thought maybe she would jinx her luck by showing no remorse for her aunt's passing. And so she solemnly toasted Aunt Flo with a Thomas the Tank Engine beaker. She knew neither Freddie nor Antonia really understood, but they affably joined in.

Anna could see the cottage so clearly in her mind's eye; although, she realised guiltily, she had been so caught up in her own downward spiral of barely scraping by, that she had only exchanged letters with Aunt Flo in the last two years and had last visited the cottage ten years ago, Aunt Flo preferring to come up to London to visit.

She brought her mind back to the here and now as she scanned the small row of houses on the main high street, her heart lifting in anticipation at each house plaque she read. Anna thought she remembered the house standing gleaming and proud at the head of Trumpsey Blazey. Half an hour later, and with no one around to ask, she tried to bring up Google Maps on her phone. It was pointless as she couldn't read maps, but she hoped for some sort of epiphany moment where all those years of orienteering the Bristol Downs at school would come into their own. Public-school education was character-building, her father had claimed when she phoned home asking – no, begging – to go to the local state comprehensive.

'Dad, I hate it.'

'You can't hate it. You've only been there a week.'

'Yeah,' she had moaned, 'but they sent us out into the countryside with nothing but the clothes on our backs and a map and compass.'

'Weren't you just on the Downs? I remember doing the same exercise when I was at the school.'

'Yeah, but we had no food for *hours*. It's clearly illegal and some form of child abuse.'

'How long were you out there for?'

'Two hours,' she had wailed, thinking she might have broken him this time. 'Then we were allowed back for tea.'

She had been greeted by the sound of a long, dead dialling tone.

Not dissimilar to the one she was hearing now. Not dead – but no signal, to her mind, was as good as dead. 'Bloody hell. What is the bloody point of a mobile if you can't be bloody *mobile* with it?'

'Mummy, bad word,' Antonia said.

'What word?'

'Buggy.' She meant 'bloody'.

Anna looked back at her daughter, who always achieved an

enviable look of disgust that Anna one day hoped to mimic when she was telling them off.

'Sorry,' Anna said, exhaling deeply. 'Only I can't find it.'

A tap on the window made her jump and she looked outside. That Horatio person stood holding his horse's reins and peering in at them. She rolled the window down.

'Hi,' she said.

'Are you lost?'

'Aren't you meant to be with the hunt?'

'Yes, but I'm taking Taittinger home.'

'Pardon?' she said, trying to hide her smile.

He looked at her disbelievingly. 'Am I speaking a foreign language?'

She inclined her head. 'Not far off.'

'Tatty,' he indicated the horse, 'needs to go home.'

'Right.'

'It looks like you're lost. Maybe I can help?'

'We've just moved here.' She lifted her chin. 'I haven't been here in over ten years and can't remember where the house is. I inherited it from my aunt.'

'What's the name of the house?'

'Primrose Cottage.'

His look changed to what she could only read as: pity? 'Oh.' He tried to recover and smiled. 'Yes, everyone's been wondering who was moving in there.'

'Well, where is it?' She fought off the rising irritation at this man's ability to make her feel so ridiculous. He seemed so supercilious considering she had only just met him; but, she knew, it was also because she hated to ask for help.

He pointed towards a narrow lane leading up towards a small cottage on the hilltop. 'There.'

'Brilliant, thank you.' As she put the car in gear, he leant in.

'Look, I wonder if we might have a chat sometime soon.' He

smiled. 'Perhaps a coffee tomorrow? I…' He stopped, as if grasping for words.

Was he coming on to her?

'Yes, maybe.' Her mind raced with excuses. 'If I'm not planting…' She tried desperately to think of something country-esque and settled on vegetables. After all, she knew it wouldn't be far off the truth: how hard could it be to grow vegetables? She would be the embodiment of *The Good Life*. 'Potatoes,' she announced triumphantly.

He smiled knowingly. 'Ah, that old chestnut, planting potatoes.'

She nodded firmly and started to move off, leaving Horatio with his horse and a strange look of amusement on his face. The lane leading to the house was steep and rough.

'Right, let's go and see our new home.' She drove along the bumpy lane to the house, about a quarter of a mile from the bridge, and at the top she stopped, her heart sinking. The downstairs windows were covered in ivy and the garden entirely overgrown with weeds. She could have cried if it weren't for the sight of Horatio and Taittinger walking up the hill in her rear-view mirror.

'Oh, why can't he get lost?' Horatio's pity must have stemmed from his knowledge that the house was in need of that man off the daytime-telly home-improvement programme. Anna vaguely remembered a female presenter prancing manically from one room of tea-slurping builders, showing their bum cleavage, to another. All before said frilly presenter, along with the poor owners, who had never actually asked for a magenta-coloured kitchen, and the builders toasted their heroism and cried at their brilliance. The owners were then forced to smile at the camera and pretend they had always wanted a hot-pink kitchen with a life-size mural of their dead hamster on the main wall.

Anna felt humiliated. Turning to Freddie and Antonia, she put on a brave face. 'How are you guys doing?'

'I'm hungry,' they chimed in unison and a lump rose in her

throat. What had she been thinking? At least, in London, she had been able to provide the most basic of care for them: warmth and food. Now, she searched the derelict cottage for any signs of homeliness. It was a shell.

'Me again,' Horatio announced, out of puff, as he and Taittinger sidled up to the car and she put the window down once more.

'I can see that. If you've come to gloat, please don't.' Her eyes smarted.

'I didn't think you'd be pleased.'

She bit back her comment and leapt out of the car, indignation flaring inside her. 'But we'll be just fine. So, Mr Horatio Spencer-what's-it, if you wouldn't mind leaving me and my children alone, instead of standing their looking on like we're some sort of entertainment, then that would be most jolly.' Jolly? Why did she use the word 'jolly'? Help. Horatio was already rubbing off on her.

'Jolly,' repeated Freddie from the back.

Horatio was staring at her intently; maybe too intently. She shifted uncomfortably under his stare.

'Listen, about that chat...' She stared at him incredulously as once again he floundered. Who was this man? 'I know what it feels like to be suddenly alone.'

'I am not suddenly alone,' she said, defensive. 'I've been alone for years.' Then she smiled, despite herself.

He grinned.

Her heart fluttered at his incredibly sexy smile but she pushed her shoulders back, more determined than ever. She was an independent woman, she said to herself, although she wasn't entirely convinced at this point in time.

'Thank you, I really appreciate your help,' she said with sincerity. She knew she shouldn't be so stubborn. Her mother's voice rang around her head: 'Anna, you are a mule, girl, a mule.'

Despite this, and ignoring the gnawing maternal guilt eating away at her stomach as she glanced in the rear-view mirror at her children giggling at Freddie's burping-on-demand, she said, 'We'll be just fine.'

He plucked a fountain pen from his jacket pocket and a gilt-edged card from another pocket. Horatio suddenly looked like an ad for some ridiculous shop on Bond Street where the rich bought diamond-encrusted hip flasks because they could. Writing quickly, he passed her the card and tilted his riding hat with his forefinger, bidding her farewell. 'Goodbye… Oh, I never got your name.'

'Anna,' she said frostily.

'Anna. Like Anna Karenina.' He laughed. 'Same fighting spirit.'

'Anna Compton.'

Anna hated coming across as the damsel in distress, but she was beginning to wonder if she had taken on too much. The cottage did not in any way match up to the idyll she had concocted in her head. She shook away her doubts. No, her aunt had left it to her and it was meant to be. She would make the most of it.

She refocused on Horatio who, she noticed, looked vaguely amused.

'Right, well, Anna Compton. I'm sure I'll be seeing you again soon.' He clucked at the horse and Taittinger obligingly followed his owner down the hill.

'Like Anna Compton,' she muttered. 'Idiot and hopeless mother.' A tear made its way down her cheek and she brushed it away. She had to be strong or, at least, find the nearest shop and buy food for the kids and Sauvignon Blanc for herself. It was the only way. She looked at her children in the back and they smiled. She wondered if it was possible to love two little people any more than she did in that moment.

'OK, it's all going to be OK.' She smiled unconvincingly.

'I'm hungry,' said Antonia.

'Me too,' said Freddie.

'Me three,' Anna joined in. 'OK, let's go and see our home.'

Anna helped them out of the car and held their hands, one

child either side of her, as they approached the cottage. She let go of Freddie's hand as she retrieved the key from her pocket and slid it into the lock. As she pushed open the squeaky door, she was hit by a musty smell and dust danced in the air at the disturbance. The three of them stared wide-eyed at the sitting room. All the furniture was in place, as if Aunt Florence had just upped and left. Anna was flooded with memories of childhood summers spent here long ago and she remembered how magical Primrose Cottage had appeared then. She had always thought she and Aunt Flo were kindred spirits and knew it was through utter generosity that she had been left the small cottage and half acre of land. Why oh why, then, was she unable to get rid of the niggling doubt in the pit of her stomach? A little voice in her head was telling her she couldn't do this; that the whole notion of idyllic country living had been barmy and out of her reach. She was washed afresh with guilt as she glanced down at her suddenly innocent and angelic-looking children: what sort of awful mother drags their children away from the safety of their – albeit incredibly poky and mold-ridden – flat, in a beaten-up Nissan Micra, with barely more than a handful of crushed, ready-salted Hula Hoops at the bottom of her tote bag? Anna Compton, that was who.

Taking Freddie's hand again, she led them carefully through to the kitchen. She caught sight of the cream Aga and the quarry-tile floor, now thick with dust, the shelves covered in cobwebs, feeling hope for the first time that day. Maybe they would be OK after all. It just needed a good spring-clean and the help of a handyman. She would make it cosy…

An almighty crash came from outside and she let go of Freddie and Antonia, told them to stay put and ran to the open front door. Her car had rolled forward into an old chicken hut. She hadn't put the sodding handbrake on, she thought, all because that stupid man had put her off.

She felt a tug at her sleeve and looked down. Freddie gazed

up at her, looked outside, and smiled. 'Mummy's a plonk-ah.'

She pulled them towards her and nodded, sniffling. 'Yep, Mummy's a plonk-ah.'

Anna realised then that she was still holding the card the Horatio person had given her. She read the address. It wasn't so much an address. Well, not the kind that required a postcode. It read: Ridley Manor.

ONE PLACE. MANY STORIES

If you enjoyed *Sunshine at Daisy's Guesthouse*, then why not try another delightfully uplifting romance from HQ Digital?